CAPTURE

CAPTURE

A SGT. DUNN NOVEL

RONN MUNSTERMAN

Capture is a work of fiction. Names, characters, places, and incidents are the product of the author's imagination or are used fictitiously. Any resemblance to actual events, locales, or persons, living or dead is coincidental.

CAPTURE – A SGT. DUNN NOVEL

Copyright © 2016 by Ronn Munsterman
www.ronnmunsterman.com

Cover Design by David M. Jones and Nathalie Beloeil-Jones
www.beloeil-jones.com

Printed in the United States of America
10 8 6 4 2 1 3 5 7 9

ISBN-13: 978-1533258915
ISBN-10: 1533258910

BISAC: Fiction / War & Military

Acknowledgments

General George S. Patton's rush across eastern France is shown through our favorite hero, Tom Dunn, as he and his men are faced with day-to-day events that aren't always under their control. A new character is introduced in this book who shows us what air superiority really meant. We also get to meet Dunn's family back home in Cedar Rapids, Iowa.

As I have said before, we owe a generation of men and women a debt that cannot be repaid. The next time you see someone wearing a veteran's hat, whether WWII or a later war, please take a moment to say 'thank you.'

My first thank you goes to you the reader. Your support of the Sgt. Dunn novels hits me right in the heart. I love hearing from you. My email address is in the Author's Notes.

Thank you to my FIRST READERS who give me honest feedback and lots of encouragement on the book, and find sometimes hilarious errors: Steven E. Barltrop, David M. Jones (Jonesy was my first novel FIRST READER back in 2006), Zander Jones (David's son; this is his first time as a FIRST READER), Nathan Munsterman, John Skelton, Robert (Bob) A. Schneider II, and Steven D. White (Steve was a FIRST READER for some of my short stories back in 2003). Thanks as always to Dave J. Cross and Derek Williams for their friendship and support.

A special thanks to my wife for her support, encouragement and love, and for her brutal, but crucial red-pen editing. A heartfelt thank you to my family for their love and support, in life as well as my writing.

Thank you to David M. Jones and his wife, Nathalie, who created the beautiful cover. Dave is the graphics artist and Nathalie the freehand artist. This is Dave's fourth Sgt. Dunn cover and Nathalie's third. Their website is on the copyright page.

Many thanks to longtime reader, Matthew Hillebrand, for his gracious help in translating selected passages of dialog from English to German. I believe it adds a terrific authentic quality to the German characters.

And last, but not least, a thank you to my friends at Rockwell Collins and Quaker Oats / Pepsi who I still think of often and appreciate even after retiring from the day job.

As always you'll find my Author's Notes section at the end of the book. Please save it until last because it has spoilers.

For my dear friend Steven E. Barltrop and his wife Kathy

CAPTURE

Chapter 1

In flight over France
6 September 1944, 1446 Hours

The P-47 Thunderbolt is a killer. German soldiers called her the "Jabo" and feared her . . . for good reason.

Armed with eight .50 caliber Browning machine guns, the P-47 could deliver 6,400 rounds of half-inch diameter bullets per minute into a target. And she could lay up to 2,500 pounds worth of bombs on the target, or fire ten rockets. And the typical Thunderbolt squadron contained twelve of these killing machines.

Captain Benjamin Banks led his squadron eastward across France at 410 miles per hour. Each aircraft carried two one-thousand-pound bombs. Their target was located just north of Verdun, France, the place of death during World War I in which nearly a million men became causalities during the ten-month-long battle. Banks' battle would likely last less than a few minutes.

The squadron flew at ten thousand feet in three flights of four aircraft. Banks was in the lead flight and his wingman, First Lieutenant Edwin Holden, kept his Thunderbolt just back and off Banks' left wing. The other two members of the flight, Second Lieutenant Ray Langley and First Lieutenant Bill Wooten, filled in the four-finger formation on Banks' right. The remaining two flights were lined up on the diagonal behind and to the right of Wooten.

The green and brown patchwork of the earth below was periodically obscured by thin clouds around 8,000 feet altitude. The meteorologist had promised good visibility over the target. Above Banks' clear bubble canopy, the blue sky stretched forever in all directions.

As a member of the Ninth Air Force, Banks had flown ground-attack missions from England for the six months leading up to D-Day. The week after D-Day, his air group, the XIX Tactical Air Command, who supported General George S. Patton's Third Army, moved to France. This immensely suited Banks and the other pilots because they would no longer have to fly over the gray, ugly, violent waters of the English Channel.

Although the Thunderbolt was a sturdy aircraft, and her gigantic 2,600 horsepower radial engine could run even when a piston was shot out, flying across the Channel with an engine in trouble was terrifying, especially in the winter months. If the pilot's dinghy didn't inflate properly and the pilot ended up in the water, the British rescue teams had no more than fifteen minutes to pluck the pilot out of the frigid waters before hypothermia set in, followed quickly by death. Banks had lost a friend back in January to the Channel. He was happy to see it taken out of the live-or-die equation.

Banks checked his map and his watch, and then keyed his mike, "Dogbone Squadron from Dogbone leader. Two minutes. Battle formation."

The squadron had been flying with a distance of about thirty feet between planes, and one hundred fifty feet between flights. They needed to increase their interval because of the threat of flak. Banks checked quickly. Everyone was sliding into their new slot.

The targets for the day were a line of six German 88s which had a commanding field of fire over the western approaches to the Meuse River. Columns of advancing American mechanized infantry had been decimated earlier in the day. The survivors had called in the 88s' positions.

"Red flight, attack." The squadron's three flights were ingeniously named Red, White, and Blue, with Red being Banks' flight.

Banks nosed the Thunderbolt over, picking out his target, the first gun on the north end of the line. Unlike Navy dive bomber pilots, who were trained to dive at a seventy to ninety degree angle, P-47 pilots came in at a much shallower angle, perhaps twenty-five degrees.

Within seconds, the six-ton plus armament P-47 hit 500 miles an hour.

The stick stiffened and Banks had to use all of his concentration to keep the plane on the right line. At what seemed to be zero altitude, but was in reality a thousand feet, he released both bombs and the Thunderbolt screamed out of the dive soaring skyward, bleeding off speed by the second, the ultimate roller coaster ride first drop.

Banks' wingman, Holden, surged ahead and dove toward the eastern ridge line overlooking the river valley. The other two P-47s followed. When Red flight's remaining planes broke through 2,000 feet, flak bursts peppered the sky with black clouds of death.

Red flight bore straight on.

Banks leveled out at 5,000 feet and would control the attack with his bird's eye view, following a racetrack oval pattern over the battle. He surveyed the result of his bombs, and was thrilled to see that gun number one was tipped over like a battleship about to go under the unforgiving waters of the ocean.

"Blue flight, White flight, attack," Banks said.

Eight more airplanes dove toward the flak and the 88s.

Two explosions struck the line of 88s. Banks had to wait until the smoke cleared. "Red two from Dogbone leader, gun number two is down." The guns had been numbered one through six, left to right, or north to south. "Red three and four target gun three."

Red's two remaining attackers shrieked toward their target.

"White flight from Dogbone leader, target guns four and five, Blue flight target guns five and six." Banks wanted a little overlap of the targets.

As Red flight approached the target, Banks spotted bright flashes along the line of 88s. He immediately said, "Dogbone squadron from Dogbone leader, be aware, three quad twenties interspersed among the eighty-eights."

The German antiaircraft gun, the *Flakvierling 38,* had four 20mm cannons on the same carriage controlled by one gunner. With a practical firing rate of 800 rounds a minute, it was a weapon to be feared.

Banks did a pilot's head roll, checking the airspace around them for German fighters. Just because the Allies had gained air superiority did not mean the Germans never sent fighters into the air.

Banks spotted his wingman approaching from the north. His recovery from the dive had taken him back to Banks' altitude. Holden would swing around to the west, and then slide back into position on Banks' left, where he would stay for the duration of the attack.

More explosions dotted the earth. Red three and four made it safely through the flak.

Banks was flying his racetrack pattern and was now at the southern end of the battlefield. This meant his White and Blue flights were coming from his left.

White one suddenly vaporized, with a fireball the only remaining clue that a living breathing human had just died. The remaining planes from White dropped their payloads and soared away. White two was now the flight leader and he banked right with the other two pilots following him.

"Blue flight from Dogbone leader. Gun three still standing. Blue one, take it out."

"Roger, Dogbone leader."

Blue one altered his trajectory to the left. By the time he reached the release point, the smoke from the previous explosions had cleared somewhat, just enough and he destroyed the last 88.

"White flight from Dogbone leader, strafe the quads south to north."

Banks wanted to destroy those weapons partly so they couldn't kill any more pilots and partly for revenge on killing his pilot.

"Dogbone leader from Red two. Possible fighters three o'clock, level."

Banks and Holden were now on the northbound part of their racetrack. Banks looked to his right and spotted two specks at the same altitude and about three miles out. "Red two from Dogbone leader. Keep an eye on them."

Banks turned his attention to the bombing attack below.

Blue flight had dropped all of its ordnance and was climbing.

White flight was firing all twenty-four .50 calibers into the line of cannons. As they cleared the ridgeline, Banks was able to take stock of the damage.

"Dogbone squadron from squadron leader. Well done! All targets destroyed. Reassemble at ten thousand. Be aware, two bogies to the east five thousand feet."

"Dogbone leader from Red two. Bogies are 109s. Two only confirmed."

Banks looked to his left now that he was heading south again. The dark silhouettes of the German Messerschmitt 109s had grown larger. Behind Banks, the rest of the squadron formed up on him. The 109s suddenly veered right, curving into a large turn away.

"Dogbone squadron from Dogbone leader. Not all German pilots are stupid. The 109s have turned tail. Let's go home."

Banks slid his stick to the right for a turn to the west and the six-ton P-47 happily responded.

RONN MUNSTERMAN

Chapter 2

Colonel Rupert Jenkins' office – Camp Barton Stacey
Andover, England
8 September, 0730 Hours, London time

A solid six-footer with red hair knocked on the door frame.

"Come in," Colonel Rupert Jenkins said.

Sergeant Malcolm Saunders glided through the door and stopped just short of the desk. He rendered a British Army salute, which his commander returned.

"Sit."

Saunders took a seat and waited.

Forty-two-year-old Jenkins gave Saunders a smile.

It was all Saunders could do not to react in surprise. Jenkins *never* smiled. Saunders wondered whether it was a good thing.

Jenkins was a gruff man by nature and had been the commander of Achnacarry House when Saunders and his men were there, which was the same time as Tom Dunn and his men.

"You and your men acquitted yourselves extremely well at Insel Riems, Saunders."

Saunders blinked. Jenkins was a no-nonsense sort of man, and in Saunders' experience had only given out criticism, never praise. Saunders was used to it and even expected it. What was this? A sudden change of heart? It seemed unlikely.

"Thank you, sir."

Insel Riems was the location of the German biological weapon facility. Saunders and his squad of commandos had captured three of the scientists responsible for the new weapon, as well as an SS major and his driver.

"I just learned that the scientists you captured are being quite forthcoming in their interviews." Jenkins leaned forward and his eyes seemed to sparkle.

Saunders couldn't help himself and raised an eyebrow.

"We're learning a great deal about their methods. They are soon going to be sent to the location where we have the canisters and provide whatever help we need."

At a Paris airfield, Sergeant Tom Dunn, Saunders' U.S. Army Ranger counterpart, had captured ten of the canisters filled with the deadly virus, which was a more efficient killing machine than the Bubonic Plague.

"Very good, sir."

When Jenkins had sent Saunders and his men to Insel Riems, it was with the knowledge that American B-17s were going to obliterate the facility at a prearranged time, regardless of whether the commandos were still on the island. He had suddenly come to realize that, in spite of himself, and of his closely held belief that a commander must distance himself from his men, he truly cared for Saunders and his men and was worried sick that they might be killed. It had been with tremendous relief that he'd taken the phone call telling him their submarine, and the men, had returned from a successful mission.

He understood he was still going to have to make life and death decisions, but he made a conscious choice to alter his behavior toward his men.

"I'm proud of you, Saunders. I just want you to know that."

Saunders sat still for a moment, taking in his commander's odd change and thinking of an appropriate response. Finally, he said, "Thank you, sir. It's our honor to serve under you."

Jenkins' lips curled into a sardonic smile, thinking *but not a pleasure*. He let it pass and said, "I hear nuptials congratulations are in order." Jenkins extended his hand and a surprised Saunders shook it.

How had the colonel found out? "Yes, sir, the twenty-third."

Jenkins nodded. "I'll see what I can do to make sure you're here."

"Thank you."

"The men have everything they need?"

"I believe so, sir."

Jenkins pinched the bridge of his long nose, the one he was often accused of looking down at others. He released his nose. "Have you drawn your replacements from the list?"

Saunders had lost two men, William Endicott and James Pickering, to German soldiers guarding the Insel Riems facility.

"Yes, sir. They should be here this morning."

"Very good. I have orders for your next mission. As I try to do, I leave the planning up to you." Jenkins lifted a set of papers and handed them to his favorite commando.

"The objective is in Belgium, Spa. It's a German Army communications center for Rundstedt's OB West Army Group. We have a spy in the city and he'll meet you and guide you to the location.

"I have a communications expert available and I want you take him along. He is there to see if the Germans have made any changes or improvements to their methods. He can also determine the value of the comm center's messages. His name is Major John Armstrong. Know him?"

"No, sir, I don't."

"I heard good things about him. Gets results. Speaks and reads German, of course."

As far as Saunders was concerned, anything or anyone who helped make a mission successful was okay by him.

Jenkins fiddled with his hands on the desk making Saunders wonder what was coming.

"There is just one little thing about Armstrong. He's never jumped before."

Saunders laughed. "Little thing, sir?"

Jenkins smiled and shrugged his shoulders. "I know you'll manage the problem."

"Certainly, sir." Saunders smiled at his colonel. "Any other little things?"

"Not really. You're due out after midnight tonight."

Saunders nodded, and started reading the papers, which included a map of the area around Spa. When he finished a couple of minutes later, he said, "I don't have any questions other than where will I find this Major Armstrong?"

"More than likely he's over at the communications center. He's expecting you."

"Thank you, sir, I'll track him down."

"I've made him aware in the strongest of terms that he's along for the ride and you are in charge operationally, no questions asked."

"Yes, sir." Saunders mentally thanked Jenkins. These kind of situations could get ugly if the officer suddenly decided he wanted to take control.

"One word of warning. He's a little low on a supply of humor."

Saunders tried to bite his tongue but lost the battle. Keeping his face deadpan, he said, "I've never had to deal with anyone like that, sir. It'll certainly be a new challenge."

Jenkins expression returned to the old Jenkins, pursed lips and a slight raising of the head to look down his long nose at Saunders.

Saunders wondered if he'd gone too far.

The corners of Jenkins' eyes crinkled, which was followed by a hearty guffaw.

Saunders joined in, wondering what had caused such a change in his commander. Finally done laughing, Jenkins stood up and reached across the desk to shake Saunders' hand.

"Good luck, old chap."

"Thank you, sir."

"Let me know if you need anything."

"I will."

Saunders left Jenkins' office and went outside. He spent a few seconds deciding whether to go ahead and walk over to the communications center, or to go grab Steve Barltrop first. He chose the latter and headed off toward the squad's barracks.

After pulling Barltrop away from cleaning his Sten submachine gun, Saunders and his best friend, and second in command, walked all the way back to the communications center. On the way, Saunders told Barltrop about Jenkins' behavior change.

Barltrop turned his blue eyes toward his friend. He was sizing up Saunders' expression to see if he was trying to pull a quick one over on him. Unable to see any clues, he finally asked, "You're having me on, right?"

"No. That's what really happened. Very strange after all this time. He even said he'd try to make sure I'd be here for my wedding day."

"Blimey."

"And then a little later, he laughed."

"He laughed? At something funny?"

"Aye."

"Blimey. He must need some rest and recreation."

"Well, I sure don't understand it."

Both men shook their heads at the changing puzzle of Colonel Jenkins.

Saunders changed the subject and gave Barltrop a brief on the upcoming mission, including the addition of Major Armstrong and his lack of humor.

"Oh goodie. A humorless Major. Just what we need."

Saunders raised an eyebrow, tilted his head to the left, and shrugged his shoulders.

"He also has never jumped."

"We have to teach him to jump in one day?" Barltrop looked askance at Saunders.

"Aye."

"Bloody hell."

When the two commandos reached the communications center and started up the wooden steps, the door suddenly burst open and a short, thin major stepped out onto the porch. He was carrying two hard briefcases. He stopped when he saw the big red-headed Saunders. His face was as thin as his body, but he had large brown eyes that gave him a sorrowful puppy dog look.

"Sergeant Saunders, I presume?"

The commandos saluted, which caused a problem for the major because he had a case in each hand. He set down the one in his right hand and returned the salute.

"Yes, sir. I'm Saunders and this is Steve Barltrop, my second in command."

"Armstrong. Pleased to meet you both. I'll walk with you."

The men started off toward the barracks, Armstrong took up a position on the right of the two commandos.

They walked along in silence for a few minutes, and then the major cleared his throat. Without turning his head, he asked, "Saunders, do you know what the Nazis eat for breakfast?"

Saunders looked puzzled at the odd question. "I'm afraid not, Major."

"Luftwaffles!"

When Saunders looked at the major, the man was grinning ear to ear. Saunders smiled, which seemed to encourage the man.

"Knock knock."

Like everyone, Saunders first learned about these kind of jokes about ten years ago. "Who's there?"

"Banana."

"Banana who?"

"Knock knock."

This was a slight breach of the rules by not giving the punchline after the first 'who.'

Saunders sighed. "Who's there?"

"Banana.

"Banana who?"

"Knock knock."

"Who's there?"

"Orange."

Barltrop was leaning around Saunders to see and hear better.

"Orange who?" Saunders asked.

"Orange you glad I didn't say banana again?"

The major laughed out loud and the commandos groaned, then grudgingly joined in.

Armstrong looked at Saunders. "Let me guess. Colonel Jenkins told you I have no sense of humor."

"Why, yes, sir, he did. How'd you know?"

"He was just setting you up. We share jokes all the time. Right now, I imagine he's cackling to himself in his office."

"I see."

Armstrong's expression turned serious. "Don't worry, Sergeant, I won't tell any jokes at inappropriate moments."

"Of course, sir. The colonel didn't mention knowing you."

Armstrong grinned again. "No, he wouldn't have wanted to give away anything."

"No, sir, I guess not."

"So which of you will be teaching me how to parachute?"

Saunders lifted a hand and pointed in Barltrop's direction.

Armstrong slowed down and stepped back up to walk on Barltrop's left.

"So what's it like staring out at nothing but sky? What's it feel like on that first step? Is it like jumping off a wall?"

Barltrop shot a frown toward Saunders and mouthed, "I'll get you for this."

Saunders just smiled.

Chapter 3

Just north of Marieulles, France
2 ¼ miles east of the Moselle River
7 September, 1445 Hours, Paris time

The assembly area for the jump off to defend the Moselle River near Arnaville was crawling with German soldiers of the 462nd Division, a member of which was *Oberfeldwebel,* master sergeant, Dieter Wittenberg. He was a platoon leader, such as it was. His entire company was made up of one-third old men, one-third young men who had just finished their time at the military school in Metz, and one-third men recovering from their wounds received on the eastern front. A hodge-podge unit.

After the defeat in and around the Falaise Gap, where the Germans had lost fifty thousand men and an untold quantity of equipment, including tanks and artillery, the German army was in disarray and Wittenberg's company was by no means an isolated arrangement.

Wittenberg had previously served in Normandy, among the hedgerows, where he'd performed extremely well with accurate fire and directing his platoon perfectly in attacks and counterattacks on the Americans, who seemed to be baffled by the monstrous hedgerows. He'd been selected for this company, as were the other leaders, because their units had ceased to exist in the Falaise gap.

At thirty-one, Wittenberg was the old man in the group of four regular army survivors, and he was two years older than the man tagged for the company commander's slot. Wittenberg was a Berlin native, but hadn't been home since late 1943, when his unit, whole at the time, was traveling west from the debacle of the eastern front. His uniform was filthy, and his face carried the week-old scruff from not being able to shave. He hoped to shave today.

Wittenberg's father taught Literature at the University of Berlin, and young Dieter grew up with world literature. His parents had made sure he had gone to college where he followed in his father's footsteps and studied German, British, and American Literature, and he'd graduated with honors in 1935. From there he began work on his advanced degrees, finishing his doctorate in 1939, the May prior to the invasion of Poland. Against his parents' wishes, he'd signed up the next month because he was sure he would have been conscripted anyway.

Wittenberg was with the company commander, *Hauptmann,* captain, Horst Alsdorf, and the other two platoon leaders, Bernard Mekelburg and Conrad Raupp. All four men were about the same height and weight. All had blue eyes and once-upon-a-time blond hair, which was now a dirt encased brown.

With all the vehicle and foot traffic on the road nearby, the commander pulled his men into someone's front yard, where they promptly sat down on the inviting grass.

The *Hauptmann* unfolded a map and laid it on the ground. "The Americans are expected to make bridges near Arnaville. Once they do that, they'll expand the bridgehead on the east side of the river. This hill," he touched a spot on the map, "is southeast of their bridgehead. You can see the hill splits the advance eastward; one route is southeast toward Arry and the other is northeast toward Metz. That's where we will stop their advance, holding them in place for our tanks and artillery."

"Where exactly is our position?" Wittenberg asked. He didn't like the looks of the path they were blocking, it was very rocky, and steep, and would be difficult to successfully perform a fighting retreat.

When *Hauptmann* Alsdorf showed the men the spot, it was far downhill.

"Isn't that too close?" Wittenberg asked.

Alsdorf gave Wittenberg a seething look. "It is where we will be."

"Yes sir."

"Any other criticisms?" Alsdorf glanced at the other two platoon leaders, who both seemed content to let Wittenberg take the brunt of the *Hauptmann's* anger as they shook their heads.

The *Hauptmann* got to his feet, putting away the map. The other three soldiers joined him. "Go get your men ready. Wittenberg, you stay."

After the two men left, Alsdorf turned to his senior platoon leader. "Don't question me like that in front of the men again."

Wittenberg started to defend himself. He was accustomed to doing that because his previous company commander had demanded it. Instead, he said, "Of course, sir. My apologies."

Alsdorf nodded. "Dismissed."

Wittenberg saluted and departed to go look for his men.

He'd walked about fifty meters when the other two platoon leaders, Mekelburg and Raupp, stepped from a doorway into his path.

Wittenberg sighed, preparing for the coming bullshit. He'd only known these two fanatical, card-carrying Nazis for a couple of days and he already despised them.

The two men looked at Wittenberg with loathing in their eyes. They had just graduated from the Officer Candidate School in Metz, but they had previously seen lots of action on the eastern front. They were good soldiers whose judgement tended to be clouded by the megalomaniacal teachings of Adolf Hitler. They would automatically default to overestimating their unit's capability while downplaying the enemy's, just like their beloved *Führer*. Wittenberg had already seen it a few times in previous meetings, although this morning they had been curiously silent. More often than not, they made Wittenberg think of the optimistic American novel character, Pollyanna, but without the charm.

Raupp spoke first, "You haven't learned to just follow orders have you?"

"Asking questions is a mark of intelligence. I note neither of you ever ask any questions."

"Are you calling us stupid?"

"Wear it if it fits."

Raupp's jaw clenched and Wittenberg spotted it.

"You make us all look bad, and disloyal with your crazy questions." This was from Mekelburg, who had slid a little closer and to Wittenberg's right. Standard procedure for a street fight.

"You are certainly capable of looking bad entirely on your own."

"You'd better take us serious."

Wittenberg scoffed. "Take you serious? You're nothing but Nazi street thugs in command of other Germans who depend on you to keep them alive."

"It isn't our job to keep them alive, but to use them in whatever way best suits the needs of the *Führer*."

"Step aside." Wittenberg had had enough. It was time to put an end to their stupidity.

"Make us." Raupp said with a sneer.

"You're both cowards. You'd prefer to fight your own countryman than kill Americans. What do you think the Party would think of that?"

At that moment, a couple of trucks rumbled by, filled with the very young faces of newly minted recruits.

"It'd be your word against the two of us," Mekelburg said.

"And so it would be."

Wittenberg took a lightning fast step toward Mekelburg, who was on his right, and simply kicked the man in the nuts.

Mekelburg collapsed holding his stuff and screaming, and then crying.

Wittenberg swung his left arm toward Raupp's throat, who blocked upward with his left arm.

With his right hand, Wittenberg grabbed Rapp's tunic and yanked the man toward Wittenberg's right.

As the man's upper body began to follow, Wittenberg swept his right leg into Raupp's left ankle, which was now bearing the over balanced load. Raupp fell onto his face with an *oof* of expelled air. To finish him off, Wittenberg rolled him over and short-punched the fallen man's solar plexus. What little air was left shot out in a grunt.

Wittenberg stood up and looked around. Amazingly, no one was in sight, the trucks were gone.

As the two men writhed on the ground, Wittenberg leaned over and said in a growl, "Don't ever fuck with me again, or you'll get worse. And just in case you idiots get to thinking about it, remember, I have more friends here than you do."

Wittenberg walked away, whistling.

Chapter 4

In the woods
2 miles west of Spa, Belgium
8 September, 0154 Hours

Saunders had been worried during the entire flight to Belgium that Major Armstrong would land badly and injure himself, but the major had landed and rolled just the way Barltrop had taught him in one afternoon.

"How do you feel after your flight, Major?" Saunders asked.

Armstrong was grinning ear to ear. "Quite exhilarating, I must say!"

The major had been an attentive student while Barltrop had taught him the basics of parachuting, and then even got in a couple of practice jumps, but those were in the daytime.

The men were gathered in a woods west of Spa. They had buried their parachutes and covered the freshly turned earth with fallen leaves.

The front line lay about sixty or seventy miles to the southwest and the German border was only fifteen miles to the east. Spa was a sprawling city covering an area one mile by a half mile in size. It was hemmed in on the north by a two-hundred-foot-tall hill whose long axis ran east-west.

The jump had been from low-altitude to reduce the Germans' opportunity to spot them on the way down. Not for the first time, Saunders wondered why the parachutes couldn't be dyed black. Being so far behind the German line had one advantage: fewer patrols. The disadvantage: lots of Germans just going from place to place, although not so much in the middle of the night.

Saunders' squad counted nine men plus himself, and one more for the major. All were kneeling under the cover of the trees, which allowed just enough moonlight in so the men could see each other fairly well, considering all of their faces were camouflaged with black grease. Only the whites of their eyes stood out clearly.

The commandos were armed with their usual 9mm Sten submachine guns with suppressors. They also carried the Webley Mk VI .455 caliber revolver. Each man carried four grenades and in special pouches on their belts, two pounds of plastic explosive. The wires, detonators, and timers were stored in separate pouches safely away from the explosive bars.

Steve Barltrop, the second in command, was to Saunders' left. Continuing left around the semi-circle were the rest of the squad. Two replacements fresh from the British Commando school at Achnacarry House in Scotland, Bernard Thurston and Francis Handford had arrived just in time to get acquainted with everyone. Thurston was a short, thick man built for power, not speed, while Handford was the opposite, tall, at six-two, and slender.

Geoffrey Kopp, a Cockney like Saunders, was gaining the reputation as a perfect mimic of the sergeant. George Mills hailed from Manchester. Edward Redington was the son of a pastor and did all the prayer leading for the squad. Arthur Garner was the master of demolitions. Tim Chadwick was a fisherman's son and could pilot anything on the water. Christopher Dickinson entertained the squad with his magic tricks.

In just a couple of months, Saunders had lost five men in battle, and two had been transferred to other squads for their personal advancement in the ranks. Of the original ten-man squad who graduated together from Achnacarry House, only five remained: Saunders, Barltrop, Chadwick, Dickinson, and Mills. Saunders couldn't take the time to dwell on the losses; too much depended on him staying sharp, but the writing of the letters to his men's parents and loved ones was always difficult.

"We're about two miles from where we think the communication center is located. We'll meet our contact about a mile from here. Only Chadwick and me will go to that meeting, just in case he's either followed or is not really on our side."

"Remind me again how we are getting home from deep in enemy territory?" Dickinson asked with a smirk.

"Oh, yes, right. Thanks old chap. We'll hook up with Monty's bunch when they come roaring through here in a few days."

Dickinson looked affronted. "You mean we're being rescued by Monty? How embarrassing."

"Not in the least. We are the advance guard!"

Dickinson put a hand over his heart. "I'm so proud."

The squad chuckled even though each man, including Major Armstrong, understood fully what Saunders and Dickinson were doing to loosen up the men. It did help, but the fact remained that they were on their own. There was no escape plan. They would have to not only destroy the communications center, but then run and hide and not get captured by the angry hornets' nest they would have poked with a stick.

"Any questions, anyone?" Saunders asked.

The men all shook their heads.

"Right. Off we go. Barltrop has point."

Barltrop took off to the northeast and the rest of the men fell in line, keeping a two-yard interval. Saunders was last and he had put Major Armstrong just in front of himself.

A man ran through the woods as fast as possible while praying he wouldn't knock himself out on an unseen tree branch and he would be in time.

Chapter 5

Rock Island Arsenal
M1 Garand Rifle Final Assembly Department
Rock Island, Illinois
8 September, 7:03 P.M. U.S. Central Time

The Rock Island Arsenal's beginnings dated back to the Civil War, when ground was broken for construction. In 1863, a prison was built for Confederate prisoners of war and eventually over 12,000 were housed there. The arsenal's first challenge was the Spanish-American War and it continued producing everything from small arms to World War I type tanks in the years since.

The Mississippi River island on which the arsenal was located was two and a half miles long by eight-tenths of a mile wide. There was one bridge that crossed north to Davenport, Iowa, and two that went south to Illinois; one to Rock Island and the other Moline.

Gertrude Dunn put the final screw in place to finish her M1 rifle. She lifted it from the work bench and with her right hand on the stock grip, she held it at port arms just as she'd been taught. With her left thumb she activated the bolt to view the chamber, which glistened with a light sheen of oil. She released the bolt and it clicked shut, and then she laid the weapon down on her workbench. She pried open the little door on the butt, and then carefully inserted the folding cleaning rod, a small bottle of oil, and a small package of cleaning pads. Before closing the door, she picked up the 'assembled by' piece of paper and signed her first name and wrote down her employee number. She thought for a moment, then added a tiny drawing of lips kissing. Smiling, she folded it carefully and slipped it into the storage space, and then closed the door.

She picked up the rifle and gently placed it on the slow moving belt just beyond her workbench. It immediately started traveling along the belt toward the quality inspectors at the end of the line. She wasn't worried about it passing inspection; she knew for certain it was perfectly assembled. She didn't even need the sheets of paper showing how to properly assemble one Rifle M1 Garand. Her memory was photographic, a trait she shared with her older brother, Tom.

The running family joke about the Dunn children's smarts and good grades went like this: If a teacher or new acquaintance would ask where the children got their brains, Mrs. Dunn would immediately answer that they all got their brains from their father since she still had hers . . . chuckle, chuckle.

Gertrude just graduated from high school the past May, and got hired at the Rock Island Arsenal in late August. She went through a week-long training program and then was assigned to the M1 manufacturing department. Almost all of her coworkers were women, many near her own age of eighteen, but some in their twenties and a few in their thirties.

They were managed by a Mr. Ted Hays, who always tried to come off gruff and no-nonsense, and even unpleasant. It didn't quite work because it wasn't truly his nature, and the girls called him Teddy Bear behind his back.

Gertrude stole a glance at the clock on the far wall; only twenty more minutes of her twelve hour shift, getting off at seven-thirty p.m. She would have ample time to complete one more rifle, and then clean her work area.

As she assembled the rifle, she thought about her mom and dad back home in Cedar Rapids, Iowa, ninety miles away. School had started, so her dad was in the first stages of the new school year. He taught math, which Gertrude had shown an aptitude for, much to her father's delight. Neither Tom nor the eldest sister, Hazel, had any interest in polynomials or geometry proofs. They did well enough in the subject to earn A's, but they were low A's; Gertrude earned high A's, in the neighborhood of ninety-eight percent.

Both parents had encouraged their kids to go to college. Hazel fell in love and got married at nineteen instead, Tom dropped out his senior year of college to enlist after Pearl Harbor, and Gertrude had explained that she wanted to do something important for the war effort. She said she would go to college after the war was over and Tom was back home. When she'd said that, she noticed the meaningful glance her dad had given her mom. She knew they were worried she was getting her hopes up. Parents up and down the street had been getting the awful War Department telegrams since 1941, including Gertrude's best friend, Margie, whose oldest brother, Sam, had been killed at Pearl Harbor, one of the more than eleven hundred sailors entombed on the USS *Arizona*. Margie had cried for weeks after, and was almost sent away to an institution, when she had suddenly recovered and vowed to join the Navy herself when she was old enough.

Instead, Gertrude and Margie cooked up the plan to go to work at the arsenal and they were roommates. Gertrude had found a rooming house in Davenport. The house was on Iowa Street, which she liked, and if she missed the bus, it was only about a two-mile walk home. Although it was uphill going home—Davenport was a river town, after all.

The shift over, Gertrude changed clothes in the women's locker room, and waited for Margie outside. Gertrude wore a pale green dress that went just below the knees. She carried a small black purse, which contained what little money she had and her driver's license, and a brush, and red lipstick, which she hadn't bothered to put on so late at night. Her shoes were simple black pumps, and her legs were bare; no one had nylons any more. It had taken some effort to get her light brown, curly hair plumped back into acceptable shape after taking off the work hat. Her brown eyes resembled her brother Tom's as did her long slim nose.

Margie joined her best friend. "Hey, kiddo," she said.

"Hey, yourself."

They joined arms and walked away from the building, took a right and followed the sidewalk a short block to the bus stop, where a large number of other tired women waited, some smoking cigarettes.

"How was your day?" Gertrude asked.

"Teddy Bear came by once when I fell behind because the trigger assembly wasn't right and it wouldn't lock into place."

"What did he say?"

"At first he tried to blame me. Said I just wasn't doing it right. I mentioned that I'd been doing it right all day with no problems. He finally had Betsy, you know, the shift lead, come over and try it. You should have seen his expression when Betsy handed the trigger assembly to him and said, 'This has to be reworked. Next time, try believing your girls.' Betsy walked off with him just holding it."

Gertrude laughed. "I would love to have seen that!"

The blue and white city bus pulled up and they got on with the crowd, dropping their tokens into the fare box. The driver, an overweight man in his fifties, said hello to each woman in turn as she boarded. They took a seat near the back; the bus was nearly full because of the end of the shift.

"I'm looking forward to Sunday dinner," Gertrude said. The Dunn's family, like most others, all gathered for a big Sunday lunch. In the Dunn family, on Sundays, lunch was called dinner, and the evening meal was called supper. The rest of the week it was simply lunch and dinner. Mrs. Dunn would do a lot of preparation the night before, so all she had to do was cook everything as soon as they returned home from church except the roast, which would go in the oven before church. The lunch tradition went as far back as Gertrude could remember. When Hazel got married, her husband joined the Dunn family on Sundays. It wasn't until Pearl Harbor when Tom, and Hazel's husband both joined up that the tradition suddenly became not the same. Mrs. Dunn insisted that the tradition would continue with whoever was available. Gertrude had missed two in a row and realized how much she enjoyed them. She would take a train to Iowa City, about thirty miles south of Cedar Rapids, and a bus the rest of the way.

"I'm sure you are."

"Are you sure you don't want to come?"

"I'm sure. I'm going on a picnic."

Gertrude raised her eyebrows. "Who with? You haven't mentioned anyone."

"I'm mentioning him now. Jack Dillard is his name. He's twenty-one and works in the machine shop. You know, the 'skilled workman' type."

"Does he have a car?"

"Yes, but he rarely uses it . . . the gas rationing. He said he would try to save up so we can drive it for the next picnic. Maybe go up on one of the bluffs over the river."

"You worked fast."

"Not really. I wasn't paying any attention to him until one day at lunch he spoke to me. Got me right here." Margie put a fist over her heart.

"Wow. What did he say?" Gertrude turned slightly.

"Pass the salt, please."

Gertrude hit Margie on the shoulder. "Oh, you!"

Margie laughed.

The rest of the bus ride home the two young women chatted comfortably, as childhood friends do.

At one point, Margie did catch Gertrude with a wistful expression on her face. "What's the matter?"

"Hm?"

"Something bothering you?"

"Oh, no. Nothing." Gertrude lied. "I'm fine."

Chapter 6

In the woods
2 miles west of Spa, Belgium
8 September, 0235 Hours, Paris time

If the British spy had thought it through more carefully ahead of time, he might have done things a little bit differently. As it was, he found himself on the ground with a huge commando on his chest and a Sten submachine gun under his chin.

He'd never even seen the British soldiers until he crashed into what he thought was a tree, but was instead actually the man pinning him to the ground. It was getting hard to breathe.

With the little air he could draw, the spy squeaked, "Chantership! Chantership!"

At the code word, Saunders immediately let go of the man and stood up. He extended his hand to help the spy to this feet. "You bloody fooking idiot! What the bloody hell do think you're doing? I could've shot you."

The spy was rubbing his chin where the barrel of the Sten had buried itself pretty deep. He held up his hands to placate the commando. "I know, I'm sorry. Thanks for not shooting me. I just had to find you before you got very far because the Germans have taken over the house where we were supposed to meet."

He looked around at the other commandos, who were simply watching him carefully.

"Well, in that case, thanks," Saunders said, extending his hand again.

The spy shook hands. "Chesley. Lawrence."

"Saunders."

Chesley was a twenty-nine year old who'd grown up in Spa and London. His father owned a machine parts company that had a manufacturing site in both locations. When the Germans overran Belgium in the early days of the war, the family had been in Spa and were unable to immediately escape to London. Through his contacts, Chesley's father had eventually arranged an escape by boat. Lawrence remembered the trip as harrowing; the family had twice almost been caught. He also thought it had been exciting, which was what drew him to Intelligence. The next summer, 1941, he'd had no trouble convincing them of his value: he spoke French like a southern Belgian native, and he knew his way around the country.

He'd started with small missions on his return by parachute to Belgium. First, working with the small, but smart and effective resistance, and then with periodic meetings with German officers gaining their trust. He and Intelligence were very careful with what information they used and how it was used so it would never be traced back to him. So far so good, three years and still alive. Far better than the six-week average life span of the Special Operations Executive men and women in France.

"I have a backup location nearby, but it's in the forest and farther from the target than we planned."

"How far from here?"

"Perhaps five minutes."

Saunders examined the British spy in the light of the half-full moon filtering through the trees. He was about Saunders' own height of six feet, but much lighter, perhaps one hundred sixty pounds. Saunders noted Chesley wore all black clothing and had applied nighttime grease to his face and hands. Nice tradecraft. Other than running headlong into a group of armed men, he seemed to have it together.

Saunders turned to Barltrop, who was standing nearby. "Take point again."

"Yes, Sarge," Barltrop said.

"Mr. Chesley, you go with Mr. Barltrop and show us the way to your backup location. What is it, a cabin?"

"Yes, an old abandoned nineteenth century hunting cabin."

"Off you go."

Within a minute, the men were on their way through the forest, following their new friend, the British spy.

Barltrop was impressed by the man's navigation skills. He made only one course change to a more northerly direction after they crossed a dry stream, and did an excellent job of using the terrain to its best advantage for stealth.

Chesley suddenly stopped and touched Barltrop on the right arm. Barltrop looked at him and Chesley lifted a blackened hand to point. Barltrop spotted the cabin, set in a small clearing just large enough to accommodate the structure. It was about five yards away. It was difficult to see through the trees and underbrush. Barltrop realized that even in daylight a man could walk right past it and never know it was there.

The column of commandos had stopped as soon as Barltrop and the spy did.

Barltrop examined the cabin, whose door faced south, directly in front of them. He checked the roof for any telltale signs of smoke from a heating stove or fireplace; nothing.

Barltrop turned to Chadwick and Mills, who were closest to him, and pointed to the west side of the cabin. The two men nodded and stole off into the trees. Barltrop beckoned for Dickinson to join him. Giving hand signals, Barltrop directed the rest of the squad to form an attack line facing the cabin. Barltrop touched Chesley and motioned for him to stay put. Chesley nodded.

Barltrop and Dickinson stepped closer to the cabin, weapons ready. When they reached the cabin's southeast corner, Barltrop looked for and found Chadwick and Mills positioned at the other corner. There were two windows, one on each side of the door. They were both covered by drapes or curtains.

Barltrop pulled out a small torch and then walked toward the door. Chadwick matched his moves, while Dickinson and Mills stayed back for the better angle on the door.

Barltrop and Chadwick reached the door at the same time. The door would swing open to the right, meaning that Barltrop would enter first to the left.

Chadwick put his hand on the metal latch.

Barltrop nodded.

Chadwick lifted the latch and pushed. The door creaked open.

Barltrop had time to wince at the sound, then rushed in and turned on the torch. He swung the light around the room and quickly discerned the cabin was empty.

"All clear," he said.

Chadwick turned to Dickinson and Mills and said, "Clear." Chadwick faced the woods where he knew the men were even though they were quite invisible and waved them forward. Soon the rest of the squad, plus the British spy and the communications expert, Armstrong, arrived. As the men filed by, Chadwick pulled Mills aside and when everyone was inside, he closed the door.

"Walk a path ten yards out," Chadwick told Mills, who nodded and took off. In seconds he disappeared from sight.

Chadwick set himself up on a circular path five yards from the cabin.

The cabin was about fifteen feet square with a cold fireplace on the east wall. Saunders, Barltrop, Chesley, and Armstrong were gathered around a square, roughhewn wooden table near the fireplace, seated on equally rough, but sturdy chairs. A narrow bed was in the northwest corner with a brown bearskin rug in front of it. Dickinson had claimed the bed, and the rest of the men stretched out on the floor, some on the rug.

"How far exactly are we from the communications center?" Saunders asked.

"About three quarters of a mile straight line." Chesley pulled a map from his pocket, unfolded it, and spread it out on the table. It was a tourist map. Barltrop shone his torch on the paper and Saunders leaned forward.

Chesley poked a spot on the map and said, "Here's the comm center." It was on the extreme western boundary of the city and on the main road that traveled roughly east through the city.

Going west, the road curved to go north as it left Spa and crossed a rail line. The tracks were on the south side of the road in the city, and on its east as it went north.

Chesley slid his finger west-northwest, and stopped about a quarter mile into the forest. "Here's where we are." He pointed to a place on the road, near the railroad crossing. "There's a checkpoint here with two soldiers on duty at all times."

"The terrain north of the city is heavily wooded, just like around us here, and is very hilly, perhaps rising a couple of hundred feet above the road."

Saunders examined the map. "So the comm center's back is to the hill?"

"Correct."

"What kind of activity does it have?"

"There are usually about ten or so people in there. Most are radio operators, but there will be the officer in charge, and two who transcribe messages for the German higher ups. Two guards are stationed outside, mostly just to make sure only authorized people get inside."

"Describe the building."

Chesley pulled a small notebook out of his pocket and tore off a page. He quickly drew the building's layout.

"One story. Used to be a lawyer's office. Two rooms, one on each side of a central hallway, and a loo."

"Back door?"

"Indeed, to the hallway."

"What's where?"

"East room is where the radios are. West room for the commander and the transcribers."

"What about in and out traffic?"

"There are often motorcycle messengers coming in and out and, rarely, officers from General Teuber's Seventh Division headquarters."

"Do you know where the headquarters are?"

"About ten miles south of the city as of yesterday."

"Hm. Right."

"Why do you ask?"

"Just curious. To get the lay of the land."

"Right.

Saunders tapped the map. "Are there sentries behind the building?"

"No, as I said, just at the front door to make sure only authorized people get in. They figure no one would try to come in from the woods."

"Daft buggers, that's the first place anyone with any brains would attack. What about in the woods themselves? Anyone setting up guard posts there, or walking around?"

Chesley looked chagrined. "I've only been through there one time, a few days ago. I didn't see anyone, though."

Saunders patted the man on the shoulder. "Don't worry about it, mate. We'll do our own checking." Saunders sat back in his chair. "Where does the phone wire come into the building?" Saunders asked.

Chesley smiled. He could redeem himself a little perhaps. "Top of the building, street side, southeast corner."

"Any ladders lying around about?"

"Er, no."

"Where's the radio mast?"

"There's one directly on top of the three-story building next door to the east. That's a hotel and houses officers. The Gestapo offices are there."

"Gestapo, huh?"

"Yes."

"How many bad guys are in there?"

"During the day not too many, just the Gestapo agents and a few officers going to and fro, maybe ten to fifteen at a time. Many more at night."

"Where are the officers from?"

"Most from the supply depot east of the city, but some of General Teuber's staff."

Saunders raised an eyebrow at this news and glanced at Armstrong who was nodding enthusiastically.

"Does the general ever go there?"

Chesley was smart enough to follow the logic. "You want to kill the general?"

Saunders ignored the question. "Does he ever go there?"

"Yes. He does. He sleeps there in the bridal suite."

"Every night?"

"Yes."

"Guards?"

"Yes, throughout the hotel."

"When does he leave to go to his headquarters?"

"Seven thirty, after breakfast at seven in the hotel dining room, which is on the street side, southeast quadrant of the first floor."

Saunders looked away for a few moments picturing the set up, and formulating a potential plan. Then he turned back to Chesley and said, "Right. Thanks. Good job on the information."

"You're welcome." Chesley didn't smile, but did appear to be pleased.

Saunders looked at Barltrop. "Any questions, Steve?"

"When is the comm center the busiest? I mean has the most people inside?"

"That's between seven a.m. and about ten o'clock. That's when the day's orders are received and passed along to the individual divisional units."

"Thank you." Barltrop nodded at Saunders, who tipped his chin knowingly. They had their attack window.

Chesley noted the small nonverbal exchange between the squad leader and his second in command. They'd obviously been together a long time. He also made one other easy-to-make deduction. "You're attacking in broad daylight?"

"Yes," Saunders replied.

"Won't that carry higher risks?"

"We want those early morning messages," Major Armstrong spoke for the first time.

"Of course, sir."

"One more question: does the general ever stop by the comm center first before going to his headquarters?" Saunders asked Chesley.

"As a matter of fact, he does drop by there first."

"Good. Thanks." Saunders stood up, and everyone else got up, too. "Time to go, men."

RONN MUNSTERMAN

Chapter 7

Southern outskirts of the village Longchamps-sur-Aire,
France
135 miles due east of Paris
8 September, 0604 Hours

Technical Sergeant Thomas Dunn and his squad sat around a
small cooking fire which warmed their morning coffee. Dunn sat
next to Dave Cross on the south arc of the circle at the six o'clock
position.

"I don't know about you, but I'm damned tired this morning,"
Cross said to his friend.

Twenty-four year old Dunn replied, "Yep, me too." He raised
his metal coffee cup as a pointer. "From the looks of everyone
else, they are, too."

"Hmm. Best keep an eye on them today."

"Yep. I think we're going to move toward the Meuse River.
We'll need to stay sharp."

Somewhere off in the distance were sounds of artillery firing.
Whose was unknown. The battlefield was always filled with
noise.

The previous day's fighting had been odd, sometimes they hit strong resistance and others none at all. The Germans had left a couple of snipers in Longchamps-sur-Aire who had killed a couple of American soldiers before Dave Jones, Jonesy, Dunn's talented sniper, took one out. The other fell victim to a direct hit from a Sherman tank's 76mm round. After that the village was secured and the armored company Dunn had attached to the week before set up for the night.

Dunn was from Cedar Rapids, Iowa. He had been in his senior year at the University of Iowa when the Japanese attacked Pearl Harbor on December 7th, 1941. Dunn dropped out of school and he and his closest friends signed up the next day.

He first saw action during the Battle of Kasserine Pass against Rommel's forces. Even though it had been a colossal American failure, Dunn had earned the Bronze Star for taking over his squad upon the death of the squad leader. He had led the men in destroying a machine gun nest that had been cutting down Americans left and right. It got him an extra stripe, to sergeant. Soon after, he was plucked from the line and sent to the Rangers school run by the British in Achnacarry House, Scotland.

It was there he first met Dave Cross. Dunn was the squad leader, and it took only a few days for Dunn to recognize Cross's talents. He promoted him to corporal and made him the assistant squad leader, a role he'd had ever since. They got along well and also became close friends right away. Sadly, they represented two of the three survivors of that first squad. Six of the others had been killed and one had received the million-dollar wound and was sent home.

Typically, Dunn's squad was assigned to special missions that involved parachuting in and destroying something or preventing the Germans from accomplishing something. Following the most recent mission, saving Paris from the Germans, who were about to release a biological weapon on the city, Dunn had been attached to Patton's Third Army. During a recent communication with his boss, Colonel Mark Kenton, who was located at Camp Barton Stacey, near Andover, England, Dunn had learned that Patton had insisted on having the "son of a bitch who thought of shooting a plane out of the sky with a Sherman tank" working for him for a while. The plane in question was about to deploy the biological weapon. Dunn had spotted the Nazi scientist board the plane with two of the weapon canisters, and as it was taking off, Dunn had convinced the tank commander he was working with to give it try. It had taken the gunner two shots, but when he hit it, the plane vaporized.

The squad was situated in a small field to the south of the village. To the west was a line of trees. Parked nearby to the north was the nine-ton M3 halftrack the squad had been using for transport. The nearest building was about twenty yards farther north, on the opposite side of the armored vehicle. To the east lay open land stretching two miles to a forest that ascended a hill whose peak was about two hundred feet higher than the open land.

Rob Goerdt, the squad's other Iowan, sat at the three o'clock position between Bob Schneider and Leonard Bailey. To Bailey's right were Jonesy and Eugene Lindstrom. Jonesy had his sniper rifle slung over his shoulder; he never left it anywhere out of sight. Lindstrom was Jonesy's spotter and the two men had also become friends.

Directly across from Goerdt at the nine o'clock spot was Clarence Waters. On Waters' left was Alphonso Martelli and the right Stanley Wickham, closing out the circle of rangers. Wickham had the dubious honor of being the third surviving member of the original squad from Achnacarry House.

The morning sky was clear and the air cool, and the men had been sleeping out of doors since leaving Paris a week ago.

"You know what I miss most about England?" twenty-year-old Lindstrom asked.

"The girls," quipped Wickham. He was from Texas and had blended his own drawl with the lilt of British speech patterns. The girls lined up to talk to him, and other things, too.

The men laughed and Lindstrom grinned.

"Okay, the thing I miss second most?"

"The food?" This came from Waters.

Lindstrom looked aghast. "Not the food."

Several men shrugged their shoulders.

"Quonset huts."

The men groaned. Back at Camp Barton Stacey, they lived in one of the metal arched wonders. Not exactly the Ritz.

Lindstrom grinned and said, "What?"

No one replied to that one.

Waters was staring at Lindstrom, trying to get him to make eye contact so he could give him a jovial finger. Suddenly, over Lindstrom's shoulder an explosion spewed dirt into the air about five hundred yards away. Waters sat up straighter. A few seconds later, another round exploded, this time only three hundred yards away and on a straight line toward them. Waters jumped to his feet shouting, "Take cover!" He pointed to the east. "They're walking them up to us!" He grabbed and pulled and pushed anyone nearby toward the halftrack. They needed to get behind it and then into the village. The men dropped their coffee cups and grabbed their weapons.

The men were running full speed away from their previous position, Waters was last after making sure all the others were safely away. A German round landed thirty yards away and exploded. The men dived into the dirt on the far side of the armored vehicle. Shrapnel pinged off the halftrack sounding like machine gun bullets striking the metal. When the shrapnel sounds stopped, the men rose and sprinted toward the buildings twenty yards away. They made it to the west side of a three-story stone house when another round struck the halftrack, leaving behind nothing but a twisted burning hulk of metal with the rubber front tires on fire.

The artillery stopped firing.

The squad gathered around Waters, staring at him with eyes wide. When Waters had first arrived in the squad, one of four replacements from another ranger squad, he'd made a poor impression on the group at dinner mouthing off about a rumor that Dunn was getting the Medal of Honor. Wickham had set him straight, but Waters was still digging himself out of the hole for it.

The men patted Waters on the back and one by one shook his hand, giving him a solemn nod before stepping aside. Dunn went last and while shaking hands, spotted red on Water's right leg.

"Here, you're bleeding. Sit down. Let's take a look."

"Huh?" Waters looked down. The calf portion of his right pants leg was soaked with blood. "Oh. Okay."

He sat down.

Dunn and Wickham knelt beside the injured man. Together they got his pants leg pulled up far enough to see the wound, which was bleeding heavily. Working as a team, the two rangers cleaned and dressed the wound, a fairly deep gash across the side of the leg. It was technically a graze because the flaming hot metal had not embedded itself, but had instead tore along the leg, leaving behind a quarter-inch wide gouge.

"You'll be okay," Dunn said when they finished. "How's it feel?"

"It burns."

"You want to go the aid station?"

"No need, Sarge. I'm good to go." There was no way Waters was going to make himself look weak.

Dunn patted him on the shoulder and stood up. He extended his hand and helped Waters to his feet. "Walk around a bit."

Waters did as he was told. He tried not to limp, but the leg *was* weak. He gave a wane smile. "I'll be okay."

Dunn nodded. "You saved a lot of lives, Clarence. I'm grateful, and proud of you." Dunn spoke loud enough for the entire squad to hear. He believed praise should be loud.

"Thanks, Sarge." Waters beamed. He glanced around at the other men and for the first time really, truly understood what it was all about. The bond of men in combat. He'd largely been going through the motions, and never felt much of anything toward the men around him. Their expressions told him he had done something important. He wondered if it was the first time in his life. He decided he liked the feeling and vowed it would not be the last. He nodded, more to himself than to the others.

Dunn let the moment sit for a bit, and then said, "Waters, did you see where the artillery was firing from?"

Waters shook his head. "No, but it has to be up on that hill."

Dunn turned to Schneider, who acted as the radioman. Dunn grinned. Schneider had had the presence of mind to grab his weapon *and* the radio.

"Come with me, let's call in some of our own artillery. The rest of you, hang out here."

Dunn and the six-foot-four Schneider made their way to a place next to a building where they could see the hill two miles away. Dunn raised a pair of binoculars to his eyes. A field ran up the hill and terminated at another tree line.

It was the tree line he was interested in. It was where he would place artillery. His guess proved right because he finally spotted a couple of men moving around. He focused on the area around them and there was the gun. He tried to locate more guns, but couldn't. He lowered the glasses and pulled out a map. After he located the Germans' position, he said, "Make the call, Bob."

When the call was answered, Dunn gave the coordinates to the artillery officer.

"Should be a few minutes."

The men waited.

A single American cannon fired from somewhere to their west. The spotting round hit the hill about halfway up.

"Plus one hundred fifty," Dunn said into the handset.

The second round landed just short of the target.

"Plus ten. Fire for effect."

About a half dozen cannon fired this time. Dunn imagined the 105mm rounds screaming overhead. Multiple explosions destroyed the German gun and shredded the trees, some of which toppled over.

Dunn waited for the smoke and dust to clear to be sure, and then said, "Target eliminated. Good job."

The artillery officer signed off and Dunn gave the handset back to Schneider.

"Good job, Sarge."

Dunn grinned. "All in a day's work."

Schneider smiled back. He admired Dunn and loved working for him. Schneider was an army brat, and had grown up on many different bases around the United States. He was only nineteen, but extremely bright, and had learned early in high school that languages were easy for him. He was fluent in German and French, and acted as translator for Dunn whenever necessary. He had been the first to understand the implications of some top secret German documents they'd found.

The squad had set up an ambush for General Erwin Rommel, but just as Jonesy pulled the trigger a lone Spitfire had strafed the general's staff car causing it to crash. Rommel had been thrown from the vehicle, but his passenger had died from the strafing.

Dunn had recovered the man's briefcase from the car's backseat. The end result of finding the papers was the destruction of the Germans' new secret weapon, an electromagnetic pulse that would render Allied vehicles inoperable.

"Let's head back," Dunn said.

When they returned to the men, the squad was busy cleaning their weapons.

Dunn waved at Cross, who finished up with his .45 caliber Thompson submachine gun, the rangers' weapon of choice. The eleven pound Thompson could fire 700 rounds a minute with an effective range of fifty yards, making it an excellent weapon for street warfare.

Cross joined Dunn, who offered him a Lucky Strike cigarette. They both lit up and drew in the nicotine. Dunn pulled on Cross's arm to put more distance between them and the rest of the men.

"I'm thinking about putting Waters' name in for a commendation. Any thoughts?"

Cross glanced over at Waters, who was talking animatedly with Jonesy, a first. "I agree. His eyes are different. I think it suddenly came together for him."

"I noticed that, too. The light bulb finally came on."

"Ayup." Cross was originally from Maine and spoke like a true Nor'easter. The son of a fisherman, he looked forward to the day he would rejoin his father on the Atlantic Ocean.

"We're going to need new transport. We'll be lucky to get another halftrack."

"Ayup."

"I'll see if I can track down logistics. Want to tag along?"

"Ayup."

Dunn punched his friend in the arm. "You need to increase your vocabulary, son."

"Ayup."

Grinning, the men took off in search of a new ride.

RONN MUNSTERMAN

Chapter 8

Spa, Belgium
8 September, 0701 Hours

It started raining not long after Saunders and his men left the hunting cabin, not heavy, but steady. All of the men put on their ponchos except Chesley, who was already wearing a long coat and broad-brimmed hat. The wet trek across the Belgian countryside, or more accurately, the hilly forest north and northwest of Spa, was at times a bit treacherous. It finally stopped raining after a couple of hours, long after the men arrived at their first stop just north of the city. The trip had been without incident and crossing the road running north from Spa had been no problem.

Spa was located in the Ardennes Forest and the German Army had established its World War I headquarters there in 1918. Henry VIII had made Spa famous for its healing waters in the first half of the sixteenth century. Royal visitors included Charles II and Peter the Great, and other wealthy Europeans visited, which eventually helped earn Spa the name "The Café of Europe." Huge numbers of British visitors in the nineteenth century led to many local names sounding English. The Duke of Wellington spent so much time there with Prime Minister Benjamin Disraeli, that one of the two hundred springs was named after him.

Saunders picked a stopping point about three hundred yards north of the city. He had sent Barltrop and Dickinson ahead to scout out the communications center and the two commandos returned to the squad after an hour.

"What'd you find?" Saunders asked Barltrop.

Saunders was crouched next to an oak tree with a trunk as wide as his shoulders. Chesley and Armstrong stood nearby trying to stay warm in the chilly Belgian morning air.

Barltrop shouldered his Sten gun's strap, letting the weapon hang barrel down under his right armpit. He tipped his head in the spy's direction and said, "It's as Mister Chesley said. One story, building next door is three. Large radio mast on top of the three-story. The comm center is last building on the west. Open ground of about twenty yards between the woods and the back of the buildings, fairly steep, but manageable. Wet ground could cause some problems on the way down and back up."

Saunders spoke to Chesley. "What's the weather forecast? We heard probably clear."

"Yes. Sunshine and about sixty degrees Fahrenheit."

Saunders nodded, then asked Barltrop, "What else, Steve?"

"Lots of windows on both buildings facing the woods. No way to prevent someone from just glancing out and seeing us. Got to move quick. No sentries in motion while we were there. Comm center's back door is middle of the building like Mister Chesley described. Wood, no glass. Opens outward. No porch. Two trash bins for burning off to our left. Building next door also has middle door, similar to the comm center. Third building is two-story, has bars across all the windows, and the back door looks to be metal." Barltrop looked at Chesley. "Bank?"

Chesley nodded. "Yes."

"What time does it open?" Saunders asked.

"Nine a.m."

Saunders checked his watch: 0707 hours. Plenty of time to get situated. Once again he pictured the buildings.

Saunders rose from his crouch. "Right. Men gather around. Here's what we're doing."

The rest of the squad joined the small group of Saunders, Barltrop, Armstrong, and Chesley.

Saunders laid out the plan. At one point he asked Chesley, "Can you do that?"

The spy nodded.

Saunders repeated the plan once more, asking the men if they had any questions. The answer was 'no.'

Saunders checked his watch again: 0712. "Mills, take point. Steve, tail end. Mr. Chesley, Major Armstrong, you're with me."

The men arranged themselves and Mills took off toward their target.

As they walked, Saunders was taken by the silence of the forest. It was as if the rain had dampened sound in addition to everything it touched.

The men carried their Stens barrel-down in case the rain picked up again, although the bits of sky they could see were clearing. Everyone eyed the forest to the right and left as they advanced, watching for any sign of Germans. It was downhill, and as Barltrop said, was getting steeper by the yard.

Eventually, Mills stopped and knelt behind a birch tree. He was a few yards from the edge of the forest. Saunders stepped closer to his commando and knelt behind Mills' right shoulder. They both examined the buildings.

All appeared to be quiet, but Saunders imagined where people actually would be at this time: radio operators sitting listening and writing, the commander in another room with the transcribers, General Teuber finishing his breakfast. He turned around to face Chesley and gave him a "go ahead" sign.

The spy nodded and took off to the east staying several yards inside the tree line. He was to work his way down to a spot where there was a small alleyway between two buildings, then come back to a point across from the comm center. He would give Saunders' man on the roof a high sign when the general entered the building, which would trigger the attack.

Saunders waved to Chadwick and Dickinson and they came forward quietly.

Saunders waited until Chesley was out of sight and checked his watch: 0721. He patted Chadwick and Dickinson on their shoulders.

The two men advanced to the edge of the forest. They eyed the ground between them and the comm center and then checked the building's windows. They saw no movement.

Chadwick whispered, "Three, two, one!"

They ran in a crouch as fast as possible to the back of the building. They stopped between the back door and a window on the west half of the building. The roof's parapet was about twelve feet above them. They shouldered their weapons. Dickinson cupped his hands and Chadwick stepped into the stirrup and launched himself up as Dickinson lifted. Chadwick transferred his feet to his friend's shoulders.

Dickinson kept his mouth shut, but promised himself to needle Chadwick later about his weight.

Chadwick realized he couldn't quite get a grip on the parapet because it was still wet from the rain. He noticed that the window frame stuck out from the wall a couple of inches, with the bricks turned skinny side out for an aesthetic appearance. He lifted his right foot and got the boot onto the small ledge.

Dickinson, who had the unfortunate view of his friend's ass from below, saw what Chadwick was doing and grabbed the man's left ankle with both hands and lifted. It was just the boost Chadwick needed. He grabbed the parapet and pulled himself up so his waist lay on the edge. He maneuvered himself the rest of the way over and gently let his feet touch the flat roof. He crouched and eyed his surroundings. The hotel next door rose a couple of floors higher. Unfortunately, there were windows everywhere and he had a moment of worry, but there was nothing that could be done about it. He leaned back over the wall and looked down at Dickinson, and gave a thumbs-up. Dickinson nodded and leaned against the wall. He looked toward where he knew Saunders was and held his thumb up in front of his chest. He crouched for the wait.

Chadwick ran toward the hotel wall and when he reached it, continued toward the street. When he was about ten feet from the front of the structure, he spotted the phone line angling down from a pole on the street. He made it to the front parapet and knelt behind it staying low. He removed his Brodie helmet and set it down quietly. Slowly he raised his head until he could see down onto the sidewalk across the street. He glanced to the left and spotted a man walking west. He was wearing a dark raincoat and a broad brimmed hat, Chesley.

Chesley walked at a slow pace, as if just out for a walk, which he had been doing for the past few days while on his reconnaissance trips. That had the beneficial side effect of getting the guards used to seeing him on the street.

Dickinson watched Chesley advance slowly toward a position directly across the street from the comm center. His ears picked up the sound of a car engine off to the east. Within seconds, a black car screeched to a halt right next to a surprised Chesley.

Two men jumped out of the car.

Chesley took a quick step back.

One of the men ran forward to grab the spy.

Chesley reached inside his coat and yanked out a revolver. He fired into the man, who fell to the pavement. The other man started to reach inside his jacket, but Chesley shot him, too.

The crack of a high-powered rifle shot sounded, coming from right below Chadwick.

Chesley dropped to the ground, dead with a bullet through the head.

RONN MUNSTERMAN

Chapter 9

British Field Hospital
4 miles southwest of the Eiffel Tower
8 September, 0715 Hours

At the first sound of the patient's hysterical screaming, Pamela Dunn took off at a run, moving as fast as possible in a tent ward filled with horribly injured soldiers. She stopped at the medicine cabinet, grabbed a syringe and a bottle, and resumed her run down the ward.

She found the terrified young man at the farthest end of the ward. He was tearing the gauze wrapping his leg stump. He'd already ripped off the end and was digging his fingernails into the flap of skin sewn over the stump.

Pamela looked over her shoulder and spotted someone who could help. "Billy! Billy!"

When the orderly looked at her, and saw she was running, he didn't wait for an explanation, he took off.

Pamela reached the patient and tried to get a grip on his wrist, but they were bloody, and her hands kept slipping off. She changed tack and stepped around the cot and pushed against his shoulders, trying to get him to lie down. He fought too hard and she couldn't do it.

Billy arrived and his additional weight did the trick. They got the man on his back, where Billy held him down, arms crossed over his chest. The soldier's face was a tear-filled mask of pain, and his eyes rolled wildly around in their sockets.

Pamela stepped back, while Billy held the patient down, and drew some morphine into the syringe. She swabbed a spot on his right bicep with alcohol and then injected the dose. The patient didn't even react to the needle stick, but in a few seconds, his eyes closed and his rapid breathing slowed.

"Right. Thanks ever so much, Billy."

"You're welcome, Mrs. Dunn. Want me to get you some new gauze and tape?"

"If you would."

"Be right back."

While she waited for the new wrapping material, Pamela got what she needed to clean the patient's leg. After washing it gently, she examined the sutures. Some of them had been torn loose completely, and was the cause of all the bleeding. She would need a doctor to re-sew them.

Billy returned with the gauze and tape, and she told him to get a doctor to fix the torn sutures.

After the doctor left and the skin flap was repaired, Pamela covered the patient with a clean sheet, tucking him in and then adding a blanket. She would have to tell Agnes, her supervisor, so everyone would be able to keep an eye on the patient to prevent him from damaging himself again.

After washing her hands, she decided to make the rounds of the other wounded men in the tent.

She stopped first to check on an American pilot who'd been wounded in flight and had barely made it back to his base south of Paris. He'd had antiaircraft shrapnel removed from his lower back, including one piece that had severed his spinal cord at the tenth thoracic disc. He didn't know yet what was in store for him.

Pamela read his chart. The numbers looked okay. She also read his name: Lieutenant Elmer Cooper.

The man was drowsy, but when he heard the rustling of the chart papers, he opened his eyes fully and stared at Pamela.

Pamela's hair was combed up and away from her face, and tucked underneath her nurse's hat. Her pale skin accented her sharp blue eyes. She wore no makeup or lipstick. Still, the man was certain she was the most beautiful woman he'd ever seen.

"Hey there," he said, smiling.

"Hello. How are you feeling?"

"Pretty groggy. You must've given me something pretty strong."

"We did. You were in surgery for two hours."

"That bad, huh?"

"You sustained some very serious injuries."

The man's eyes narrowed.

Pamela saw the sharp intellect in them, but she also spotted the fear.

"How serious?"

Pamela moved around to his right side, and sat down in a chair next to the bed. She grasped his right hand with both hers. His dwarfed hers, the same way Tom Dunn's did.

"You will survive, Mr. Cooper."

Cooper raised an eyebrow. " 'Survive.' Not 'recover.' "

"You have a spinal cord injury."

Cooper immediately yanked his hand from Pamela's and using both hands, pushed himself to a sitting position. He swayed for moment, then steadied himself. He stared down at the end of the bed. His face and neck turned red from his effort to wiggle his toes.

He collapsed backwards onto the bed.

"Paralyzed." Not a question.

"From the waist down we think."

Cooper's respiration sped up and Pamela took hold of his hand again. "You're alive and will remain so."

"Only half of me, though. A wheelchair for me, huh?"

"Probably. Although in rare cases, some people do learn to walk with braces. Only time will tell."

"God Almighty. I never thought it would happen to me."

"I know."

"Can't be fixed?"

"No."

"How long before I ship out?"

"I'm not sure. I'll let you know as soon as I find out."

"Okay, thanks."

"Where are you from?"

"Wyoming. I bet you don't even know where that is." He smiled because he didn't mean any harm by it, no one in Europe had yet. Even a couple of idiots during flight training in Florida, who had been from New York, thought it was somewhere around Arizona.

Pamela nodded. "I do, too! It's west of Nebraska and South Dakota, and south of Montana."

Cooper's mouth dropped open. "How did you know that?"

Pamela held up her left hand and waggled her wedding finger. "My husband is from Iowa."

Cooper got a lopsided grin on his face that Pamela would learn over the next few days meant he was about to be ornery. "Oh, sure, that's the state back east by Kentucky and Pennsylvania."

Pamela frowned. He was obviously thinking of Ohio. Dunn had told her that people mysteriously mixed up Iowa with Ohio and, even more weirdly, with Idaho. Maybe it was all the vowels.

Cooper couldn't keep a straight face and cracked a smile.

"Right. You're having me on. You are a cheeky one, Mr. Cooper."

"Guilty."

Pamela got up from her chair. "May I get you anything?"

Cooper shrugged. "I'm okay for now."

"I'll see you sometime later today." Pamela turned away.

"Um, nurse?"

Pamela looked over her shoulder. "Yes, Mr. Cooper?"

"Thanks for being honest about this." He waved a hand toward his legs.

"You're welcome."

"I just thought of something I need."

"What's that?"

"Paper and a pencil. I want to write my dad. We need to figure out how I can still work the ranch from a wheelchair."

Pamela had to work very hard not to lose it in front of this brave young man. She swallowed the lump in her throat, and replied, "Coming right up!"

Later, Pamela happened to walk by Cooper and he was busy writing, occasionally wetting the pencil tip with his tongue. At first glance, it looked like he already had four pages written, front and back.

Chapter 10

Spa, Belgium
8 September, 0725 Hours

As a mortified Chadwick watched Chesley fall, a German soldier, probably the one who'd fired the killing shot, ran across the street. When he reached the fallen spy, he kicked him over on his back. Satisfied that the man was dead, he turned back to Chadwick's building and raised a hand, presumably to his partner guard at the front door. Chadwick ducked below the parapet, and crouch-ran to the back of the building.

He leaned over the edge and found Dickinson looking up expectantly. Chadwick drew his finger across his throat to give the abort mission sign.

Dickinson turned around to face the hill and gave the same sign to Saunders.

Chadwick waited until Dickinson returned his attention to him, and then slipped over the side of the building, his feet dangling about six feet from the ground. He let go and dropped. Dickinson helped him retain his balance on landing. They both checked the area behind the buildings and then took off toward the woods.

When they made it to the trees they found Saunders and Barltrop kneeling behind a large oak tree.

"Mister Chesley's dead, Sarge," Chadwick reported.

"What the bloody hell happened?"

Chadwick told him about the car and the two men. "Had to be Gestapo. It looked like they recognized him immediately, so they had to be searching for him. They came from far down the street, and not right from the Gestapo headquarters in the hotel."

Saunders gave a sigh of relief. Although saddened by Chesley's death, he was glad it didn't seem to be related to the current mission. Chesley would have known that if he was taken alive, the Gestapo would have eventually found out Saunders and his men were there. He'd done the only thing he could: take some German bastards with him.

Major Armstrong sidled up to the four men. "What's happening?"

Saunders filled him in and finished with, "We have to abort the mission for today. The place will be crawling with krauts."

"We shouldn't have tried to get the general. If Chesley had stayed back here with us, this wouldn't have happened."

Saunders eyed the major for a moment, then said, "What's done is done. I viewed it as an additional opportunity for the mission."

"But—"

Saunders held up his hand. "Sir, please. Colonel Jenkins told me he told you I would be in charge operationally." Saunders spoke with an expression saying he would not brook any further discussion.

Armstrong started to say something, but changed his mind. He looked away briefly, perhaps gathering himself. When he looked back at Saunders, he said, "He did. I apologize. I know we can't have two commanders." He gave Saunders a slight bow with a nod. "Forget I said anything."

"Done, sir."

Saunders started walking toward the rest of the men a few yards away saying over his shoulder to Barltrop, Chadwick, and Dickinson, "Time to move out."

The three men followed in his footsteps.

When he reached the rest of the squad, Saunders said to Redington, "Take point. Lead us north about a half-mile to the top of this hill."

"Right, Sarge," Redington replied. He shouldered his pack and strode off. The rest of the men fell in line, with Garner taking up the rear.

Saunders walked with Barltrop and Armstrong on either side of himself.

The going was difficult on the wet ground and the steep uphill, but they broke through to a more gentle slope and their speed picked up.

"We'll go again in the morning, Major."

Armstrong's face brightened. "You changed your mind?"

Saunders gave the major a quizzical look. "What do you mean?"

"I thought you were aborting the mission." Now Armstrong looked confused.

"No, sir. I said we're aborting it for *today*."

"Oh, I say. That's wonderful. I must have misunderstood you."

Saunders shrugged. "Nothing to worry about."

"Do you think the Germans will have increased their security?"

"Unlikely. I'm pretty sure they got who they were looking for when they killed Chesley. Nothing there to link him to us or the mission."

Armstrong nodded. "Right. Thanks."

"Sure."

The squad walked steadily through the thick woods and eventually Redington held up a fist. Everyone else took up kneeling defensive positions alternating which direction they guarded: west, east. Garner turned around to face their rear.

Redington advanced toward a clearing that appeared to be surrounded by evergreen trees. He disappeared briefly, then came back into view. He gave a thumbs up sign.

Saunders grabbed Handford and Kopp and gave them instructions. They each took off in opposite directions, Handford to the northwest and Kopp northeast, their Sten submachine guns at the ready.

Saunders waited patiently, and about five minutes later Handford and Kopp reappeared on the north side of the clearing. They marched up to Saunders.

"It's all clear out to three hundred yards Sarge. We did a half circle each and came straight back," Kopp said. "Saw no one, and didn't see any evidence of anyone coming through here at all, soldiers or hunters."

"Right. Everybody up. Let's find comfortable spots. Handford, Kopp, Redington, and Thurston, set up a picket line around the clearing, a hundred yards out. I'll send replacements in two hours."

The four commandos nodded and each one took off in a different cardinal direction.

Saunders led the way toward the soft layers of pine needles covering the ground under a particularly big pine tree. He shrugged off his pack and put it down, then flopped down to the ground where he sat cross legged. Barltrop joined him, as did Major Armstrong. The rest of the squad found places to roost for the upcoming long hours of waiting

Saunders took a drink from his canteen and offered some to the major, who declined with a thanks.

After a few minutes of silence, Saunders laid out his new plan for the next morning. Barltrop, sitting to Saunders' left, poked a few holes in it, and they settled on the final plan.

When they concluded the plan discussion, Barltrop asked, "Remind me, when's the date?"

"September twenty-third."

"Sadie will be out of the cast by then?"

"Aye. Most likely next week." Saunders held up both of his huge hands. They both had the first two fingers crossed.

"You still up to be my best man?"

"Wouldn't miss it for anything," Barltrop replied, grinning wide. He liked Sadie very much, and was even from the same city, Cheshunt, north of London, although he hadn't known her in school, but had seen her around.

"When are you getting hitched, Steve?" Saunders asked with a boyish grin that made his red handlebar moustache twitch.

"Ah, you know, someday."

"You haven't met the right girl, Mr. Barltrop?" Armstrong asked. He seemed serious to Barltrop, who didn't take offense at the man stepping into the personal conversation.

"Oh, sure I have. Kathy. She just doesn't know it yet."

"Well, good luck to you, then."

"Thank you, sir."

The men settled back into silence for a few minutes, and then Armstrong broke it.

"Knock, knock."

Saunders sighed, and then glanced quickly at Barltrop. "Your turn, mate."

"Who's there?"

"Amos."

"Amos who?"

"A mosquito just bit me. Knock, knock."

"Who's there?"

"Andy."

"Andy who?"

"Andy just bit me again. Knock, knock."

Barltrop sighed in exasperation, but played along, "Who's there?"

"Ida."

"Ida who?"

"Don't you think Ida better kill him 'fore he bites me again?"

Saunders and Barltrop groaned, and then chuckled softly at the neatly ordered sequential jokes. The other men nearby laughed lightly, enjoying seeing their sergeants the target of a master knock, knock joke teller.

Armstrong grinned happily.

Chapter 11

French countryside
141 miles east of Paris
8 September, 1412 Hours, Paris time

General Patton's Third Army advanced toward the next natural impediment, the Meuse River, which was about one hundred forty-three miles east of Paris. It was also only fifty-four miles from the nearest point on the German border, which was northeast at the tri-country point where Germany, France, and Luxembourg met.

Dunn's mechanized platoon was assigned to sweep the woods west of the Meuse clear of Germans. Dunn's squad was the leftmost of three, each riding on or sometimes marching alongside its own halftrack. The halftrack carried a .50 caliber Browning, which provided tremendous firepower to each squad. Dunn's squad was responsible for a front about two hundred yards wide. Two miles to their south, the Sherman tanks were roaring down the main road toward the bridges at Chauvoncourt and Maizey. Dunn's platoon would advance on Dompcevrin. If needed, and if at all possible, a tank platoon would join them from the south to clear that small river village.

Dunn's immediate problem was a large farmhouse. The halftrack driver had done a terrific job of following the narrow road, almost more of a trail, but straight ahead, between them and the farmhouse, was a large field. Dunn and Waters had dismounted the halftrack and worked their way carefully through the wooded area to the edge where they knelt to examine the field and the house. The house was near the northern edge of the woods across the field.

Dunn raised binoculars and focused, not on the house, but on the woods to its north, looking for Germans setting a trap. Satisfied they weren't there, he inspected the house, which was about a quarter of a mile way. It was a two-story building with the front door and small porch on the south side. All windows were open, which didn't necessarily mean anything. A French family could be living there still. They'd already run across a few houses just like that.

Dunn could not advance across the field; that could be certain death. Dunn estimated the distance through the woods to a spot north of the house to be about a half mile's trek. The halftrack would have to stand fast, or would it?

Dunn looked to the south following the edge of the woods and pictured where the road through the forest would lie.

"Stay here," he said to Waters, who nodded. Dunn backtracked a few yards to make sure he was well inside the woods and out of sight of anyone in the house. He walked south until he found the road. Taking a few steps to the east he stopped and peered through the trees at the house. No good. He strode a few yards father east and tried again. There it was: a lane just a few yards wide with a perfect vantage point on the house. Dunn stepped off the road to the south and rooted around until he found two roughly six-foot-long branches lying on the ground. He snatched them up. They were a little more than an inch thick. He found the spot where he wanted the halftrack, and created an 'X' on the ground in the center of the road with the branches.

Dunn rejoined Waters and the two men made their way back to the others.

Dunn stood outside the halftrack and waved at everyone to get out, including the driver and the corporal manning the .50 cal. When the men formed up around him in a semicircle, Dunn first spoke to the driver and the gunner.

"There's a farmhouse up ahead in a large field. We're going to have to go through the woods to the north of it. I need you to provide fire support up ahead on the road. I put a couple of big sticks on the road in an 'X' for you."

"Okay, Sarge. I got it," the driver replied.

Dunn looked at the gunner. "You'll see a narrow opening with a direct shot at the house at a range of four hundred yards. Remember, we're going to be to the north, so do not go farther down the road or you'll put us in your crossfire."

"Yes, Sarge. What's my target?"

"Any krauts coming out the front door, or I guess, for that matter, any windows, too."

The gunner chuckled. "Okay. Doors and windows, got it."

Dunn turned to his men as the driver and gunner boarded the vehicle. A moment later the halftrack trundled away.

"We're going to have about ten yards of clearing between us and the house. We'll split up into two teams and use fire and advance. I'll take point."

Dunn took off and his men followed.

Dunn made a path carefully through the forest, treading softly and making sure he was avoiding noise-making objects, sticks and dry leaves. His route was ten yards inside the forest. The pace he set was methodical and about three miles an hour. Plenty of light filtered through the trees, as did a southerly breeze.

After a little more than ten minutes, and after they had turned east, Dunn raised a fist and the squad stopped. He pointed toward the southeast, where the house was partially visible through the trees about seventy-five yards away. There was no German movement in sight. Pointing a finger at Cross, who was right behind him, Dunn took off again, and Cross followed. The rest of the squad took a knee and raised their Thompsons, aiming at the house.

Dunn kept one eye on the house and the other on the ground in front of him. He came to a halt at a point directly north of the house, still ten yards from the forest's edge, putting Cross and himself twenty yards away.

What could be considered to be the house's back yard was covered by tall grass. Rain barrels sat at each of the back corners under the rain spouts. The back door was closed and a blind pulled over its small head-high window. Four windows, two on each floor on either side of the door, gave the house dark eyes and a smile. A rust-covered pitcher-style water hand pump stood fifteen feet from the house. To the east of the back yard was the barn, whose main door faced south. All of the small doors, five of them, that would lead into livestock stalls, were closed.

Dunn and Cross watched the house for five minutes.

Suddenly, the back door opened and a German soldier stepped out carrying a silver water bucket. The door's spring slammed it shut behind him. He wore his uniform trousers, but had shed the tunic, and his upper body was covered only by a gray sleeveless undershirt. He carried no weapon and his head was bare.

Dunn and Cross raised their weapons out of habit, but held back on pulling the trigger. Dunn checked all of the windows again, but there was nothing moving. An idea popped into his head and he examined it quickly. It seemed sound enough, so he nudged Cross and using his hand told Cross what he was going to do. Cross shook his head and raised an eyebrow. Dunn nodded to accent his intentions, but Cross put a hand on Dunn's arm and shook his head again. Dunn nodded once more and gave a double eyebrow lift, as if to say, 'yes, I am!'

An exasperated Cross rolled his eyes, but tilted his head in acquiescence.

The German soldier reached the pump and set the bucket down under the spigot. The handle clanged against the side of the bucket after he let go. The position of the pump handle was on the north side, nearer to Dunn, which meant the soldier had to turn his back on a U.S. Army Ranger. Not the greatest place to be, and potentially fatal.

Dunn eyed the ground in front of him, picking out the best pathway. As soon as the soldier started working the pump handle, Dunn took off.

Cross raised his weapon, aiming at the back door, where he thought trouble would appear.

In a half dozen strides Dunn hit the tree line.

The soldier was intent on the pump.

With a few more quick running steps, Dunn was right behind the soldier. With his left hand he covered the man's mouth and with his right, jammed the Thompson's barrel into his back.

"Shh." Dunn figured that would translate.

The soldier struggled to free himself and reached a hand around clawing at Dunn's face.

RONN MUNSTERMAN

Chapter 12

French countryside
141 miles east of Paris
8 September, 1455 Hours

Dunn jammed the barrel harder into the German's back and whispered, "Halt!" Dunn knew that would translate, too.

The soldier stopped struggling and raised his hands. Dunn pulled with his left arm, while still covering the enemy's mouth, and the soldier had no choice but to backpedal with his captor.

Cross rose and ran to the woods' edge.

Dunn got the German to Cross without them falling down. He spun the German around so he faced Cross, and would know he was outnumbered.

Cross held his finger to his lips and then grabbed the German by the undershirt. He pulled the man forward and pointed to the ground. The man complied and got down on his knees. Cross motioned for him to get farther down and the soldier dropped all the way to a prone position.

Dunn took over again and knelt next to the captive, pushing the barrel of the Thompson into his back.

"Go get the guys," he said to Cross.

"Okay."

A few minutes passed, and the rest of the squad showed up. Some of them raised their eyebrows when they saw Dunn with the German.

Dunn pointed at Schneider and beckoned with the same finger.

Schneider joined Dunn on the opposite side of the prone German. Dunn rolled the prisoner over onto his back. The prisoner was met by the black eyes of Dunn as well as the dark muzzle of the Thompson just inches from his face.

"Tell him if he wants to live, to answer my questions."

Schneider repeated what Dunn said as he leaned down to be in the German's line of sight.

"Ask him to nod if he wants to live."

The German nodded, eyes wide with fright.

"How many in the house?"

No answer from the German, who tried to look away. Dunn grabbed him by the chin and repeated the question.

"I won't tell you."

Dunn wouldn't have told a German anything either if the tables had been turned. The men in the house were the man's family. He couldn't betray them.

Dunn nodded acceptance of the reply, smiled and clapped the solider on the left shoulder. "What's your name?"

"Karl Appler."

"Well, Karl, it looks like you got stuck as a lonely rearguard who is about to be overrun by the American army. There are only two possibilities here: one, you all surrender and get sent to a nice prisoner of war camp with hot food and a warm place to sleep, plus medical care."

Dunn paused while Schneider translated. When Schneider got to the part about hot food, the German's face brightened.

"The second possibility for you and your friends is . . ." Dunn raised the Thompson and pressed the cold muzzle between the German's eyes.

The German closed his eyes.

"How many in the house?"

"*Drei.*"

"Three," Schneider said.

Dunn said, "Huh, just three."

"What about the barn?" Dunn tipped his head in the building's direction.

"No one."

Dunn turned to look at the back door. Just maybe. He helped the German sit up. He gave instructions carefully and when he asked if the German would do it, the reply had been "*Ja!*"

Dunn spread out his squad in the tree line half on either side of Dunn, Schneider and the German prisoner.

Dunn spoke to the prisoner, "Make it sound convincing, or I *will* hurt you and you'll be screaming in pain for real. Do you understand?"

The German nodded enthusiastically. Perhaps he was thinking of the hot food.

"Now." Dunn was counting on two things: the prisoner knew Schneider would tell Dunn if he said anything he wasn't supposed to, and two there really were only three men in the house.

"Ralf! Help me! Help me! Please help me!"

The back door flew open and another German similarly dressed to Appler ran out looking around for his friend.

"Again. Softer."

The prisoner complied and Ralf zeroed in on the sound and then took off at a run toward the woods.

Dunn had stationed Jones and Lindstrom kneeling behind two large trees at a point between the prisoner and the house. As the second German ran right between Jones and Lindstrom, they yanked up on a rope hidden by leaves. The German's front foot snagged on the line and he pitched forward onto his face. Cross and Wickham rolled up the second prisoner and hauled him farther into the woods, where they tied him up and gagged him.

Dunn got everyone resituated along the tree line. He told Appler to call out again.

This time when the man came out, a worried look on his face, Dunn realized that in addition to being perplexed, the enemy soldier was armed with a Mauser. Dunn gave a soft whistle. This did two things at once: the soldier turned his face toward the sound, and suddenly eight American soldiers, who all had their

Thompsons aimed at him, stepped out of the woods. He dropped his rifle and raised his hands.

The back door burst open and the last German dove out of the house, when he got to his knees he brought up a Schmeisser MP40 submachine gun.

Jonesy, who was closest, saw the ugly snout of the German weapon swing his way.

The two men's eyes met.

Jonesy squeezed the Thompson's trigger and a three-round burst tore through the German's center chest, who dropped the Schmeisser as he folded in on himself and fell to the ground backwards.

Dunn and Schneider got the first prisoner up on his feet.

Dunn called for Waters and when the man stood in front of Dunn, the sergeant said, "Make your way around the west side of the house. Better hold out something white to get the driver's and gunner's attention. When you do, get them to drive over here."

"Okay, Sarge."

Waters pulled off his uniform top and then yanked off his brown undershirt, the closest thing to white he had. He took off toward the spot Dunn suggested.

Meanwhile, Dunn and his men got the three survivors together, their hands bound behind them. Waters returned to Dunn and said, "Halftrack is on its way. Looks like they'll have to go farther east and come back for us."

"Thanks." Dunn spoke to Schneider, who was standing near the prisoners, "Ask if they have food in there."

The first German captured, Appler, said, "Some bread and cheese in the kitchen. Wine in the cupboard."

Since neither had their uniform tops on, Dunn sent Wickham into the house with Goerdt, and Martelli to see what they could find, and to bring back the uniforms, and all the food and wine they could find.

While his men were scavenging, Dunn spoke to Appler, "Sorry about your friend."

Appler snorted derisively. "He was an idiot. Always trying to be the hero, always getting someone else killed. I wanted to shoot him myself."

Dunn raised an eyebrow when Schneider translated this dissertation by the prisoner.

"Why didn't you?"

"He was SS. Check his pockets."

Dunn did that and found the SS identification papers. He checked the man's other pockets, but found nothing of interest. Dunn waved at Schneider to bring Appler with him. Dunn entered the house and the other two men followed. They walked through the kitchen into the living room where backpacks and sleeping gear were spread out.

Dunn turned to Appler. "Show me his stuff."

"He doesn't have anything you would be interested in."

"Show me anyway."

Appler shrugged and pointed to a pack closest to the window.

Dunn tore it open, finding a few letters. He handed them to Schneider, "See if these are just from home."

Schneider scanned them quickly. "Yeah. They are."

Dunn continued searching and was about to stop when his fingers felt something hard. He felt around but couldn't see what it was. After a moment he figured out it was something in the lining of the pack. He felt around some more and discovered a vertical opening. Slipping his fingers inside the hidden pocket, he felt and then grabbed the hard object. He withdrew it and held it up. A small notebook. He flipped it open and found it was filled with text. He handed it to Schneider.

"Is this a diary?"

Schneider read a few pages briefly. "Yeah. Places he's been." He skipped to the middle. "Huh. He was keeping track of men he killed. That's creepy." He went to the last page. "They were in Thillombois yesterday, which is about five miles northwest of here. That's the end of it."

"Nothing useful?"

"Not that I see."

Dunn held out his hand. "If I get the chance I'll hand it off to battalion S-2, just in case."

Schneider handed off the book.

The three men left the house and waited for Dunn's men to finish what they were doing.

About ten minutes later, the men came out of the house, their arms laden down with food and the German uniforms. Dunn took the latter from Goerdt and went through the pockets of one. He found the identification card. It didn't match the name for captive number one. He read it out loud and captive number two nodded. Dunn continued his search and found a few coins, French francs, but that was all. He put the money back in the pocket and handed it to Schneider, who draped it over the owner's shoulders. He repeated the process with the second tunic and the identification card said Karl Appler. He also found a couple of letters and a picture of a man and woman in their forties.

Dunn handed the letters to Schneider, who skimmed them.

"Just more letters. These are from his parents. One is dated in June and the other July."

Dunn nodded as his translator folded the letters carefully back into their original form.

Dunn held the picture. "Your parents?"

Schneider translated.

"*Ja.*"

Dunn slid the letters and the picture back into the pocket where he'd found them.

"Your parents will eventually get a letter from the Red Cross that you are a prisoner of war, but are well and healthy. Your war is over."

The solider nodded. "*Danke.*"

"You're welcome."

"Jonesy, you, Lindstrom, and Bailey check out the barn. It's supposed to be empty, but be careful."

"Right, Sarge."

Engine and clanking treads sounds drifted to the men and soon the halftrack roared up and stopped on the west side of the house.

Dunn got the rest of the squad and the prisoners into the vehicle, and then he walked into the back yard, eyeing the barn apprehensively. Jonesy and the others strolled out of the barn, and Jonesy gave Dunn a thumbs-up.

A relieved Dunn waved his arm and the three men ran over to join him.

"Nothing there, Sarge."

"All right. Let's get loaded up."

As Dunn watched his men load the three prisoners, and then board the halftrack, he did what most soldiers did. He thanked God for getting his men and himself through another contact with the enemy.

He also wondered what the hell was in store for them in the coming weeks and months.

Chapter 13

900 meters north of Arry, France, and
1,000 meters east of the Moselle River
9 September, 0615 Hours

Platoon leader *Oberfeldwebel* Dieter Wittenberg organized his three squads in their positions facing the Moselle River. He would be with the second squad in the middle slot of the three. He liked their position as far as cover went, lots and lots of big boulders and rocks, as if there had been a rockslide centuries ago. He didn't like his position because the same rocks went all the way back up the hill to the northeast, which was their only path of retreat.

The sky was overcast with clouds at about three thousand feet. This suited Wittenberg immensely; it meant they were less likely to come under air attack. It had rained for about an hour or so before sunrise and the ground was wet, making the rocks slippery.

Wittenberg's platoon was the northernmost of three. Mekelburg's was to his immediate south and Raupp's the last one south. *Surrounded by idiots*, thought Wittenberg wryly. He hadn't had any more trouble with the other two platoon leaders since their brief and one-way fight the other day. He did occasionally see one or the other of them staring daggers at him. Figuring they would be plotting revenge, he was careful and always knew where they were.

Each platoon had a couple of heavy MG42 machine guns attached. Wittenberg placed one in the center of his third squad and the other with the first squad on the north end of the platoon. The second one could cover both the river and the woods to the north. The rest of the platoon's men were armed with the Mauser K98, including Wittenberg.

Walking down the line of his men, he spoke to each one, giving encouragement and a pat on the back. He'd managed to acquire a couple of cartons of cigarettes at the cost of some chocolate he'd found a few days ago, so he dispensed those to the men.

A pimply-faced seventeen year old named Odis Andler from Holzkirchen, a small city south of Munich, cleared his throat and when Wittenberg paused, asked, *"Wann kriegen wir die neuen Waffen, die Herr Göbbels uns versprochen hat, schätzen Sie?"* When do you think we'll get the new weapons *Herr* Göbbels has been promising us?

Wittenberg did a mental sigh. He'd heard the rumors, which had been running rampant through the men for some time. It was as the boy had said, all due to Göbbels' propaganda machine. He made promises of super weapons, such as a super bomb capable of destroying an entire city, and the use of mustard gas on the enemy cities. All coming to save the fatherland just in time. Just be patient until they arrive, Göbbels repeatedly said. All horseshit as far as Wittenberg was concerned.

"Meinst du nicht, OKW würde uns sofort damit aufrüsten, wenn sie sie hätten? Um die Alliierten auf ihrem Marsch nach Deutschland zu verhindern?" Don't you think OKW would release them now if we had them? To stop the Allies from reaching Germany?

"Aber Herr Göbbels hat gesagt, wir sollen Geduld haben," the boy persisted.
But *Herr* Göbbels said to be patient. *"Und er hat uns versprochen!"* And he promised!

Wittenberg patted the boy on the shoulder and glanced around. A couple of the other youngsters were listening intently, waiting to hear what their platoon leader would say.

"Ich sag' dir, was wir tun, Andler. Wir konzentrieren uns auf unsere Aufgabe—im Moment müssen wir diese Lage halten. Und wir überlassen Herrn Göbbels seine Aufgabe. Kannst du das?" Let's do this, Andler. We will focus on our job, which at this moment is to hold this position. Let's allow *Herr* Göbbels to do his job. Can you do that?

"Ja, Herr Feldwebel. Ich tue mein Bestes." Yes, Sergeant. I'll do my best.

Wittenberg nodded, and glanced around at the other boys. They nodded back at him and he smiled.

Wittenberg left them and continued on down the line. After making contact with all of his men, he scrambled back to his position, not far from the third squad's MG42. He took a knee and examined the river valley in his view. His position lay over a hundred meters above the river, which flowed north to south with an S-curve. The southern part of the city of Arnaville lay to Wittenberg's right just across the river. Roads followed the river's curves on both sides.

Straight ahead, the remnants of a blown bridge lay partially submerged in the Moselle. Battalion intelligence had expressed the idea that the American engineers would build a pontoon bridge to the north of the broken bridge. Artillery would already have that area pre-targeted, as well as the river road on the west side to interfere with the Americans ability to bring up the materials for the bridge. Of course, the Americans would anticipate this and would place their own artillery on the ridges overlooking the river valley for counter-battery fire. And if the skies cleared, the dreaded American P-47 "Jabo" ground attack airplanes would pound the panzers and artillery.

Wittenberg's company's responsibility was to contain any infantry forces that made it across the river by keeping them pinned in place so other units could race from Arry on the south to overrun them on the flank. He lifted a pair of field glasses and methodically examined the area across the river. There were no enemy units in sight, although intelligence had reported some of Patton's forces were getting closer. He wondered why battalion command had decided not to harass the enemy's approach to the river and concluded they believed German losses would weaken the eventual defense of the river.

The fact that the spot where he knelt put him just fifty kilometers from the Fatherland's western border was not lost on him. Nor was the fact lost that the Moselle River was the last natural impediment to Patton's Third Army until the Rhine River.

Chapter 14

Spa, Belgium
9 September, 0745 Hours

Saunders and his men, plus Major Armstrong, had spent a marginally comfortable near twenty-four hours on the hill under the pine trees. All they'd seen come by their area were a few rabbits and two deer, which had made everyone's mouths water to no avail.

Kneeling behind the same tree as the day before, in the woods just north of the communications center, Saunders and Barltrop eyed the back of the buildings for anything suspicious. Major Armstrong was just behind Barltrop. They'd been there for an hour. The men were a few yards farther into the woods, waiting. It was quiet, although they did hear a motorcycle come from the west around seven a.m., which stopped in front of the communications center. Five minutes later, it had gone back the same way it had come.

"I think we should go now," Saunders said softly.

"I agree," Barltrop said.

Saunders had reviewed the attack plan with the squad prior to leaving their hideout.

Saunders got to his feet and turned around. He gave a high sign to the men behind. They rose as one, and moved toward him, forming a tight line running parallel to the buildings, with Saunders in the center.

Saunders checked the line then held up three fingers. He did a countdown, and when he folded down the last finger, the men took off, running low.

Dickinson made it to the door, stopping on the doorknob side. Chadwick knelt to Dickinson's left, in front of the door. Dickinson waited until the others were in position. Some of the men had to duck down because they were directly in front of a window.

Thurston helped Mills climb up onto the roof, where Mills would go cut the phone wires and remain to keep an eye on the street.

Dickinson put his hand on the doorknob and tried to turn it, but it was locked. He reached over his shoulder and pulled a two foot solid steel pry bar from his pack. He carefully inserted the flat tip between the door and the jamb and then slowly began pulling, putting his weight behind it. The door began to give. When a gap appeared, Chadwick grabbed the doorknob and pulled. The door opened a quarter inch with a slight snicking sound.

Dickinson put his pry bar back in his pack, and lifted his Sten.

Chadwick stood up and pulled the door open a few inches while Dickinson peeked into the hallway.

Dickinson gave a thumbs up sign and Chadwick opened the door fully, stepping back out of the way as he pulled. Saunders stepped through the door, and Redington and Mills followed.

A door on the right was partially open, and Saunders moved toward it, keeping an eye on the long hallway ahead of him. He peeked in quickly. It was the loo, empty. The doors leading into the rooms Chesley had mentioned, one on each side of the hallway, were near the front door. They were closed.

The hallway was about five feet wide, so Saunders motioned for the rest of the men to get inside. The squad formed into two lines, against each wall. Saunders was in the lead on the right and

Redington on the left. Saunders checked over his shoulder to make sure the men were ready, then looked at Redington and nodded.

They began to move down the hall, slide stepping smoothly along the wood floor.

The immediate problem for the squad was determining where each German was in the building, and the second problem was what to do with them. The only safe assumption to make was that everyone in the building would be armed at least with a sidearm. Another problem was keeping each German from firing his weapon. While Saunders' men all carried suppressed weapons, the Germans would not. Shots ringing out from inside a communications center was bound to attract attention. Lots of it. Saunders had made his decision long before the squad entered the building: no hesitation, shoot.

As Saunders moved closer to the set of doors in the hallway, he kept an eye on the front door, knowing there were two sentries on the other side. He wanted to keep them out there. Saunders had two rooms to get under control, plus a front door to guard. On top of that, his men had to be aware of a general officer who might be present, and to keep him alive. A tough challenge during a split second decision.

Saunders and Redington stopped when they reached their door. Both doors would swing open to the right. Chadwick stood to the right of Saunders' door, and Barltrop did the same for Redington; they would be the first in the rooms.

Saunders put his hand on the doorknob and turned it slowly until it stopped. He looked at Redington, who nodded, and did the same thing with his doorknob. A glance at Barltrop and Chadwick earned Saunders more nods.

Saunders pushed the door open just enough to see in. In one second he took in everything he needed to know. On the opposite side of the hall, Redington was doing the same thing. Saunders pulled the door so it touched the door jam, but was still open. He gave hand signals to explain what he seen. Redington relayed his information.

Saunders nodded and held up three fingers. All eyes were on his hand. He ticked off the countdown, and then pushed the door open all the way.

Chadwick darted in firing two quick bursts into the two soldiers standing behind the general.

Saunders crossed over to the right and shot the communications center commander, who was sitting behind his desk, facing the door. He spun to his right, toward the area he couldn't see from the door. A male typist jumped to his feet, so Saunders shot him.

Dickinson followed Saunders in and ran past Chadwick to the general who was turning to see what was happening. Dickinson put a hand over the high ranking officer's mouth and shoved the Sten's barrel into the man's right ear. "Shh," Dickinson said.

Redington put his hand on the door to push it open, but it suddenly swung open to reveal a German officer who stared at the British Commando in surprise. You could say the officer was surprised to death because Redington shot him.

Barltrop rushed into the room. Another officer sat behind a desk across the room, and Barltrop shot him.

Redington ran inside the room and turned left, followed immediately by Garner and Kopp.

A row of five radio operators sat at a long table against the south wall. The one closest to the commandos spotted movement out of the corner of his eye and turned his head toward the source. His expression turned to shock, but he recovered quickly and stabbed a hand out for a phone. He picked it up and then his expression changed to disbelief when the dial tone didn't come on.

Redington, Garner and Kopp opened fire, killing all five, including the one with the dead phone in his hand.

Thurston and Handford had hung back in the hallway, and Major Armstrong waited behind Thurston on the south side of the hallway. Armstrong's eyes were wide at the metallic clicking sounds of the Sten guns' receiver action, the disgusting wet slapping sounds of the bullets striking flesh, and the thumps on the floor as the bodies fell over.

Handford moved closer to the front door.

Redington came out of the office and waved at Armstrong, who ran into the radio room where he set to work examining the equipment.

In the other room, Saunders stepped closer to the still seated general and aimed his Sten at the man's forehead. Saunders nodded to Dickinson, who removed his hand slowly, and his gun from the general's ear.

"Do you speak English?" Saunders asked.

The general was in his mid-fifties, with a little gray in his dark brown hair. He had a cleft chin, and a scar along his left cheek, undoubtedly from sword play in his youth. A badge of strength and courage. Even with the 9mm Sten's round hole staring him in the eyes, he seemed calm, and determined.

"Certainly," the general replied.

"Your war is over, general. You're my prisoner."

A small smile touched the general's lips. "We shall see whose war is over."

He started to draw in a deep breath to call for the guards, but Dickinson was too quick and clamped his hand over the man's mouth again.

"Tsk, tsk," Saunders muttered. He nodded to Chadwick, who had joined the two commandos. "Gag him and bind his hands."

Chadwick did that quickly with Dickinson's help.

Saunders walked around behind the desk and rolled aside the dead commander, who had slumped back in his chair. Saunders took off his backpack and set it on the floor. He searched the desktop for maps, picking up the few papers there and sifting through them. He didn't find any maps, so he just grabbed all the papers he could find, including those inside the desk drawers, and shoved them all into his pack.

Across the hall, Armstrong had finished with the radios and was now doing the same thing as Saunders: grabbing everything that he could from code books to completed messages. He instructed Kopp to help.

In the meantime, Barltrop and Garner were busy setting plastic explosive charges. Barltrop was placing a few against the south wall, to cause damage to the Gestapo headquarters in the hotel on the other side. The resulting fire, a byproduct of the explosions, would cover up the deaths by bullet and the theft.

Handford and Thurston were standing a few feet from the front door. They could see out the small windows set at about eye level. Handford, who was on the right, could see one of the guards, the one on the left side of the door. He was facing toward the street.

Suddenly they heard the sound of a motorcycle engine roaring closer. Handford moved so he could see the street. A German messenger parked his motorcycle and got off, then stepped up onto the porch, where he showed his identification papers to the guards.

Handford waved at Thurston to move. Both men backed away from the door and then slid through the office doors on their respective side of the hallway. Handford had moved into the office where Saunders was holding the general prisoner.

Handford and Thurston faced each other. Handford made a guess and waved at Thurston to close his own door. Thurston did so, staying close to the door.

Handford peeked around the door jamb when he heard the front door rattle open, then close. Jackboots clunked across the wooden floor. The messenger walked a straight line toward the radio room. He opened the door and stepped in. All he got was one boot inside the room.

The door was flung open and Thurston jammed his Sten into the man's chest. He squeezed off two rounds and the man collapsed. Thurston pulled him the rest of the way inside the room and dragged him over to the side where a couple of other bodies were lying.

Handford ran quietly up to the front door. The guards were back in position on each side, completely unaware of the death taking place behind them. He raised his eyebrows and tilted his head in recognition of the fact that the building was pretty damn solid if they hadn't heard anything happening inside.

Thurston noticed the messenger's bag, which had fallen to the floor, and was still by the door. He picked it up and carried it over to Major Armstrong.

"Sir, these just came by messenger."

"Oh, good. Thanks."

"You're welcome."

Thurston got a plastic explosive package out of his pack and set it to go off at the time Saunders had said earlier: 0802 hours. He ran quietly down the hallway and slid the package under the bathroom toilet.

When he stepped back into the hallway, Saunders and his small group were already heading for the back door, dragging their prisoner with them.

Right behind Saunders' group came Barltrop and the men who'd been working in the radio room.

Saunders checked his watch: 0759 hours. "Let's hustle men. Three minutes. Chadwick, you cover everything until one minute then get the bloody hell back to the woods."

"Righto, Sarge!"

Mills leaned over the edge of the roof and Thurston helped him descend.

Chadwick took up station right at the back door after the rest of the commandos and the major had departed. His job was to shoot anyone coming through the front door in the next two minutes.

When the last of his squad mates made it through the door, he backed through the door, and knelt, using his body to hold the door wide open. He was only partially visible from inside the hallway, plus the bright backlight behind Chadwick would make it hard for anyone coming in the building to see clearly for a few seconds.

He checked his watch: two minutes to go.

The front door opened and the two guards stepped through into the gloom of the hallway. They advanced down the hallway and one turned to his right and opened the door to the radio room.

He shouted something in German and started to enter the room.

Chadwick shot him.

The other guard figured out the shot had come from the far end of the hallway and raised his weapon.

Chadwick shot at him, but missed as the man suddenly ducked away, turning to go back out the front door. He just managed to get the front door open when Chadwick drew another bead and fired a three round burst that struck the guard in the back. He fell forward, blocking the door from closing.

"Shite!" Chadwick checked his watch: one minute. He ran down the hallway, grabbed the dead soldier's boots and pulled him back inside the building. The door swung shut.

Chadwick ran toward the safety of the back door as fast as possible. *Please let the clocks be accurate*, was his thought.

When he was a few feet from the door, he considered diving through it, but realized he would need a lot more distance than that, so he pumped his legs furiously. He was five yards from the tree line and the rest of his squad when the, as it turned out, accurate timers sparked the plastic explosives.

The building's walls seemed to bulge out as if it had taken deep breath. The roof shattered into pieces and then fell in slow motion back into the inferno below. It was as if the building had taken a direct hit from a one hundred pound bomb, which was the rough equivalent of the plastic.

A pressure wave shot through the open back door and caught up to Chadwick, flinging him face first into the ground.

The explosions against the hotel wall adjoining the communications center punched two holes big enough to drive a car through. The upper portion of that wall, with little below it for support, began to crack. After a few more seconds, the entire wall fell into the hotel, taking several floors and Gestapo agents along with it.

Chapter 15

Meuse River, west bank, just east of Dompcevrin
143 miles east of Paris
9 September, 2050 Hours

Dunn had handed off the three surviving prisoners from the farmhouse to the MPs and was glad to be rid of them. They'd kept pestering Schneider and Goerdt, who'd let it slip he also spoke German, with questions about POW camps, and whether they would be sent to America. It made Dunn wonder whether POWs in the U.S. were somehow passing the word over here about how good it was there. In any case, Dunn had finally told the Germans to save their questions for the MPs because his guys didn't know anything.

Dunn decided he'd better have his men trade in their Thompsons for M1 Garands. In the upcoming fighting in the river valleys the firing distances were going to increase well beyond the Thompson's fifty yard effective range, and the M1's effective range was ten times that. Jonesy had asked to keep his Springfield 1903 sniper rifle and Dunn agreed. The doubled effective range over the M1 and accuracy that Jonesy could provide with the scope outweighed the loss of the more rapid-fire M1.

On top of that, Dunn had managed to hold on to the two .30 caliber Browning 1919 machine guns he'd requisitioned for the bridge capture in Chartres a couple of weeks ago. These were the newer versions that used the newly designed disintegrating belt. This gave them a theoretical rate of 1,200 rounds per minute, but barrel heating and the potential for runaway cook-off firing without pulling the trigger, held that to a lower more practical 600. The effective range of 1,500 yards was three times the M1's capability.

"Dave, let's get the thirties set up one each on the ends of our area of responsibility."

"Right, Sarge."

Cross got busy assigning two-man teams to operate the machine guns.

The area Dunn referred to was a line on the west bank of the Meuse River which ran about forty yards, with ten yards between pairs of men. Dunn believed the men reacted and felt better with a foxhole buddy. As the men dug themselves shallow foxholes, just deep enough for lying or kneeling, Dunn walked up and down the line snapping off encouragement.

The engineers were working on building a bridge to cross the river, because all the other bridges had been destroyed as the Germans retreated, at a point two miles down river, to the south. Dunn's platoon extended to the south about a half mile. The Sherman tanks they were attached to, fifteen of them, were positioned behind them about two hundred yards. The platoon's assignment was to prevent German flanking attacks and counterattacks across the open fields that lay to the northeast of the bridge site.

Farther south of the bridge site, other Shermans, as well as Tank Destroyers, were set up to act as bombardment artillery on the ridgeline across the river where the German artillery was suspected to be.

After everyone got settled, Dunn jumped down to share a foxhole with Jonesy just north of the rightmost machine gun manned by Lindstrom and Bailey. The other machine gun was manned by Schneider and Wickham. North of Dunn were

Martelli and Goerdt, and on the other side of them were Cross and Waters. This put each team of two within yards of Dunn or Cross for control.

"You hungry, Jonesy?"

"I'm always hungry, Sarge." Jonesy grinned.

Jonesy grew up in south Chicago, and had a touch of tough street kid in him. He had blue eyes, and already had the start of a widow's peak at the age of twenty-three. He hadn't set out to become a sniper, but deer hunting trips with his dad and two brothers had taught him the necessary skills and most importantly, the patience to eventually become the best shooter Dunn had ever seen. When Dunn had first witnessed Jones shoot on the firing range, Jones had placed groupings of his shots at 600 yards within a seven and one-half inch diameter circle. Even the range master said he'd never seen anything quite like that. Ever since, Jones had a standing order to take his Springfield along on their missions.

Dunn broke into his pack to get at the K-rations. "You want dinner or supper?"

"I'll take the dinner, I like it better. Today anyway."

Dunn handed over the small box and picked up a supper box for himself. He wanted the chocolate. He'd been giving away a lot of it lately to kids—a little girl in Italy and a boy in Chartres, France—and wanted to have a bit for himself.

The men settled down in the foxhole, which was mostly dry, even though it was close to the river. They used the attached twist key and opened the round can of mystery meat. They ate silently, using their little metal spoons.

When they were done, they threw everything back in the box and tossed it in the foxhole out of the way.

The sun was going down and Dunn noticed a buildup of clouds in the west. Five minutes later the first German artillery round exploded near the bridge site. The dusk sky was soon aflame with American tracer high explosive rounds arcing toward the German guns from the Shermans and the Tank Destroyers. Dunn and Jonesy could hear the supersonic roar of the 76mm rounds as they flew overhead.

Dunn checked on his men from his foxhole. They were staying low, but watching the fireworks display, too. An hour passed before the German guns finally fell silent. The Americans stopped firing, their gunners waiting and watching for other plumes of cannon fire from across the river. It was soon evident that the Germans had either been destroyed or had retreated.

The sun finally gave up the day and slid under the horizon.

Dunn was grateful that none of the German artillery shells had fallen short of their target and hit his men.

He was about to say something to that effect to Jonesy when the screaming started.

Chapter 16

American airfield, XIX Tactical Air Command
20 miles south of Paris
9 September, 2055 Hours

"Chief, I think there's an oil leak in the cockpit. I can smell it."

The crew chief nodded to Captain Banks. "I'll get right on it, sir."

"Thanks, chief."

As always, the aircraft's crew chief firmly believed that the plane belonged to him and the pilot only borrowed it. Any chief worth his salt knew every bolt, every fitting, every line in the airplane.

Ben Banks turned and walked away toward the tents that served as home. After about ten yards, he looked over his shoulder at his aircraft. The setting sun was behind the plane, so she looked black, but her true colors were the same horrible brown-green as the B-17s, with white trim around the cowling and one white stripe on each elevator and the tail. *She's beautiful*, thought Banks. The requisite painting of a blond woman in skimpy clothing adorned the area just forward of and below the cockpit. Her name was *Gorgeous Mary*, named after a girl Banks met during pilot training in Texas. She'd written to him for a short time after he'd left for England so he went with her name. Then she'd "met someone else," another pilot in training, of course. Banks hadn't bothered to change the name.

His wingman caught up with him. "Hey, Skip."

"Hi Ed."

The two men were the same height, five-nine, and weighed about the same, perhaps one hundred fifty-five pounds with their gear. Where they differed the most was their hair color, dark black for Ed Holden and light brown for Banks. They'd known each other just over six months, with Holden coming in as a replacement. Banks was already the squadron leader and he picked Holden as his wing man when he'd lost his to antiaircraft fire.

"What was the score today?" Holden asked, as he always did.

"Three Panzer Mark IVs, a couple of trucks, and a staff car."

"Hm, not too bad. I prefer hitting Tigers."

"Who doesn't?" Banks asked with a grin. "But we'll take whatever the krauts give us."

"Want to go to Paris tonight? Can we get passes?"

Banks thought about the idea. It had been a week since their first foray into the City of Light. Add to that the stress of losing a man a couple of days ago when they'd attacked the German artillery on the ridge overlooking the Meuse River valley near Verdun. Mike Osborn and his Thunderbolt had been vaporized.

Banks decided quickly. "Okay. We aren't scheduled to fly tomorrow. I'll see if I can wangle a few from the old man."

Banks loved Paris. Even with all the commies running around spouting some proletarian bullshit, it was still a great place for drinking, eating, more drinking, and if you played your cards right, a night of great sex.

They reached the tents and split off with Banks promising to talk to the colonel.

Banks headed toward the colonel's headquarters tent, which was only a hundred yards from the sleeping area. So far they'd been lucky and there hadn't been much rain. Whenever there was, though, the paths through the tents could turn into a quagmire.

The sides of the colonel's tent were rolled up to let the breeze in. Banks ducked under the edge, and walked over to the colonel's map table, where the group commander was standing. Another officer was standing on the other side of the table. Both were looking at a map.

"Evening, sir." Banks saluted. "Evening, Major Jackson."

Colonel Bill Walker returned an abbreviated version as did the major.

"Hello, Banks. How did things go?"

Banks repeated the score he'd given to Holden and added, "All accounted for, sir. Although Bill Wooten got clipped in the undercarriage by ack-ack. Luckily, his gear was undamaged and he got the bird on the ground okay. My chief is checking the oil line around my cockpit. I thought I smelled oil when I landed."

Major Jackson wrote the score down on a clipboard, then pulled over another one and scribbled the damage and repair report. He glanced up at Banks. "All ordnance dropped?"

"Yes, sir."

"Well, done," Colonel Walker said.

"Thank you, sir." Banks cleared his throat. "Sir, I was wondering if we might be able to get a few passes to Paris for tonight. We aren't flying tomorrow."

The colonel glanced at the major, then back at Banks. "Sorry, Banks. No passes. You *are* flying. We have to hit some targets that are building up around Metz."

"Oh, I see. Very good, sir. Just thought I'd ask. Do you need anything from me tonight?"

"No, nothing I can think of. Go get some chow and rest."

"Yes, sir."

Banks exchanged salutes with his superior officers and left.

On the way back to the tents he hoped Holden hadn't already said something about Paris to the men. He wished he'd said something about that.

He found his men sitting outside in an open area that had become the unofficial back yard, complete with chairs and logs on end for low tables.

Judging by the fact that the men weren't busy shaving and slicking back their hair, it appeared that he was safe, Holden hadn't spilled the beans after all.

Banks spotted Holden over by the coffee pot chatting with a couple of the guys.

Benjamin Banks was the old man of the squadron at twenty-five. He had a complement of thirty-five pilots, down one due to the loss a few days ago. He also had twenty-four P-47s and about 200 men to support the aircraft and the pilots. With more pilots than planes, a pilot could expect to fly every three missions, except the squadron leader who generally flew more often, taking fewer breaks from combat.

Banks grew up near Wathena, Kansas, a small farming community of about a thousand people. It was located five miles west of St. Joseph, Missouri, which was famous for the short-lived Pony Express. The son of a farmer, Banks lived northeast of town. He had learned work ethic from his no-nonsense father. Farm chores before anything. An average student, mostly because he got bored daily, Banks made it through high school and graduated in 1937. Wiry and physically tough, he got a job at the Armour and Company meatpacking plant in south St. Joe, in the center of the stockyards. It was grueling work, but it paid well. And you did get used to the smell.

Banks caught Holden's eye from across the way and jerked his head for Holden to join him away from the other men.

"What's going on?"

"Paris is out."

"Ah shit."

"Did you mention it to the men?"

"What? Oh, hell no. I know better than that, Skip."

"I know, just had to ask."

"Where are we going to tomorrow, since it's not Paris tonight?"

"Targets around Metz."

"Oh boy."

"Yeah."

Metz was known to have lots of antiaircraft guns around the city.

"Keep it to yourself. No need to worry the boys."

"Okay, Skip."

"Let's join in and get a drink and some dinner. I'm starving."

"After you."

Chapter 17

Meuse River, west bank, just east of Dompcevrin
143 miles east of Paris
9 September, 2100 Hours

Following the scream, the heavy sound of a single .45 caliber Colt shot rang out from north of Dunn.

Dunn jumped out of his foxhole with the grace and speed of a 100 yard hurdler and ran toward the sounds. He didn't have to go far. At the very next foxhole he spotted Al Martelli standing outside of the hole, his eyes wide, and a hand over his heart. He appeared to be checking to see if it was still beating.

Martelli's foxhole buddy, Rob Goerdt, was still in the hole, standing there holding his Colt in his right hand, and a long object in his other. When Dunn got closer, he could see in the dimming evening light that Goerdt was holding a snake. A quite dead snake. It was at least three feet long and had a thick powerful body. Dunn looked more closely and noticed the snake was headless.

Goerdt holstered his .45 and threw the snake toward the river. Drawing his combat knife, he bent over and was out of Dunn's sight momentarily. When he stood up again he held out the snake's head, impaled upon the knife, the jaws were open, revealing twin fangs.

To Dunn, it looked like a rattlesnake, but not quite.

Martelli had calmed down and stepped closer. He reached a hand out toward the head, but Goerdt yanked it out of reach. "Uh, I wouldn't do that."

Surprised, Martelli asked, "Why? It's dead."

"Yes, but there could be venom on the fangs. You get some on you and it finds a cut, you could be in real trouble."

"Oh." Martelli snatched his hand back, and examined the snake's head from a safe distance.

Dunn asked, "So what happened exactly?"

Martelli spoke first. "Well, we were watching the fire show, and praying nothing fell short on us. Afterwards, I felt something on my shoulder. I glanced over and there it was staring me right in the eyes. I started shouting and jumped out of the foxhole. Then Rob there, pulled out his forty-five and shot the thing's head off."

Goerdt was smiling. "You're lucky he wasn't coiled up. He'd have bitten you in the face."

"Really?"

"Yep."

"It's really poisonous?"

"Yep. See the little hoods over the eyes?"

Martelli looked at the snake head. "Yeah."

"Sign of a viper. Always poisonous. I don't know what kind it is, so it might not be potent enough to kill, but you can't take chances."

"I've never seen a viper before. Not too many of them in the Bronx, I guess." Martelli laughed nervously.

Dunn and Goerdt laughed lightly.

"Thanks, Rob. How did you know about this?" Martelli asked.

"Hunting in Iowa. We find rattlesnakes once in a while out in the timber." Goerdt got a mischievous look on his face and said, "I could retrieve the body and we could have snake steak, if you like."

"No snake for me," Martelli said with a shudder.

Dunn chuckled to himself and walked off to the north. He would let everyone else know everything was okay.

Goerdt jumped out of the foxhole and went to a spot about ten yards east. He knelt and, using the ground, carefully disengaged the head from the knife. He dug a small hole about a foot deep and used the knife tip to scoot the head over the edge into the hole, which he covered up and tamped down with a boot. It was getting darker by the second and he had just enough light to examine the blade. Digging the hole seemed to have cleaned off the blood. To make sure he jammed it into the earth a few times all the way to the hilt. He wiped the blade against the tall grass, then sheathed it. He'd examine it more closely in the morning light.

Back at the foxhole, Goerdt settled into his spot.

"Thanks, Rob."

Goerdt glanced over at his buddy. "You're welcome, Al."

Martelli seemed to want to say something else, but was having a little trouble with it.

"What is it, Al?"

"I didn't scream like a little boy, did I?"

Goerdt recalled the high-pitched screeches that Martelli had loosed as he was trying to get away from the viper. It had been quite funny since Martelli had a pretty deep voice. To give Goerdt credit, he merely smiled as he patted Martelli on the shoulder. "No, Al. You didn't. Not at all."

"Okay."

Goerdt got the same mischievous expression on his face as earlier, but Martelli couldn't see it very well. "Maybe a little bit like a teen-aged boy."

Goerdt didn't mind the punch in the shoulder. It was worth it.

After Dunn let everyone know what had happened, which caused a few chuckles at Martelli's expense, he jumped back down in his own foxhole. He'd given the order for one man in each foxhole to take the first two hour shift, the other one should get some shuteye. Dunn told Jonesy to go ahead and sack out.

The sun had set fully and the moon was rising in the northeast. It had been a full moon a few days ago, and so it was very bright. Anything moving in the fields across the river would stand out black on white. The air was getting cooler, a pleasant break from the day's warmth. It wouldn't get cool enough for discomfort, but Dunn knew that was coming in the months ahead. He was accustomed to Iowa winters, but it was one thing to go out for a few hours and come back in to the roaring heat of a fireplace, and another to spend every day and night out in the miserable and dangerous weather. Just thinking about it made Dunn shiver.

Alone with his thoughts, Dunn recalled Pamela's wonderful revelation that they were going to have a baby. They'd had a special dinner at a fancy Paris restaurant within sight of the Eiffel Tower. Dunn had received the meal as a gift from a grateful French Resistance fighter, whose uncle owned the restaurant.

Dunn had been stunned by Pamela's news and then delighted. They figured the baby would be born in May of the next year. It had been a sobering moment to realize that at the age of twenty-four he was going to be a father. His own birthday was the next month, on 15 June. He supposed that the baby could be born near his birthday, if it was late. It? Pamela seemed sure it would be a boy, and when she told Dunn she wanted to name him Thomas, Junior, Dunn felt something, but he wasn't sure what it was. It was only later he recognized it as pride and joy.

He'd written a letter to his Mom and Dad back in Cedar Rapids. Their house was on the outskirts of the city. To Dunn it had always felt more rural than city because from his second floor window he could see cattle and corn—the two big C's of Iowa. He'd kept the letter's information simple, Pamela was expecting, due in May, and was feeling fine.

The family already knew she was working as a nurse on the continent with the Queen Alexandra's Nursing Service, but Dunn hadn't expressed his fears for her safety to them—why make them worry about that? One thing he was glad about: now that she was expecting, she would have to tell her supervisor. Pamela had told Dunn she would probably have to go back to England in October. He carefully hid his relief at this news.

Dunn wondered what kind of father, dad, he would be. He thought he had a great role model in his own dad. Mr. Dunn was prone to periodic pithy advice and Dunn hoped he could do as well with his own child. Mr. Dunn was a math teacher and had always encouraged Dunn to do well in school. Dunn was an excellent student, but was uninterested in math, although he earned A's in it. He discovered in junior high school that he loved history. His dream job was to teach it, and he was majoring in History and Education when he dropped out of college on December 8th, 1941 to enlist.

Pamela and he and had discussed where they might live, and had agreed that it would be in the States, probably in Cedar Rapids, or if they felt adventurous, Chicago. In the light of the French moon, Dunn wondered whether he could really raise a family in such a large city, with its big-city problems. He shrugged his shoulders. Just have to wait until it was time to choose.

He checked his watch and was surprised two hours had already passed and the moon had risen farther into the sky. He rousted Jonesy and settled down into a sitting position for his two hour nap.

His last waking thought was, *I'm a lucky man.*

Chapter 18

North of Spa, Belgium
9 September, 2115 Hours

No one had followed Saunders and his men after their adventure at the communications center. Barltrop and Handford had stayed behind in the woods. They kept an eye and ear out for the explosions, which went off at 0802 hours as planned. Handford had run out to help Chadwick get to his feet and into the woods.

The three men had watched as the comm center quickly became engulfed in flames, the collapse of the joint wall with the hotel containing the Gestapo headquarters, and finally the fire jumping to the hotel. They waited and watched for over an hour as the Spa fire department futilely fought the impossible roaring flames. The firemen had finally retreated and concentrated on saving the rest of the buildings on the same block, something they just managed to accomplish.

The communication center collapsed in on itself, and as the smoke began to clear, Barltrop could see through to the street, where fire personnel, Gestapo agents in their black suits, and curious Spa citizens watched the action. At one point, one

Gestapo agent began gesturing and appeared to be shouting at the other agents. After a full five minutes, the cowed agents scuttled away, presumably to discover what had happened. Was it a gas leak, which might account for the explosion, or did someone set the fire and it sparked a gas explosion?

When he was satisfied that no one was searching for enemy soldiers, Barltrop tapped Handford and Chadwick on the shoulder and nodded to the north.

Upon their return, Barltrop had Handford provide the report to Saunders, and the new man did an excellent job; Barltrop hadn't needed to add anything at all.

Saunders accepted the report, and sent Kopp and Mills back to keep an eye on things. They would be relieved every two hours.

Over twelve hours later, the men were still in the same pine tree covered and surrounded clearing. They'd spent most of the day sleeping in turns, cleaning their weapons, and taking stock of their dwindling food supplies.

Major Armstrong had gone into his own world, reading his way through the messages that they had taken from the communications center. The men left him alone except to offer food and water periodically, because the man seemed to forget he needed both.

Saunders had assigned two men to guard the general, who seemed resigned to his fate, and offered no trouble. Saunders had not bothered to question the man and instead opted for psychological pressure. He'd instructed Armstrong to do his reading from a point fairly close to the general and in his eye line. He was to periodically hold up a message, shake it at the general, and laugh, saying something in German along the lines of "You've got to be kidding," and "Well, we already know this," and "Do you really think we're that stupid?"

After an hour of this, the general had closed his eyes and turned away from Armstrong. Armstrong continued anyway, knowing the general couldn't cover his ears.

Saunders got up from his resting place and walked over to stand in front of the general, who looked up with pleading in his eyes.

"Are you ready to talk to me?"

The general shook his head.

"Well, what do you want?"

The general mumbled through his gag. "Uhn, uhn." He tilted his chin up in an attempt to draw attention to the gag.

"You want me to undo your gag?"

Enthusiastic nods.

Saunders raised his suppressed Sten and aimed at the general in an offhand sort of way. "Will I have any problems with your trying to shout for help?"

"Mmm, mmm," the general replied, shaking his head.

Saunders called out, "Dickinson?"

Dickinson looked up from where he was lying on the ground. "Yes, Sarge?"

"Undo his gag. Be sure to stay out of my line of fire."

The general's eyes nearly bugged out at the last remark.

Dickinson removed the man's gag, carefully staying out of Saunders' line of fire.

The general opened his mouth wide and took in a deep breath, and let it out, and worked his mouth as if exercising the muscles unused all day.

"Thank you."

Saunders leaned over, crowding the general's space. "What do we get for taking off your gag?"

The general blinked, and then replied, "I can tell you nothing. Surely you know this."

"Well, maybe we can just start simple. What's your name?"

"You already know my name. I saw you read my identification papers."

Saunders shrugged and nodded for Dickinson to replace the gag.

"Manfred Teuber."

Saunders smiled. "Manfred. Very good, that wasn't so hard, was it? Here's another easy one. Are you married, Manfred?"

"*Ja.* Twenty-one years. "

"Long time. How about kids?"

"Two daughters."

Saunders sat down in front of the general, his Sten held in his lap. With the general's hands still tied behind his back, the commando had no cause for concern.

"Which army group are you from?"

"I will not answer."

"Who do you report to?"

"I will not answer. You know I cannot answer. I am not required to answer."

Saunders gave the general a chilling smile. "Manfred, Manfred. You seem to be under the misapprehension that the rules apply to you."

Before the general could think of a rejoinder, Major Armstrong said, "Sergeant Saunders! I need you to see something." The major held up a message and waved it.

Saunders held the general's gaze for a long moment, and said softly, "Perhaps we don't need you anymore, Manfred. That would be a shame. I've grown to like you in a short time." He turned to Dickinson and nodded.

Dickinson replaced the gag on a suddenly meek and frightened general.

Saunders sat down beside Armstrong.

"What'd you find, sir?"

"A couple of messages referring to a top level meeting. Lots of generals are supposed to be there. Thought you'd be interested to know about it."

"Where?"

"Aachen."

Saunders got out a map and asked, "I assume that's in Germany?"

"Yes, should be near the Belgium border."

Saunders examined the map briefly. "Right. Here it is." He laid his fingertip against the scale for the map, saw that the width of his finger was ten miles, and then used that to measure the distance to Aachen. "A little more than twenty miles."

Saunders thought about it for a few minutes, trying to find a way to attack the meeting. Twenty miles, though, through a contracting German army, would be ultra-high risk, and likely unsuccessful. And worse, fatal to his men. A different idea occurred to him. "Does it say where in Aachen? Like what building?"

"It doesn't. For that matter, it could be just outside the city. I'm sorry, just not enough information."

Saunders glanced at the German general, who was watching them closely.

Saunders got up, patting Armstrong on the shoulder. "Thanks, Major."

"Sure."

Saunders made to walk back over to the general when Garner stepped into the clearing. He and Thurston were on Spa guard duty. Saunders changed directions and met Garner, making sure they were far enough away from the general.

"What is it?" Saunders asked.

"It looks like the Germans might be retreating, and leaving the city. The Gestapo all got in their cars and drove off to the east. A column of fifteen trucks came though carrying troops and some pulling artillery."

Saunders smiled. This was good news. Relief might be just hours away instead of a few days. Montgomery must be advancing much faster than expected. He checked his watch. "You're due for relief soon anyway. Grab some grub, I'll send someone back for Thurston."

"Okay, Sarge."

Saunders sent Redington and Chadwick to relieve Thurston. He gathered his men away from the general. "It appears that the krauts are leaving the city. Monty might be arriving soon, maybe tomorrow. Let's stay alert. No sense getting into trouble at this point."

Saunders dismissed the men and they resumed their places. Saunders still had a couple of men outside the clearing acting as a moving picket line.

Saunders sat down in front of the general after removing the man's gag. "Are you hungry, sir?"

"Yes."

"Before you have some dinner, I thought you should know something. Your friends are leaving Spa. They're also leaving in droves from the front line, retreating, presumably back to Germany."

The general gave no reaction to the news, which caused Saunders to say, "You already knew this was happening, didn't you?"

"I will not answer."

Saunders shrugged. "Hope you like English weather."

"I despise everything English."

Saunders laughed, a deep rolling thunder. "Of course you do. That's all right by me. I despise everything German. How you guys thought you'd actually win this war is beyond any logic I've ever known. Ironic, don't you think, that your famous German logic and efficiency can't win the war?"

Instead of waiting for an answer, Saunders got up and left.

A few minutes later, Barltrop and Dickinson untied the general's hands and gave him a tin of meat and a canteen. They sat nearby, ready in case the man tried to escape into the darkening woods.

Barltrop noted the Iron Cross hanging at the general's neck. His eyes narrowed as he hoped the general would try.

Chapter 19

Meuse River, west bank, just east of Dompcevrin
143 miles east of Paris
10 September, 0626 Hours

When Eugene Lindstrom stood up to stretch, a squelching sound came from the bottom of the foxhole. He glanced down to find what he already knew would be there: an inch of mud water sitting in the bottom. He was lucky he'd put his poncho on for some extra warmth, otherwise the rest of him would be soaking wet. Or more likely, his buddy, Leonard Bailey, would have awakened him so he could cover up against the rain.

Bailey was leaning against the muddy top edge of the foxhole's east side, staring out at the river valley. He heard Lindstrom's rustling sounds and turned his head to say, "Morning."

Lindstrom gave a mock two-fingered salute and said, "Morning. Any coffee yet?" Lindstrom was feeling a bit cold even with the poncho. Damp air could do that to you.

"Schneider brewed some. I'm off for another. Want one?"

Lindstrom held up his metal cup. "Quickly, please."

Bailey laughed and took the cup with the hand already carrying his own. "Be right back."

As Bailey passed Dunn's and Jonesy's foxhole, he was surprised to see his sergeant already up and staring across the river with his binoculars.

"Good morning, Sarge, Jonesy."

He waved and the two men replied in kind, Dunn still looking through the binoculars.

All the men he passed were up and around, some already had coffee and some had broken into their food supply.

While filling the two cups with the black and wonderful smelling coffee, Bailey asked Schneider if anything had come over the radio overnight.

"Not a thing, sorry."

"Okay, just thought I'd ask. See you guys later."

He bee-lined back to Lindstrom and handed off the hot coffee, then jumped into the muddy foxhole. The two men drank their coffee in silence while facing the east, enemy territory. They finished the coffee about the same time and then got some C-Rations out for breakfast.

With his mouth still partly full, Lindstrom asked, "What's winter like in Denver?"

"Not too bad, really. Everyone thinks we get snowed in all the time, but because we're just over five thousand feet, the snow we get tends to melt quickly. The temperature rises and we have a lot of sunshine. My mom told me that last March we got a foot and a half, but it was back into the forties soon after. Compared to other places, it's pretty mild. What about Eugene, Eugene?" The guys had fun with Eugene's name after learning he was from Eugene, Oregon.

"Well, let's see, the winter highs are around upper forties to lower fifties. Maybe we get six inches of snow, although it does rain quite a bit in the winter. Sounds like both our home towns are going to be a lot better than a winter here."

"Yeah, I've been hearing it can get brutally cold and snow somewhere around two or three feet."

Lindstrom shook his head.

The men settled back into silence.

Dunn came by a few minutes later. "Hey guys, we're moving out in thirty."

"Okay, Sarge. Where we headed?" Lindstrom asked.

Dunn shrugged. "East is all I know."

"Okay."

Lindstrom and Bailey finished their meager breakfast and then packed.

Not much later, their halftrack drove up and parked near Dunn's foxhole.

Before everyone climbed into the vehicle, Dunn gathered his men and said, "I just got the word for the day. We're twenty-five miles from a place called Arnaville and that's where we're headed next. It's on the Moselle River and battalion is expecting the Germans to make a strong stand when we try to build a bridge, and then try to secure a bridgehead on the east bank. Where we'll be positioned won't be known until we get there and battalion makes a decision.

"On the way, we need to be ready for German units bypassed by the speed of the Shermans."

"So we're the mop up crew?" Wickham asked.

Dunn nodded. "Us and a couple of squads from third platoon."

Cross glanced up at the clouds. "Any chance of air cover?"

Dunn shook his head and sighed. He was unhappy about it. "Nope. Very unlikely. Not impossible, so if we think we need it, or if we find viable targets like artillery or tanks, we'll go ahead and call in for an airstrike."

Dunn glanced around at his men. They looked tired, but as always carried themselves well. They were getting their determined expressions set on their faces. He loved seeing that.

Dunn, with Cross's help, had actually handpicked each man, including Clarence Waters. Dunn had known of Waters' proclivity for smart mouthing at the wrong time, as well as pulling a few stunts while assigned to his previous squad leader, Bagley. Dunn also knew the man could shoot with the best of them, which was important since Dunn's men *were* the best of them. Dunn had heard about Waters' first incident at the first squad meal together at Camp Barton Stacey nearly three weeks ago. Wickham and Martelli had handled it. Since then, Cross had made sure Waters was paired with him whenever possible. Waters had done well in Chartres at the bridge they had to secure for Patton's forces, and later at the Paris airfield where the bioweapon was captured.

"Any questions, men?"

Dunn got a chorus of 'No, Sarge.'

"Very good. Load up."

While the men tossed their gear and equipment up into the back of the halftrack, Dunn got into the cab on the passenger side. He greeted the driver, and the gunner manning the massive .50 caliber Browning and got 'Hellos' back.

A few seconds later, Cross hollered, "All set back here."

The driver didn't wait. He put the nine-ton vehicle into first gear and the beast lumbered away to the south to join the rest of Patton's Third Army.

It took ten minutes for Dunn's halftrack driver to find the proper spot in the lengthening line of armored vehicles heading east. At the front of the miles-long column were two companies of Shermans with the mechanized infantry following.

Dunn had carefully checked his map. The route to Arnaville was primarily in the east-northeast direction, following a pretty good road that didn't go through any other villages.

Dunn guessed their speed at about twenty miles an hour. He kept an eye on both sides of the road and in the distance he watched for any signs of Germans. The countryside reminded him quite a bit of eastern Iowa, with some rolling hills, the farm fields, and the woods. He rarely had time to miss home, but after driving fifteen minutes through this area it was starting to hit him.

To distract himself from the thoughts of home, he spoke to the driver, "What's your name?"

"Jack Eastman."

"Tom Dunn. Nice to know your name, Jack. Where you from?"

"Tulsa. You?"

"Iowa."

"Cold up there in the winter, I hear."

"Yup."

"Don't think I could live there."

"You get used to it."

"Yeah, but why bother?" Eastman laughed.

They drifted into friendly conversation about family as they drove along.

Dunn figured they'd traveled eleven miles when the shit hit the fan.

The first sign of trouble was a series of explosions far ahead of Dunn's halftrack. A Sherman tank a quarter mile ahead on the road exploded. The halftrack driver immediately turned off the road and headed for a wooded area five hundred yards away zig zagging like a Navy destroyer.

Dunn held on tight as the halftrack bounced over the rough terrain.

Up ahead, Shermans turned left at a forty-five degree angle to get off the road and started firing at targets unseen by Dunn.

Explosions rocked the earth and shattered the air. The clouds above had moved away earlier, and now the blue sky was turning brown and gray from the dirt particles and smoke.

A round exploded just fifty yards away from the halftrack. The driver continued his zig-zag path.

Dunn had plenty of time to wonder if this was going to be it.

When the halftrack reached a point about ten yards from the woods, the driver slewed the vehicle around so the back pointed south. "Get your men out, Sarge." The driver opened his door and ran around to the back to help.

Dunn jumped out and yelled, "Everybody out!"

The men were already on the move.

The gunner scrambled out after Dunn.

In seconds, Dunn's entire squad was on the run. Dunn pushed each man that ran by to give him a boost. The men dispersed and ran to a point about fifty yards deep in the woods. With no time to dig into the earth, each man got down as far as possible.

To the north, artillery rounds were exploding, seemingly everywhere. One landed not far from the abandoned halftrack and the shrapnel hitting the vehicle sounded as if someone was striking the armor with ball-peen hammers.

It seemed to Dunn that the artillery was lessening. He lifted his head and listened. Suddenly, it all stopped. He rose to his feet, but kept the tree he hunkered behind between himself and the open field. He checked his watch and let a full minute go by.

He spoke to the ranger closest to him, Goerdt, "Tell everyone to stay here."

Grabbing Jonesy, Dunn took off toward the open field. Jonesy was a step behind.

Dunn edged up to the field and looked around. Smoke was everywhere. One halftrack lay on its side and numerous smoldering Shermans dotted the road. They'd never had a chance.

Chapter 20

American airfield, XIX Tactical Air Command
20 miles south of Paris
10 September, 0644 Hours

"Colonel, please. We need to get airborne," squadron leader Ben Banks pleaded.

"The reports say the ceiling is at three thousand. That's risky."

"We can take the risk, sir. We've done it before, you know."

Colonel Walker shook his head. Here he was the commanding officer and he felt like he was losing the argument.

Banks held up a hand and ran outside of the tent. He looked up at the sky and ran back in. "It's starting to rise, sir. By the time we get up and over the target, we'll have another thousand feet. At least."

Walker glanced at Major Jackson, who nodded.

"Okay, you're a go. Now get out of here."

"Yes, sir."

Banks ran all the way to the tents where his men were waiting for word. When they spotted him running their way, each man picked up his flight helmet and took off for his plane. They were already wearing their flight gear, trusting that Banks would carry the day with the colonel.

Banks grabbed his own gear and ran to *Gorgeous Mary*. He climbed aboard and the crew chief helped him get situated in the cockpit. Banks loved the size of the cockpit. Compared to a P-51 Mustang, it was enormous with lots of room for legs and shoulders. The Thunderbolt was carrying two one-thousand-pound bombs and the eight .50 caliber Browning machine guns were loaded and ready.

The crew chief jumped off the back of the wing and ran around in front where Banks could see him. A crewman sat on the forward edge of the port wing and he would act as Banks' eyes helping guide the plane to the airstrip because Banks could not see over the extraordinarily long nose while taxiing. Two other crewmen waited outside the edge of each wingtip.

Banks saluted the chief, who returned it, and the pilot started the massive engine. It coughed a couple of times, then the four-bladed propeller began to spin. Banks gave her some more throttle and adjusted the choke. The engine settled into a happy rumble. Banks gave the chief a thumbs up. The two crewmen darted underneath and yanked out the chock blocks as the chief ran to the port side out of the way.

Banks gave her more throttle and the plane rolled away toward the grassy airstrip. Since it was wet, Banks would be cautious on his turns. He followed the crewman's hand signals and maneuvered the P-47 into the right place at the north end of the airstrip to take advantage of the southerly wind. When the P-47 stopped rolling, the crewman slid off the back of the wing near the fuselage, waving at Banks.

Banks glanced left. His squadron was lining up for takeoff.

Banks raised a hand and closed the canopy. He pushed the throttle forward and the engine roared. The plane rolled, picking up speed, pressing the pilot into the back of his armored seat. Once he was airborne, he put the aircraft into a slow climb to two thousand feet and banked over into a wide turn. He and the rest of the squadron would form their flights one by one and circle the airfield until all were in the air.

When the last pilot to take off slid his aircraft into position, he radioed Banks.

"Heading eighty-one degrees at angels twenty-two," Banks told his squadron. Angels was for altitude, and the minus factor for the day was ten, so he meant twelve thousand feet. "Twenty-six minutes." At four hundred miles an hour, the Thunderbolt would cover one hundred seventy-five miles of ground very fast.

Banks settled into his seat and made himself comfortable for the short ride.

The low pressure center moved farther north putting it over Belgium, and the barometric air pressure dropped some more. This increased the southerly winds and the southern edge of the cloud cover began to race northward, with the skies clearing behind it.

RONN MUNSTERMAN

Chapter 21

In flight over France
10 September, 0722 Hours

When the sky had cleared a few minutes ago, Captain Banks had changed his squadron's altitude to five thousand feet. Suddenly, just to his right, he spotted an ongoing battle on the ground. He recognized right away the shape of the Sherman tanks and the halftracks that were coming under fire. He searched the ground ahead of the American column and quickly found the source of the attack.

"Dogbone Squadron from Dogbone leader. Change of plans: new targets just ahead. Follow me in."

Banks would tell the colonel later he'd come upon the battle and decided to eliminate the new targets of opportunity.

Banks was pretty certain the eight German artillery guns would be solely focused on the American armored column, and not on the sky. He also doubted they would have any additional antiaircraft weapons around them.

He rolled the Thunderbolt to the right and aimed for the line of artillery.

Banks targeted the guns at the farthest end of the line as he came in from the north. *Gorgeous Mary* screamed as her airspeed hit almost five hundred miles an hour. He released both bombs and soared off to the south. He banked left so he could climb back to five thousand feet and survey the results of his squadron's attack. In short order, the squadron destroyed all eight artillery guns.

Banks gave the order to return to base and the squadron formed up on Banks at the low level of five hundred feet. He glanced down and could make out that men were waving. He waggled his wings. He couldn't hear their cheers, but he knew they were shouting their heads off.

Suddenly, aircraft engine sounds drifted down.

Dunn stepped out from under the trees and looked up as did Jonesy. Dunn recognized the black silhouettes of the Thunderbolts as they roared overhead, seemingly right on top of him.

"Oh my God, those guys saved our bacon," he said. He raised his arms and waved as did most of the men still out in the open. Dunn saw the Thunderbolt squadron leader waggle his wings. Dunn shouted his head off.

It was impossible for Dunn and Banks to clearly see each other's faces. Just as it was impossible to foresee a person-to-person meeting.

Chapter 22

None of Dunn's men had been wounded, although Cross had a close call during the artillery strike on the column when shrapnel glanced off the top of his helmet as he dug himself into the ground as far as possible in the woods south of the road. His helmet suddenly sported a shiny metal scratch about an inch long. Shiny things on your person in combat were bad, so on the ride into Arnaville he'd taken his Zippo lighter and held the flame under the bright silver mark until it turned black. After the metal cooled, he'd rubbed the charred area with his finger, the way an artist used charcoal. When he was done he held the helmet at different angles. He was satisfied with his work and promptly went to sleep.

It had taken close to an hour to reorganize the column, and care for the wounded. In all, four Sherman crews had been killed and three halftracks had been hit either directly or close enough to kill all aboard. One such vehicle was the one carrying the platoon's first sergeant and the mortar squad. Another sergeant in the platoon would take over. Dunn had seniority, but the first lieutenant platoon leader told Dunn the other man had been with the platoon for six months. Dunn had said he understood, and it was not a problem for him. And it wasn't. He was happy leading his squad of rangers, but he was not particularly interested in rising up the command food chain. Too much bullshit accumulated the farther you climbed.

He accepted the role his squad had been assigned: plug a hole in the platoon for Patton, but if he had his druthers, he'd be happier on a special mission, at which he felt his squad excelled. But since it wasn't his call, he'd do what he was told.

When Patton's Third Army column rolled into the tiny river village of Arnaville, most of the armored units pulled off the road west of the village, but Dunn's halftrack, and several other vehicles rolled into the center of the French community.

Dunn's halftrack had stopped next to a building that appeared to be a general store, which reminded Dunn of Mr. Gavino's store in Ville di Murlo, Italy. The men piled out, stretching their cramped muscles when they hit the street. When Dunn got down, he looked around. The road going through the village was narrow, but plenty wide for the American equipment. Buildings and houses were one- and two-story affairs, and most were either stone or covered with stucco. A few villagers seemed to be going about their business. Two middle-aged women walked west on the opposite side of the street, each carrying what might be small sacks of groceries. An old man with a limp—Dunn wondered if it was from a World War I injury—made his way slowly but steadily down the street away from Dunn. There was one notable exception: no children were in Dunn's view. Had the French decided to keep them inside and out of sight, or had they evacuated them? Dunn shrugged to himself and sidled up next to Cross.

"I'm going to grab the platoon leader and see if we have any information on the day. Keep the men close to the halftrack, don't let them wander around."

"Okay, will do."

Dunn started to leave, but stopped and put a hand on his friend's shoulder. "I'm glad you're okay. Gave me a scare, old buddy, when that one hit your helmet."

Cross took a deep breath and let it out slowly. "Me, too. It was really loud on the inside."

"I bet it was." Dunn squeezed Cross's shoulder and nodded, then turned and walked away.

As Dunn walked east, he passed the next halftrack and that vehicle's squad leader, a small man by the name of Red Lancaster, fell in step with him. He was a skinny, freckle-faced kid called 'Red' for the obvious reason. He looked seventeen, but was actually twenty-three.

"Everyone all right in your squad, Red?" Dunn asked.

"Yes, we're okay. Yours?"

"We're okay. One close call, shrapnel hit my second's helmet a glancing blow."

"Whew. I heard McKay and the weapons squad got it."

"Yep. There's the new first sergeant." The two were approaching the lead halftrack and the platoon leader was standing outside his vehicle conversing with the replacement first sergeant. "There he is with Lieutenant Carver." Carver was facing their way and the first sergeant had his back to them.

"Yeah . . . I know."

Something in the man's voice made Dunn glance over. Lancaster did not look happy.

"What's wrong?"

Lancaster stopped walking so they wouldn't get within earshot of the lieutenant and sergeant, and turned to face Dunn. "He's ambitious. He steps on people. Watch your back."

"Thanks for the heads up."

"I mean it."

"I believe you. Thanks."

Lancaster nodded and marched off. Dunn kept pace and they joined the lieutenant and first sergeant.

"Sir," Dunn said.

"Sergeant," the lieutenant replied. "You've met Sergeant Kinney?"

"Yes, sir." Dunn nodded at the man who he knew he couldn't trust.

Kinney nodded back with no real expression on his face, although he did steal a glance at Dunn's right shoulder where the five stripes for a Technical Sergeant rested. Dunn noticed the glance. It supported Lancaster's comments.

Dunn offered his hand and Kinney hesitated, then shook it brusquely.

"I'm meeting with the CO soon and will tell you what I know ASAP, but in the meantime, have your squads do an equipment check. We lost our heavy stuff, so Kinney, I want you to scrounge around and find us some fifties and a bazooka. Trade whatever you have to, to get them," the lieutenant said.

"Sir, we've got a bazooka," Dunn said.

The lieutenant looked at Dunn and was clearly about to ask Dunn where he'd come by the weapon, but in the end said, "Great." To Kinney he said, "See if you can still get another one."

"Absolutely, sir."

"That's all, men."

"Yes, sir," said all three sergeants.

Kinney unnecessarily said to Lancaster, "You heard the lieutenant, go get your men started."

Lancaster nodded and turned away.

Dunn started to follow, but Kinney said, "Dunn, wait a minute."

"What is it?"

"I want you to track down the equipment the lieutenant wants."

Even with Lancaster's warning, Dunn was surprised by the request and hesitated briefly.

"You don't understand the order, Dunn?"

Dunn smiled, and said, "Sure, I recall the order. It was given to you."

Kinney frowned at the resistance. "And I'm giving it to you."

"We disagree on the validity, don't we?"

"You're refusing a direct order?"

Dunn thought over the question. Typically, a squad leader would just do what the first sergeant said, but Dunn felt this was an example of a man in position trying to push his men around. Dunn knew if he refused, he was starting down a path with this man from which a recovery for either would be unlikely in terms of working well together. On the other hand, Dunn knew a bully when he saw one. Backing down wasn't going to happen.

"I'm refusing to do your work for you, Kinney."

Kinney's jaw clenched, and he said, "I can put you on report for this."

"You do that. It'll make interesting reading for the lieutenant."

Dunn turned away and felt a hand grab his left arm. He turned back to face the sergeant.

"Oh, no. You're not gonna do that, Kinney. Take your hand off me now if you ever want to wipe your ass again."

Kinney removed his hand, but said, "You're going to regret this, Dunn."

"We shall see, Kinney."

Dunn walked away a few steps, and stopped and turned around. "Good luck with the weapons. Don't want to disappoint the lieutenant, do we?"

By the time Dunn got back to his men, he'd put the troubles with Kinney aside. He was pleased to see his men sitting on the curb, already doing their weapons check. Cross had taken the initiative once again. He walked over to where Cross was sitting on the curb with his M1 broken down.

Cross was running an oiled swath cloth through the barrel. When he pulled out the long folding rod, he put his thumb in the open gutless breech, and then turned the barrel to look down it. He positioned his thumbnail so it reflected light up the barrel. Satisfied the barrel was clean, he put everything back together and snapped the trigger guard into its locked position. He folded the rod by first pulling each joint apart and then snapping it over. He slipped all of the cleaning gear back into its storage spot in the rifle's butt, and closed and locked the lid. Last, he reloaded the eight round clip and shoved the bolt forward, ramming a cartridge into the chamber.

He looked over at Dunn, who had been watching. "Pass inspection?"

"Looks good from here," Dunn replied with a grin.

"So what's the news?"

"Nothing. No one knows anything yet. Lieutenant's going to meet with the CO. He'll let us know what he finds out ASAP."

"Figures."

"Yeah." Dunn glanced around, noting that Schneider and Goerdt were both too close for a private conversation. Dunn tipped his head toward a spot back to the west. Cross got up and followed, carrying his M1 in his right hand.

When they were far enough away, Dunn said, "We're going to have a problem with the new first sergeant, Kinney." Dunn filled Cross in on what Red had said, and the exchange Dunn had with Kinney.

"Terrific. Just what we need."

"Make sure to keep an eye out for him at all times. We'll keep this between us, but if he tries to interact directly with the men, make sure you either let me know or you get over there with them."

"Okay, I will. What's his deal, anyway?"

"Like Red said, Kinney's an ambitious, stab you in the back kind of guy."

"A real gem."

"Yep."

Dunn glanced down the street to the east, where he could see Kinney. The man had his hands on his hips and was leaning forward and jawing at his former squad.

"Dave, it's fucking hard enough to fight the Germans and now we have to fight one of our own."

"Ayup," Cross replied in his nor'easter accent.

Chapter 23

British Field Hospital
4 miles southwest of the Eiffel Tower
10 September, 1230 Hours

Pamela handed Dr. Kittell a scalpel and he began the process of trimming some dead skin from the wound. After that work, he would stitch it closed. Pamela thought the bullet wound in the patient's stomach would eventually heal okay, but it would make him less interested in taking his shirt off at the beach: the deep puckering would give him two belly buttons. Or maybe he had a wonderful sense of humor . . .

A roaring buzzing sound seemed to come from nowhere and everywhere at the same time. Pamela had time to wonder what it was. And then her world disappeared.

Dr. Kittell watched helplessly as his nurse collapsed, narrowly missing hitting her head on the surgical table.

"Help over here! Someone help Mrs. Dunn!"

Agnes, who had just finished with her last patient a few minutes ago and was washing her hands, grabbed a towel and dried them off as she ran over to kneel beside Pamela. Pamela was lying on her stomach, unconscious. Agnes checked for respiration and was relieved to find Pamela breathing steadily. Agnes placed her two middle fingers against her friend's neck and was rewarded with a strong pulse.

Agnes raised her head to look around. She spotted who she wanted. "Billy, bring over some pillows. And the smelling salts. On the quick!" Agnes looked at Dr. Kittell, who was trying to concentrate on his stitches. "Doctor, do you need help?"

Without looking up Kittell said, "No, I can finish this and clean the patient. You take care of Mrs. Dunn."

Billy arrived with three pillows.

Agnes gently rolled Pamela over onto her back.

"Put them under her legs, I believe she's fainted."

Billy complied.

Agnes undid Pamela's top button and pulled her blouse farther open, and then waved her hand in front of Pamela's face. She held her hand out toward Billy, who promptly dropped a vial of the smelling salts into it.

Agnes snapped it open under Pamela's nose, and Pamela reacted immediately, trying to get her nose away from the bitter smell. Her eyes fluttered open. When she was able to focus on Agnes and realized she was on the ground, she asked, "What?"

Agnes patted Pamela on the cheek. "You've had a faint, dear. Do you think you can sit up?"

Pamela looked as if she was trying to solve a difficult math problem. "Er, yes, okay."

Agnes put a hand on Pamela's back and helped her try to sit up.

Pamela screamed and fell back. "Oh, ow. Oh, it hurts."

"What hurts Pamela?"

At the sound of Pamela's scream a few more nurses arrived, but stood around helplessly.

"My tummy. Oh." Tears rolled down her face.

"What kind of pain is it? It's important to know."

"It's like monthly cramping, but it seems worse."

To Billy, Agnes said, "Stretcher."

"Yes, Ma'am." Billy took off toward the front of the tent.

"Okay, Pamela, we're going to get you to bed."

Pamela's face was filled with sudden fear. "Is everything all right with the baby?"

"We'll check just as soon as we can."

Billy arrived with another orderly and they put the stretcher on the ground next to the fallen nurse. Quickly, but gently, they loaded her onto the stretcher. Soon they had her on a bed toward the back of the tent. They pulled a couple of wood framed canvas privacy dividers into place around her. Billy covered Pamela with a wool blanket, but when doing that he noticed something that made his heart nearly stop. He stepped out from behind the privacy divider and ran to go get Agnes.

Agnes arrived within seconds with Irene and Edith, Pamela's new friends who'd joined the hospital with her nearly a month ago.

"Hello, Pamela," said both Edith and Irene.

Agnes walked around to stand on Pamela's right side.

"Hi, girls."

"How are we feeling?" Edith asked. She took Pamela's left hand in hers.

Irene removed Pamela's white hat, which was rather askew, and brushed back Pamela's hair with her hand.

"Better. The pain is still there but not as bad. More like a tummy ache now."

"Let us have a look, shall we?" Agnes said. She pulled the blanket down knowing already what she would see, thanks to Billy.

The red spot on Pamela's white skirt seemed a terrible blemish and harbinger of something awful.

Agnes put her hand on Pamela's shoulder. "It appears you've a bit of bleeding. Mind if I take a look below?"

Pamela raised her head to look, but Agnes pushed her back down and said, "Let me take care of you. Edith, hot water, soap, and cloths and towels."

"Right," Edith said as she ran off.

"Did I have a miscarriage?" Pamela's voice carried panic as her mind reeled at the prospect. What would she tell Tom? He'd been so happy. They'd been so happy.

"Let's not get ahead of ourselves, dear."

Agnes helped get Pamela's skirt off and then she said, "Okay. Now for the underwear."

Pamela nodded as she gripped Irene's hand tightly.

Edith arrived with everything and set them on a table nearby.

Edith washed Pamela's blood off and patted her skin dry.

"I don't see any evidence of a miscarriage in your underwear, Pamela, so that's good news, but I need to examine you to be sure. Are you ready?"

Pamela nodded. "Quickly. I have to know."

Agnes spent several minutes on Pamela, feeling inside carefully, taking her time to ensure she didn't miss anything.

At last she withdrew her hand and smiled at Pamela. "No miscarriage! Your baby is safe."

Pamela let out a cry of relief and Edith and Irene joined in as Pamela sobbed. Irene patted Pamela and dried her tears.

Agnes cleaned Pamela and pulled the blanket back up to Pamela's chin. "Let's get Pamela's sheets changed, and we'll move her to her tent."

"Right," Edith said.

While Edith and Irene did that, Agnes moved so she could kneel beside Pamela's head.

"You understand what this means, don't you?"

"Yes, but I need to hear you say it."

"Right. You are to stay in bed until I can arrange for you to fly home."

"I so wanted to make it to next month."

Agnes touched Pamela's shoulder. "I know. I know. But your job is to keep that baby safe. We're going to need all the babies we can get, don't you think?"

"Yes, but I'm still sorry to leave you."

"No need. You just take care of yourself and the baby. Do you have a family doctor?"

"Yes. I'll go see him straightaway when I get home."

Agnes patted Pamela's arm. "Good. We'll get you some clean clothes, and then have Billy get you moved to your tent so you can rest."

"Thank you, Agnes."

"Think nothing of it."

"But I do."

"Then you're welcome."

Irene Alsbury and Edith Lockwood sat on either side of Pamela's cot. She was tucked in, with her blanket under her chin. She was frowning.

"I'm going to die of boredom," Pamela complained.

"Terrible way to go, I'm sure," Irene replied.

"You're supposed to be on my side."

"Think of the new skills you'll learn between now and baby's arrival. Sewing, knitting, nappy folding, and proper washing. You won't have time to be bored."

"The doctor will let me work, don't you think?"

Irene glanced at Edith. They had discussed this exact thing with Agnes.

"Look, being on your feet ten or twelve hours a day is hard on your body."

"But I'm used to it."

"That was your body before baby. Now it requires more rest. You've got to take this seriously."

Pamela sighed deeply. "I know."

Edith's face brightened. "Maybe . . . maybe you could visit the hospital at Barton Stacey and read to the men, or help them write letters. You'd be able to sit down for that."

A smile crept onto Pamela's face as she considered the idea. "I like that. I could do that. The doctor couldn't say that was too much exertion. Could he?"

"No, he could not," Irene said. "Then it's settled. No boredom for you."

Pamela grasped each young woman's hand. "You are such good friends. Thank you."

"We'll miss you," Edith said, as tears welled up.

"Yes, we will," Irene said.

Both women leaned over and hugged Pamela, who started to cry. Before long, all three women were crying.

After a few minutes, Irene sat up. "Goodness, this is hard. We need to talk about something else."

Edith sat up, and reached for a box of tissues. She held it out for the other two. The women dabbed their eyes and cheeks.

Pamela winked at Irene, and said, "So, Edith, how are things with Doctor Kittell?"

Edith tried to look innocent. "I don't know what you mean."

The doctor had taken a shine to Edith shortly after their arrival, as she had for him. They spent as much time together as was reasonably possible at a field hospital. While they tried to be discreet, it was still a closed community. They weren't the only couple, which helped keep the gossip down and harmless.

Irene laughed, and said, "I bet there's some serious snogging going on."

Edith chuckled. "Could be. Yes, I believe there is."

"Is he a good snogger, then?" Irene asked.

"If I said he was absolutely terrific at it, would that be kissing and telling?"

"Oh, I'm sure it would be," Pamela said.

The three friends shared a good laugh.

Chapter 24

Spa, Belgium
10 September, 1520 Hours

The liberated citizens of Spa lined the streets as the British forces streamed through. Vehicles of all kinds rolled through slowly. Sometimes, the people would crowd so close the drivers feared they would accidentally run over someone, but so far it hadn't happened.

Saunders had moved his squad west through the woods and to the north-south highway they'd crossed just a couple of nights ago. His men stood along the roadside and watched the traffic and the Belgians.

A little girl of about seven, who had short brown hair, worked herself through the crowd to stand alongside Dickinson. Her mother stood behind her. When the commando finally noticed her, he smiled and knelt down beside her. He was rewarded with a shy smile. Dickinson smiled back and then held up his hand for her to wait for something. He dug into his pocket and removed a shiny shilling. He held it up before her eyes and then with his magician's hand did a flourish and then opened his hands to show the coin had disappeared. Her mouth formed the letter O. He raised his left hand and her eyes watched it closely, expecting the coin to appear there. Instead, the commando slid his right hand behind her left ear and produced the coin. He moved it in front of her face and she clapped her hands and giggled.

Dickinson handed her the coin and she jumped into his arms, giving him a bear hug. He hugged her back and looked up at the girl's mother, who was smiling. The woman nodded her thanks and Dickinson nodded back. The girl let go and held out the hand holding the coin, intending to give it back.

Dickinson smiled at her and shook his head. He gently grasped her hand and closed her delicate fingers over the coin. He pointed at her and nodded. She looked up at her mother for permission to keep the gift, and when she got it, she kissed Dickinson on both cheeks.

Suddenly overcome, Dickinson stood up quickly and faced back toward the street. The little girl stepped up to stand beside the big British soldier and grasped his hand. Dickinson looked down at her and she smiled at him. As he thought of his own nine-year-old sister, a tear rolled down his cheek.

Saunders watched the jeeps carefully, and when a promising one finally came by he stepped out on the road, waving his arm attract the driver's attention. As soon as the British jeep stopped, Saunders approached the passenger, a colonel.

Saunders saluted and said, "Sir, Sergeant Saunders. I have a German general in custody and want to turn him over." He pointed toward his men.

When the colonel realized Saunders really did have a general, he broke into a smile. He told the driver to pull off to the side and Saunders followed.

After the jeep stopped again, the colonel got out and asked, "And you're prepared to just hand him over to us?"

"Aye. Yes, sir. We're glad to hand him off so we can get back home."

The colonel raised his eyebrows at this. "You're going back home?"

"Yes, sir."

"What's your unit?"

"Special Operations under Colonel Rupert Jenkins at Camp Barton Stacey."

"Hm. Don't know of him. How are you getting back?"

"Just need a ride to the nearest airfield and a radio. Someone will come pick us up."

The colonel seemed to be digesting this, and must have decided it wasn't worth digging into. "Okay, Sergeant Saunders. What's your first name?"

"It's Malcolm, sir."

The colonel turned back to his driver. "Call in a request for some RMPs. And also get someone to give the sergeant and his men a ride back to Remouchamps. They can pick them up right here."

"Yes, sir."

Saunders noticed that the colonel pronounced it Ree-moo-champs, and was pretty sure that wasn't right, but of course said nothing.

"Does the prisoner speak English?"

"He does, sir." Saunders could see the man's wheels spinning as he began thinking of questions.

"Tell me how you came about capturing him."

Saunders thought briefly about whether he could tell the colonel the full story, then decided an abridged version would do. He told the colonel everything except Armstrong's role and that they had indeed gotten away with lots and lots of German messages. Those would go back with Armstrong to his unit where they would analyze them further and decide what was valuable.

"Indeed. Right, Sergeant. Bring your general over."

"Right away, sir." Saunders saluted and ran back to the men. With Dickinson assisting, Saunders guided the general back to the colonel. The colonel frowned when he saw the general with his hands tied behind his back. Saunders had removed the gag on the trip back to the road.

"Untie him, Sergeant. What's the idea of tying him up? He's a general officer for God's sake. Show some respect."

"Dickinson, untie the poor general's hands, would you please. And do be gentle about it."

Dickinson smiled and untied the general.

"Don't be smart, Sergeant," the colonel said.

"I wouldn't dream of it, sir. He's all yours."

Saunders saluted once more and he and Dickinson beat it before the colonel thought of something else to say.

Officers, he thought, refraining from shaking his head. *In a class in and of themselves. The fooking bastard general was lucky I didn't just order him shot along with everyone else at the communications center.*

Saunders went back to his men and filled them in.

An hour passed, as well as seemingly hundreds of vehicles, and then a truck pulled up beside them. The driver leaned out the window and hollered, "Saunders?"

"Aye."

Saunders got the men loaded with little effort. Going home was always better than leaving it.

By seven-thirty p.m., the men were on a C-47, headed back to Hampstead Airbase. From there, it would be a short drive to Barton Stacey, and hot food and a comfy bed.

Chapter 25

Moselle River, east side
10 September, 1935 Hours

A clear sky had held for the day. At two a.m., after recon units had crossed the hand-built pontoon bridges put in place by the engineers and held a small bridgehead on the east side of the river, Shermans had followed thereafter and targeted enemy tanks. A late morning German armored counterattack from the south, from Arry, had driven the bridgehead forces back several hundred yards. Quick thinking on the part of the company commander had led to an air strike by a squadron of P-47s, who in turn drove back the enemy tanks, taking out three that were closest to the Americans.

Late afternoon found Dunn's platoon crossing the pontoon bridge. Enemy fire plunked against the halftracks, but no casualties were taken. As soon as the halftracks hit the end of the bridge, they turned left. The squads jumped out of their vehicles and set up a perimeter facing east, digging in just inside a long strip of trees and shrubs that ran along the west side of the north-south river road. The first squad, still operated by Kinney, took up a position to Dunn's right, and the third squad, Red's was the next one over. Overall, their line covered about sixty yards. The platoon leader was with the company commander farther south.

Dunn divided the squad in half and placed himself in the center of the group on the right, while Cross was in the center of the other group. This would help him direct fire during a firefight.

Dunn looked around at his immediate surroundings. The river road running north to south was about five yards away. Kinney's and Red's squads were positioned behind the levy-like berm the road ran across. In essence, they were in a ditch not unlike a World War I trench. They could stand and lean against the top edge to fire their weapons. Dunn had been forced to select the trees as cover because the terrain changed and his squad had no berm to settle under.

Next, he checked out the enemy position. They were part way up a pretty sizable hill, which became rockier as it went up. Dunn wondered about the wisdom of selecting that position. To the north of the Germans were heavy woods that came down hill and stopped about two hundred yards from the road. There were some scattered trees between the road and the denser woods that Dunn thought his men could use if needed. Nighttime would still be the preferred time, but the need to advance didn't always wait for dark.

Dunn rotated in place, making sure his body stayed behind the tree trunk he was using as cover. More troops and equipment were pouring over the pontoon bridge. The engineers were working on another bridge about four hundred yards farther south. They appeared to be about fifty percent the way done.

Jonesy was to Dunn's left, and Lindstrom, the sniper's spotter, was to Jonesy's left. Jonesy was scanning the rocks with his Unertl 8-power scope that was attached to his M1903 A1 Springfield.

They began taking sporadic fire.

The Germans were at about five hundred yards, right at the M1's maximum effective range.

"See where they are Jonesy?" Dunn asked.

"Uhm, I'm finding some but not many. They're concentrated around that rock that looks like a face. Do you see it?"

Dunn lifted his field glasses to his eyes and searched until he found the face rock. "Yeah."

"Okay, they pop up like prairie dogs from just in front of it."

"Okay, pass the word to the left to target that area the next time they fire."

"Will do."

While Jonesy did that, Dunn gave the order to his right. He settled down and aimed his M1 at the face rock.

A minute passed and then twinkles of light appeared in front of the face rock. Dunn's men opened fire. Some incoming rounds zipped over Dunn's men's heads, and a few found their mark in the trees, making loud slapping *thunks* as they struck the wood. By the time the men's M1 empty clips twanged as they flew out and the men reloaded, the Germans had stopped firing.

With reloaded weapons, the men raised their heads to peek. Dunn and Jonesy used their optical instruments to survey the target. A few Germans popped up again after a minute, and Dunn ordered his men to fire. The German helmets disappeared as rock chips flew just above their heads; the M1 .30-06 rounds were in the neighborhood.

"Cease fire."

Dunn could hear other M1s firing just to his south. Kinney was exchanging fire with the Germans, too.

Suddenly Schneider scooted up next to Dunn. He held out the radio handset. "Sergeant Kinney for you."

Dunn took the hand set. "Dunn here."

"Just got a report of four Panzer Mark fours coming toward us from the north. Get your bazooka team in there and stop them."

"Will do, Sergeant."

Kinney didn't say anything for a moment, then said, "Aren't you going to ask 'don't we have any armor to take care of them?' "

Dunn could see the sneer on the man's face.

"If you were doing your job, you would have already told me we do have some armor, but to get ready in case they run into trouble."

"I can report you for this."

"So you already said. Dunn out."

Dunn handed the phone back to Schneider, although Schneider thought he could hear screaming still coming over the line. "Sarge, I don't think he was done."

Dunn smiled at the big man. "Yeah, he was, he just didn't realize it."

"Okay." Schneider started to put the handset back in place, but he could definitely still hear Kinney shouting. He handed it back to Dunn.

"The more time you waste talking to me, Kinney, the closer the Panzers are getting." Dunn handed it back to Schneider, who put it away again while Kinney continued to shout something unintelligible.

"If he calls again, tell him I'm busy."

"Okay, Sarge," Schneider replied, wondering what the hell was going on between Dunn and Kinney. There was no doubt in his mind that Dunn must have been provoked earlier. There was also no doubt on whose side Schneider would be.

Dunn slid down the line to the north and found Goerdt and Bailey. He knelt between them, putting a hand on Goerdt's shoulder.

"Grab your bazooka, Rob. We've got four Panzer Mark fours coming from the north. See if you can change their mind. Bailey, you're up. Stay low as you move into position."

"Got it, Sarge," Goerdt replied.

Goerdt grabbed the bazooka and took off, M1 in his right hand and the antitank weapon in the other. Bailey picked up a pack containing the rocket propelled armor-piercing rounds. The pack weighed in at about forty pounds, and Bailey shrugged it onto his back carefully, then followed Goerdt.

Dunn worked his way back to his position and wondered why the Germans had stopped firing. It had been a few minutes, so he once again raised his binoculars. As if he personally had been the cue the Germans were waiting for, they opened up, this time, the bullets came in furiously, tearing into the trees. Smaller branches were sliced apart and fell onto the men huddling behind the tree trunks.

Dunn recognized the weapon, the MG42, called Hitler's buzzsaw. The thing could spew 1,200 rounds a minute, by far the most of any weapon on the battlefield. It felt as though there might be at least two of them firing, based on the number of bullets streaking through the woods.

Dunn dropped to a prone position and took a peek. Movement on the left of the rocks told him what he'd been thinking. The Germans were trying to make it to the woods so they could slide down and flank the platoon. Their problem was that the ground was open for almost one hundred yards.

Dunn passed the word, and in spite of the German rounds, his squad began firing at the ten or so Germans on the move.

Jonesy sighted on the lead enemy soldier, and squeezed the trigger. The bullet raced uphill and met the soldier, who crumpled. The squad's M1 rounds were getting close, but not hitting anyone. Suddenly, two more Germans fell. The advancing squad stopped, turned around and scurried back to cover behind the rocks. Dunn's men kept firing to keep the Germans in place.

The MG42s ceased firing. Dunn figured the commander was trying to think of something else to try.

"Everyone okay?" Dunn called out. He was relieved to get a bunch of affirmative responses.

Suddenly, the booming sounds from American artillery came across the river from the west.

Explosions bloomed on the hill, blowing rocks everywhere. In some places small rockslides started moving downhill for a short distance.

Chapter 26

Goerdt and Bailey did stay low as they advanced northward, being careful to check their position against the rocks from where the Germans had been firing. They covered a distance of two hundred yards before they heard the clanking of the tanks' tracks off in the distance. The ditch along the road had returned and they were below the roadbed.

Goerdt picked his ambush point, which was another ten yards ahead. Scrambling quickly to get into position, he settled in amongst a stand of young trees surrounded by waist-high shrubs that ran north along the road, like a front yard hedge. The trees were twenty yards west of the road, pretty much an ideal position for a side shot.

"Here," he said to Bailey.

Bailey took off the pack and set it on the ground.

Goerdt shouldered the bazooka and Bailey loaded a rocket, and then tapped Goerdt on the helmet.

The lead tank came into view fifty yards away, and the other three followed, with about ten yards between them. They moved slowly, perfectly aware of the American proclivity for using the bazooka. All the tanks were buttoned up to protect the crew from small arms fire. To Goerdt, it seemed as though the coaxial machine gun on the lead tank's right front was aimed right at him.

Closer and closer the tanks came.

Then they stopped ten yards short of where Goerdt needed them to be.

Goerdt didn't have a shot and muttered, "Shit."

The lead tank's turret slowly rotated to its right, toward Goerdt and Bailey.

The barrel depressed.

Goerdt thought he was simultaneously staring into a tunnel and death.

The tank fired.

The supersonic round screamed overhead.

Goerdt realized the tank was firing at the completed pontoon bridge. He rose to a crouch and ran along the hedge line until he was perpendicular to the lead tank. He shouldered the bazooka, got his target, and pulled the trigger.

As soon as the rocket was away, Goerdt took off running again with Bailey on his heels.

The lead tank exploded and caught fire.

The last tank in line reversed and began backing away. The second tank had to wait for number three to move. It began firing its coaxial at the position Goerdt and Bailey had just vacated.

Goerdt stopped when he parallel to the second tank, which was now moving north, now that number three was finally backing up.

Bailey loaded a round.

Goerdt aimed and fired. The rocket struck the second tank just beneath the turret and another explosion rocked the world around the two rangers.

Tanks three and four were firing their machine guns. Hot rounds zipped through the hedge, narrowly missing the Americans, who had immediately started running north again.

Tank three was now almost twenty yards away and would be out of effective range soon.

Goerdt decided to take the shot from where he was. Maybe the angle would be good enough to blow a sprocket and track off, stopping the tank. Then he could get closer for a flank killing shoot.

He knelt and raised the bazooka. As soon as he felt the tap on the helmet, he fired. He watched the rocket streak away. It struck the front drive sprocket and the tank's tread unraveled along the road before the tank came to a stop.

The fourth tank had spun in a one hundred eighty degree rotation and was now charging off to the north as fast as possible.

Goerdt hollered, "Yeah!"

"Nice shooting, Goerdt."

"Thanks."

Goerdt debated expending another rocket on the disabled tank, but before he could decide, the top hatch opened and a hand appeared holding a white cloth.

"Huh," Goerdt said. He turned to look at Bailey. "Want to capture a tank crew?"

"Sure, why not?"

Goerdt laid down the bazooka and picked up his M1, which he had placed on the ground for each rocket shot.

"Let's go."

The tank commander was now fully visible from the waist up.

Goerdt and Bailey made their way to a point about ten yards from the tank.

Goerdt whistled and the commander looked around until he found Goerdt just back in the shrubs.

"Wir wollen kapitulieren." We wish to surrender.

"Kommen Sie raus! Waffen auf den Boden. Hände hoch und stellen Sie sich neben den Panzer." Come here! Take off your weapons. Come out with your hands up. Line up next to the tank.

The commander didn't seemed surprised at all by Goerdt speaking German. He spoke into his radio headset, took it off, and then climbed out of the turret. Soon, all five crewmen were lined up facing Goerdt and Bailey. One of them was bleeding heavily from a scalp wound. Goerdt figured the man was the coaxial gunner who would be on the front right, closest to the explosion. It was a wonder he wasn't dead.

"Hände hinter den Kopf." Hands behind your heads.

The crewmen complied.

"Hier lang." Walk this way.

The men slowly advanced until they were right in front of Goerdt and Bailey.

The Americans backed up and waved for the Germans to come though the shrub, keeping their M1s aimed at the men.

Once all were on the west side of the shrubs, Goerdt held his M1 on each man in turn as Bailey quickly frisked him. The crewmen were unarmed, and Goerdt told them to start walking, but to stay down so their own people didn't shoot them.

Goerdt and Bailey made the Germans wait while they recovered their bazooka and rockets. By the time the seven-man parade made it to Dunn's position, the wounded man had needed the help of two of his crewmates to stay on his feet.

Dave Cross was first to see Goerdt and Bailey return, herding a gaggle of Germans ahead of themselves. Cross turned toward Dunn and whistled. When Dunn looked, he immediately saw the line of Germans over Cross's head. He raised his eyebrows.

To Schneider, Dunn said, "Tell Kinney we have prisoners."

"Yes, Sarge,"

Cross helped Goerdt and Bailey get the German prisoners seated on the ground, where the bazooka team stood guard over them.

Lindstrom knelt beside the injured man and treated the wound, wrapping a bandage around his head. When he was done, he offered the man a cigarette. The prisoner accepted it and after he stuck it in his mouth, Lindstrom lit it for him with his Zippo lighter. Lindstrom moved around the other tankers and soon they were all smoking, savoring the American Camel cigarettes.

Dunn made his way over to check on the prisoners. He noticed they were smoking and looked at Lindstrom. "You gave them Camels?" Most of the rangers smoked Lucky Strikes.

"Yes, Sarge."

Dunn shook his head. "Horrible way to treat prisoners," he said somberly.

"Yes, Sarge."

The prisoners were watching the brief conversation, trying to discern whether it was bad for them.

Dunn suddenly laughed at Lindstrom, and the Germans relaxed.

"What do we have here?" Sergeant Kinney asked, popping into view from the south.

"Tank crew," Dunn replied.

"What's their unit?"

"They just got here. Don't know yet."

Kinney gave Dunn a derisive look, and said, "They've been here long enough to get cigarettes from you, but you don't know what unit they're from?"

"That's about the size of it."

"I heard you got a couple of guys who can speak kraut. Give me one. Now."

"Sure." Dunn pointed at Goerdt. "Here's one. Rob, meet Sergeant Kinney. Kinney, meet Rob Goerdt."

Goerdt held out his hand and said, "Good to meet you."

Kinney ignored Goerdt's hand.

Goerdt lowered his hand, steaming on the inside, but staying impassive on the outside.

"Lindstrom, go back to your position. Bailey, you, too," Dunn said, with a nod of thanks.

"He's all yours, Kinney."

"Ask which one is the commander," Kinney said.

"Oh, I know which one it is," Goerdt started to raise his arm to point, but Kinney slapped it down.

"I said ask," Kinney snapped.

Goerdt glanced at Dunn, who was standing to Kinney's left. Dunn rolled his eyes, but nodded.

Goerdt suppressed a sudden urge to laugh. Clearly Dunn didn't think much of Kinney. Goerdt looked at the tank commander straight in the eyes and asked, "Who's the tank commander?"

The commander's mouth dropped open a little. He knew Goerdt knew. He raised his hand and said, "I am."

Kinney turned his attention to the commander. "What's your unit?"

The commander watched Goerdt as he translated, then shifted his eyes back to Kinney. He rattled off something.

"He will only give his name, rank, and serial number."

Kinney shouted at Goerdt to repeat his question. He got the same response.

Kinney stepped forward and backhanded the commander. "What unit?" he shouted.

The commander shrugged and repeated everything a third time.

All eyes were on Kinney, including the rest of Dunn's men on the line.

Kinney suddenly drew his Colt .45 and pointed it, not at the commander, but the man next to him, who looked to be all of nineteen. Kinney thumbed the hammer back.

Dunn flew across the distance, grabbing Kinney's gun hand and shoving it upward.

Kinney pulled the trigger, but the barrel was pointing at the sky. The *boom* made the Germans duck and scramble away.

Dunn got a grip on the Colt's barrel and twisted with his right hand. The weapon popped out of Kinney's hand, and Dunn handed it off to Goerdt. With his left hand he twisted Kinney around to face him, snatching the man's shirt front in his fist.

Dunn had his right fist pulled back ready to launch a haymaker.

"That'll do, Sergeant Dunn," Lieutenant Carver said as he joined the group. He seemed to have just appeared out of nowhere.

Dunn let go of Kinney and lowered his arms.

Kinney, already over some kind of mental edge, slugged Dunn, who was looking the wrong way at the lieutenant, on the side of the face, knocking the six-two ranger to the ground. Schneider, who was closest, tackled Kinney and pinned him to the ground. Kinney struggled, but the six-four Schneider held him fast.

The German prisoners' eyes were wide, clearly wondering what was going on. What kind of American unit was this anyway?

Dunn got to his feet, his face a mask of anger. He took a step toward Kinney, but stopped himself. He backed up and stood there breathing hard, his hands at his side clenching and unclenching.

Lieutenant Carver walked over to Dunn and said, "Well done. We can't have mistreatment of prisoners of war. Not in my unit."

Dunn looked at the lieutenant and said, "No, sir, we can't."

"Let's get some MPs over here to take the prisoners off your hands, and Sergeant Kinney, I'm afraid."

"Yes, sir." Dunn started to move toward the radio Schneider had left at his position.

"Dunn?"

Dunn turned to face the lieutenant, whose expression seemed to be one of sadness blended with one of relief at having a man like Dunn available after the fuckup by Kinney, who would likely be on his way back somewhere west, way west.

"Sir?"

"You're my new first sergeant."

"Yes, sir." Without missing a beat, Dunn asked, "Who can take over first squad?"

"That'd be Earl Finley. Staff Sergeant. Good man."

Dunn didn't say what he was thinking: *You probably thought Kinney was a good man, too.*

RONN MUNSTERMAN

Chapter 27

The Dunn family home
Cedar Rapids, Iowa
10 September, 12:57 P.M., U.S. Central time

Gertrude Dunn climbed out of her dad's black 1937 Model 74 Ford four-door sedan and stood in the driveway admiring her childhood home. The driveway led to a one car unattached garage sitting past the back of the house. The front yard was expansive, almost fifty feet from the sidewalk to the porch. The house faced south and two old maple trees provided deep shade from the sun. The first floor was brick, and the upper story wood. A porch covered the entire front and wrapped around to the east side, where the dining room was located.

Gertrude knew there would still be a wooden swing set in the backyard. She recalled many a day playing on it with Tom and Hazel, as well as all of them earning a few ankle injuries from the practice of launching out of the seat at its highest point on the forward swing. Gertrude wondered whether that led Tom to jumping out of airplanes.

"Nice to be home, isn't it?" Henry Dunn asked his youngest child from in front of the car.

Gertrude looked at her dad and smiled. He was a tall, lanky man with the same brown hair and dark brown eyes as all his kids. At fifty-one, Mr. Dunn was fit and strong. Mechanically inclined, he fixed everything that broke, whether it was a favorite toy or the family car. In the summer, when he was off work from his teaching job at Benjamin Franklin High School, he worked on his brother Walter's farm southeast of Cedar Rapids, near Mount Vernon.

Gertrude stepped around the front of the car and hugged her dad. "It sure is." She pushed back and looked him in the eye. At five-eight, she was the tallest girl in her class, and had come by it honestly because Mr. Dunn was six-two, so she didn't have to look up very far.

"I know it's only been a few weeks, but it really seemed longer not seeing you and mom, and Hazel."

Henry nodded and said, "Sometimes it is like that. When you reach my age, though, it can seem to fly by."

Henry offered her his right arm and they walked across the soft green grass, and up the steps to the porch.

Gertrude glanced around. The same old comfortable chairs were still in the exact same spot as always. One of their three cats, the black one called Smokey, rolled over onto his back and stretched, and curled up to go back to sleep, completely ignoring the humans a few feet away.

Just as Gertrude reached for the screen door, it opened and her older sister Hazel burst through to give her a giant hug.

"Sissie!"

"Sis!" Gertrude shouted back.

Henry extricated himself from Gertrude just in time as the two young women hugged and hopped up and down together while he stayed out of harm's way, smiling.

The hopping ceased and the two women let go, grinning at each other.

"How is it?" Hazel asked.

"I love it. It's hard work, but I feel like I'm helping the war effort. More than just following the rules on rationing or gathering metal or rubber. How are things at Smulekoff's?"

Smulekoff's was the best furniture store in the city. Located downtown, it had moved to a brand new five-story building just two years prior, down by the Cedar River.

"It's great. I sold a beautiful sofa yesterday to a newlywed couple. It was really fun."

Gertrude patted her older sister on the arm. "That's fantastic."

Mrs. Dunn appeared at the door wearing a white cotton dress with a blue apron on. She stepped through the door and hugged and kissed Gertrude.

"It's so nice to see you, sweetheart! I'm so glad you could come today. Are you hungry?"

"Starving! Breakfast seems like yesterday."

Gertrude had arisen early, eaten two pieces of toast, and headed out to catch the train.

Henry pulled the screen door open and said, "Let's go in. I believe dinner is ready."

Mrs. Dunn said, "Dinner *is* ready. Beef roast, mashed potatoes, gravy, and . . . canned peas!"

Hazel and Gertrude squealed in delight and ran inside shouting, "Peas!"

Henry looked at his wife, Elizabeth Ann, and grinned. "How many rationing points for the peas?"

"One can, sixteen points."

"Ouch. Out of forty-eight, right?"

"Yep."

"It was worth it hearing their screaming."

"Sure was." Mrs. Dunn smiled.

Henry blocked the door open with his back and drew his diminutive wife into his arms. He hugged and kissed her. "Love you."

"You, too, Hank."

The two had married in 1915, when Henry was twenty-two, and had just started his first teaching job. Elizabeth Ann was one year younger. The two had met during his senior year in high school, and dated all the way through his college years at the University of Iowa, where'd he'd earned his degree in mathematics with a teaching certificate. Hazel was the eldest of their three, and was born in 1917. Thomas followed in 1920, and Gertrude in 1926.

The family was seated at the oak dining room table, large enough for eight. The group gathered around one end to be close to one another, Henry at the head, Elizabeth Ann to his left and the girls across from their mother. They held hands while Henry said the prayer. He ended with, "And Lord, we just ask that you keep all our boys safe from harm overseas, and for us especially Tom and Danny. Through Jesus' name we pray. Amen."

Danny Young was Hazel's husband, who was aboard a submarine somewhere in the Pacific. She hadn't seen him for two years.

The ladies all added their own, "Amen."

Henry quickly sliced the beef, and handed the platter to Hazel, sitting closest to him.

The family soon had their plates full. Henry and Elizabeth Ann took small portions of the peas so their daughters could have more.

Elizabeth Ann lifted the cover off another dish and handed it to Gertrude, who took it, her eyes gleaming.

"Cottage cheese," she said, almost moaning with pleasure. She spooned out a double portion onto her plate, right next to the mashed potatoes. "Hmm." She turned toward Hazel and held the dish almost under her sister's nose.

Hazel immediately said, "Ugh. Get that away from me, you meanie!"

Everyone laughed. Hazel couldn't stand cottage cheese, saying the texture just felt creepy on her tongue. Tom and Gertrude had teased her mercilessly over the years, but Gertrude was the best at it.

Gertrude set the dish on the table away from Hazel, but said, "One of these days, Hazel, you'll crave this!"

"Not ever happening."

"Any news from Danny?" Henry asked, thinking it was time to change the subject.

"Nothing this week. Maybe tomorrow." Hazel seemed unperturbed. Letters from her husband sometimes came in little flurries, and sometimes a few weeks could go by. She had to believe as long as no telegrams came to her house, things were all right.

The meal continued, and the conversation wandered comfortably from topic to topic.

When the last food was scraped off the plates, Elizabeth Ann rose to begin clearing the table. Gertrude immediately jumped up to help.

"Why don't we wait a minute for that?" Henry said.

Elizabeth Ann looked at Henry, who tipped his head in the direction of the large walnut buffet against the wall.

"Oh, how could I have forgotten? Gertrude, dear, would you get that letter off the buffet?"

Elizabeth Ann sat down and gave Henry a little smile. He winked at her.

Gertrude picked up the envelope and when she saw who it was from, nearly shouted, "It's from Tom!"

She tore open the letter, not realizing it had already been opened. "Shall I read it?"

"Of course," Elizabeth Ann said.

Gertrude unfolded the papers—there were two pages—and started reading. "Gosh, Tom's handwriting is worse than ever! Let's see, 'Dear Mom and Dad, We've been moving around a lot in France. Last mission a success, no losses.' " Gertrude looked at her dad. "Does he mean his men?"

"Yes."

"Okay, thought so. Okay, he goes on to say how much he misses us, especially at Sunday dinner." She wiped away a tear at this. She turned to Hazel, "He wants to know how Danny is doing."

Hazel nodded, making a mental note to write Tom a letter that evening. "What else?"

Gertrude smiled. "His British friend Malcolm Saunders is engaged to Sadie. They hope to get married as soon as Sadie can walk down the aisle with her dad." She looked at Henry again. "She got injured in a buzz bomb attack, right?"

Henry nodded. It wasn't hard to imagine how Sadie's parents would have felt at the news.

Gertrude shuffled the papers to bring the second sheet to the top.

"Okay, he says, 'A bit of fortuitous luck,' . . . huh, just like Tom to use a word like that . . . 'I was able to have dinner with Pamela in Paris.' Oh my, that is so romantic."

In his last letter, Dunn had mentioned Pamela's new job working as a nurse in France.

Gertrude continued, reading the next line and she suddenly stopped. She began to cry. She handed the letter to Hazel with her hands shaking.

Hazel scanned the page to find what had provoked her sister's tears.

"Oh! Hallelujah! Pamela is expecting! Sissie! We're going to have a niece or a nephew." Hazel put an arm around Gertrude and hugged her tight.

After the hug, the girls looked at their parents. Henry and Elizabeth Ann had tears of joy streaming down their cheeks.

Hazel and Gertrude jumped up and ran to a spot between their parents and gave them both a hug. "Your first grandbaby." The family shared the happiness hug and then the girls sat back down.

"When is she due?" Gertrude asked.

Hazel read, " 'We think the baby will come next May. Pamela will be going back to England in a few months.' "

Hazel handed the letter back to Gertrude who read the important lines again, to herself.

As the family started chattering about Dunn's and Pamela's coming bundle of joy, Hazel seemed to be having trouble gathering herself. Suddenly, she burst into tears and sobs. Elizabeth Ann leapt to her feet and ran around the table.

Hazel had her face buried in her hands as Gertrude hugged her from one side and her mother from the other. The sobbing subsided.

Elizabeth Ann knew what had triggered the outburst, but asked, "What's bothering you, honey?"

"I feel so silly. I'm supposed to be happy for Tom, and I am, but I'm upset that Danny and I weren't able to start a family before he shipped out." She stopped, afraid to say what she was really thinking.

"Go ahead and say it, dear," her mother prompted.

Hazel looked at her mother and saw love and concern.

"I'm afraid Danny will die and we'll never have children." She started crying again, and from under her hands covering her face, said plaintively, "Oh, Almighty God, when is this war going to end?"

No one had an answer.

Gertrude thought about her problem, the one she'd lied to Margie about not having. She was worried that she wouldn't find a man of her own. It seemed all the good ones were older and married already or were overseas.

Gertrude swallowed heavily. Compared to Hazel's fears, it seemed so small, and she kept her mouth shut.

RONN MUNSTERMAN

Chapter 28

Moselle River, near Arnaville, France
10 September, 2200 Hours, Paris time

"Sarge?" Schneider held out the radio handset.

Dunn took it and answered, listening for a short time. "Yes, sir, be right there."

Dunn gave the handset back and said, "Gotta go see the lieutenant. Be back soon."

"Okay."

Dunn walked north a few yards and stood behind Cross. "Lieutenant wants me. Take over will ya?"

Cross glanced at his squad leader / first sergeant. "Will do."

When Dunn reached Lieutenant Carver's location, behind the third squad, he joined the other two squad leaders.

Lieutenant Carver started talking as soon as Dunn arrived.

"Our target is what seems to be a company up there in the rocks. We have to get them moved out because they're in range of the bridges. If we can't get them out, you need to destroy their machine guns and keep them occupied so they can't spend much time shooting down here." He went on to lay out the basic idea for the upcoming attack, where each squad would be advancing. There was no use of maps because the moon hadn't quite risen yet, so locations were identified verbally and with care. The lieutenant asked several times if everyone understood where whatever he had just mentioned was located. When he was satisfied they knew exactly where he meant, he would move on to the next item.

"Artillery will commence pounding the enemy at twenty-three fifty hours, and cease at moon rise, which is a minute after midnight. You wait one minute, then launch the attack at two minutes after."

When he was done, he added, "We expect more armor and infantry to cross over tonight at the same time we attack to fill our emptied slot here, so we have to stay on our time table. If for some reason you fall behind, you must make it up." He looked around at his men in the darkness. "Any questions?"

Three 'no sirs' were the replies.

"Okay. Good. Back to your men. If you need any equipment, see Sergeant Dunn. I'll be back shortly. That is all."

The lieutenant turned around and took off for the company headquarters.

The men dispersed, but the third squad's leader, Red Lancaster, stopped Dunn. "Sergeant Dunn, we're short on grenades. Can you help us get some more? Maybe a dozen?"

"Sure, go see Finley and get them from his squad. He has lots of extras for some reason."

"Great! Thanks."

"That's what I'm here for, Red."

Red laughed and left. He caught up with the other squad leader, who listened to what Red was saying. He looked at Dunn and nodded, grabbed Red by the shoulder, and they marched off together.

Dunn turned away, letting them work out the details.

When Dunn returned to his men, he pulled everyone off the line except Jonesy and Lindstrom. Dunn gathered the men behind the two still on guard and gave them the plan.

"I estimate the distance we have to cover to be about eleven hundred yards and it should take us around twenty minutes. Adding fifteen for unexpected problems puts it at a total of thirty-five. We'll leave here at twenty-three-ten hours to get in place before the artillery starts firing. Any questions?"

No one said anything.

Schneider held out the radio handset to Dunn. "It's the CO."

"Dunn here, Captain Stafford."

"Lieutenant Carver just got hit. He's alive but out of action. I need you to take command of the platoon. Your attack plan remains the same."

"Understood. Will do, Captain."

The two men signed off.

To the squad, Dunn said, "The lieutenant got hit. Still alive but out of it. I have the platoon. Bob, go pass the word to Red and Finley."

"On it, Sarge."

"Okay, get your gear together. You guys might eat a little something before we leave, too. We may or may not have time for breakfast, depending on how it goes."

The men nodded, and dispersed to eat and pack.

At 2310 hours, Dunn's men led the way north staying low on the west side of the road. Red's and Finley's squads followed keeping an interval of five yards between squads. Cross had point and Wickham was second. Waters was last.

Dunn was just too damn busy to worry about suddenly being in charge of the platoon. He simply got to work. He'd determined that they needed to travel just over four hundred yards along the road before crossing it. Even in the cover of darkness, there was enough starlight to make out motion on the road, and that could get the men killed. By going the four hundred yards, they would be hidden behind the western tip of the woods that ran down the hill to the north of the German position in the rocks.

When Cross reached the point Dunn wanted, he stopped and the line of men halted. Dunn moved up to join Cross. Together they eyed the tip of the woods and followed a visual line up the hill. The rocks, which had been white blobs in the starlight, were invisible.

"This is the right spot, Dave. Let's get on across."

Cross stood up and took off at a run. They had almost two hundred fifty yards to cover to get into the woods. Dunn expected the men to cover that distance in two minutes. Dunn stood at the crossing spot, acting as traffic cop as each man went by, patting them on the arm and saying encouraging words like 'you got it' or 'good man.' When his last man had crossed over, Dunn handed off traffic control to Red, and Dunn ran to catch up with Waters.

Dunn and his men waited ten yards inside the woods for Red's squad to enter. A couple of more minutes passed, and then the third squad arrived. Dunn pulled Red and the other squad leader, Earl Finley, to the side. "Close the interval to one step—we can't afford to lose each other in these woods."

The platoon went on the move again. The going was tough, uphill combined with the trees, but Cross reached the line of departure at 2345 hours, right on time.

Dunn dispersed the men into a line facing south. The relative position of each squad was the same as along the road: Dunn, Finley, and Red. They were twenty yards deep in the woods, to make sure they stayed out of the way in case of an errant artillery round or two.

After the men were all in the correct position for advancing toward the enemy, Dunn grabbed Red and Finley.

"Let's scout ahead. See what we can see."

The men nodded and Dunn strode off. When he reached the edge of the woods, he stopped and knelt carefully, so as not to make any noise. He estimated they were a hundred yards from the nearest rocks, with most of it open ground between them. He stared a long time across the area, but could see no movement.

Whispering, he asked, "You guys see anything?"

"No," Red replied, also whispering.

"Nothing," Finley replied quietly.

Dunn turned away from the rocks and lifted his left arm so it was right in front of his chest. With his right hand he slid back his sleeve, keeping the palm over the luminous watch to hide any light. It was 2349 hours.

"We'd better get out of here. Shelling about to start."

Dunn and the other two squad leaders were still a few paces from their men when the night turned to day and the earth shook.

Chapter 29

900 meters north of Arry, France, and
1,000 meters east of the Moselle River
10 September, 2345 Hours

Oberfeldwebel Dietrich Wittenberg moved carefully along the line of his soldiers, stopping to pat each on the shoulder and say a few words to help keep their spirits up.

When he reached the second MG42 two-man team, he knelt behind them. "Moonrise in fifteen minutes, men. Do you think you can lay some rounds on the bridge?"

"No doubts, *Oberfeldwebel*. Easy."

"Good. See if you can make the Americans scurry like rats!"

The two men laughed and Wittenberg patted them both on the back, and continued moving down the line. When he finished with his unofficial inspection, he headed back to the south.

He found his preferred spot at the midpoint of the platoon's line. The boulder he crouched behind was nearly as tall as himself, reaching his shoulders, making it a convenient height for firing his Mauser K98.

He stared downhill at the river, which in the starlight was merely a darker ribbon than the surrounding countryside. He could picture the layout even if it was still mostly blotchy at the moment. The Americans had set up a perimeter along the river road, just inside a long string of trees and a levee. He thought there was only a platoon in there based on the fire his position had received periodically during the daytime firefights. He doubted there had been many casualties down there; he certainly had only a few. He imagined the two MG42s created some consternation among the men hiding there. The thought made him smile.

Quite a lot of American armor had roared across the bridge and headed south toward Arry, and he thought, probably beyond. He hadn't bothered with the armor, what good would it do? No, he'd wait for the follow up infantry, and start cutting them down, first on the bridge with the MG42s, then for those who made it onto the east bank, right there at that spot.

He glanced to his left, wondering whether the idiots Raupp and Mekelburg would conduct some kind of stupidity like a charge down the hill to overwhelm the infantry. They hadn't bothered him since he'd taken them both down two days ago, but he imagined they were cooking up some kind of revenge. Best to be vigilant until they got themselves killed.

Returning his attention to the river he lifted his eyes when a series of bright flashes lit up the hillsides beyond the west bank. He immediately yelled at his men to take cover, and word spread in both directions.

Wittenberg ducked behind the boulder and tucked in making himself as small as possible.

The sound of the cannons firing never reached the German soldiers' ears because the 105mm rounds arrived one second sooner.

The ground shook and rattled. Men screamed. Sometimes the screams were cut off.

All Wittenberg could do was stay in place. Moving to another spot was a crapshoot. A round could land on you as you ran. Or when you got there. Or if you stayed, a shell could hit you. It was fate, nothing more.

Round after round hit the hillside. Rock chips turned into shrapnel. Wittenberg thought he had figured out the American firing pattern. The shells landed farther and farther south of his position as they were in essence raking the hillside with 105mm bombs instead of machine gun bullets. Which meant they would come back.

They did.

One round landed a few yards on the downhill side of Wittenberg's boulder and he thought for a moment he was going to suffocate as it felt like the air in his lungs was being sucked out. His ears hurt. When at last he was able to draw in a breath he was relieved, but sound was nothing but a dull roar.

He wondered whether the shell's crater would cause his boulder to roll downhill, leaving him naked. It didn't, but he thought about it a long while.

He felt a man run past him to the north. He lifted his head to see a medic running toward a fallen man. He couldn't see who it was. He wondered if it was one of the younger men.

Time seemed to stand still as explosion after explosion rocked the hillside.

And then it stopped.

Wittenberg's ears were ringing and he knew his men's would be, too. It could take hours for hearing to return to near normal. He waited almost a minute, and then raised his head to look around. Other men were raising themselves to their knees while others lay still. This worried Wittenberg. He stood up, feeling wobbly in the knees, and woozy in the head. Did he have a concussion? He steadied himself with a hand on the boulder that, for now, had likely saved his life. He scanned the western horizon in the moonlight. He was surprised by the sudden appearance of the moon and checked his watch. Ten minutes had passed. And he hadn't even noticed. There were no flashes of artillery on the other side of the river. He turned his attention to the river road and wondered if the Americans were still there. He knew the artillery could have been meant to soften his men up for an attack. The question was, from where? They wouldn't charge up the hill any more than he would charge down it. He looked to his right. The woods. They would come through the woods.

Wittenberg shook his head and that mysteriously seemed to make him feel better. The men were out of position for an attack from the woods. They would be flanked. With some difficulty, he started rearranging his men on the hillside, getting them to slide into a better defensive position facing north. An MG42 loader was dead, so Wittenberg picked another man to take his place.

He didn't quite get the men moved in time.

Heavy fire came from the woods. Wittenberg couldn't hear well enough to determine what the weapons were, but thought the Americans were firing their M1s based on the frequency of the muzzle flashes.

His men began to return fire with their slower rate of fire Mausers, but were taking casualties from the onslaught of the M1s.

Wittenberg ran back and was able to hurry up his third squad and get them onto the line. They began firing.

Even in the moonlight, it was hard to spot the men firing at them.

The Americans on Wittenberg's right, slightly uphill from his firing position had stopped shooting. This was bad news.

Wittenberg directed his first squad, which was farthest to the right to be prepared for a charge from even farther uphill. He believed the enemy would try to increase the angle of the flanking attack because he had his men in the correct defensive position. He was positioned about five meters from his MG42 crew. Out of the woods, a rocket streaked right at the machine gun team. The bazooka round exploded right on them, blowing them skyward. The weapon itself was destroyed.

Just as Wittenberg expected, he spotted movement in the trees a hundred meters northeast. He gave the order to open fire and was rewarded when the movement changed directions back into the trees.

Fire soon resumed from the northeast.

Just as Wittenberg was thinking about calling for additional help, the Americans ceased firing. He gave the same order and waited.

Five minutes of silence passed without another shot being fired.

Still unable to see into the woods, Wittenberg kept his men on high alert.

After another ten minutes, it was clear the Americans had decided to hold a truce for the time being. Perhaps they were thinking of what else they could try. Wittenberg turned his attention to the terrain to the northeast. The woods hiding the enemy ran along his men's position for perhaps forty meters, then the tree line turned north. The distance between the enemy and his men was about one hundred meters. It looked like they might be at an impasse.

He hoped.

He could tie up an enemy platoon for quite some time. A one-to-one ratio always favored the defender.

He hoped.

RONN MUNSTERMAN

Chapter 30

In the woods 1000 yards north of Arry, France, and
1,000 yards east of the Moselle River
11 September, 0601 Hours

Dunn was pissed off. The attack had fizzled right from the get go.
The ten-minute-long shelling hadn't done much of anything. The
Germans had reacted quickly to the flanking attack. At first, it
looked like Dunn's platoon was going to break the German line,
but the opposing platoon leader had gotten his men turned and
brought an MG42 to bear on the attackers. The weapon had killed
two men in Red's squad, tearing their heads right off their bodies.
That was when Dunn ordered Goerdt and Bailey to take out the
machine gun with the bazooka. Finley's squad had two wounded,
serious enough that they would have to be sent back to a field
hospital.

Dunn was mourning his own loss: Clarence Waters got shot
as they were retreating from their position on the secondary
attack. He'd been hit in the neck and bled to death in a matter of
seconds. Wickham, who had been closest to him, had tried to stop

the blood loss, but no one could have, and Waters had died in his arms.

Dunn had helped Wickham carry Waters deeper into the woods. Wickham's shirt was covered with Water's blood, and at first Dunn thought Wickham had wiped his face with a bloody hand, but when he took a closer look, Dunn saw that he had a two inch gash on his left cheek that was bleeding heavily, as face wounds always do. Dunn got Wickham seated and had Martelli patch him up. The rest of the men were all okay, which Dunn took as a good sign. He hoped the Germans had taken it as bad.

Dunn had called in an after action report, which included the losses and the fact that the attack had been beaten back, to the company's executive officer shortly after the firefight. He had been ordered to stay in place and to continue looking for an advantage. When Dunn asked if any other platoons would be coming, the XO had said 'no.'

In the daylight, Dunn and Red, who had made their way near the edge of the forest, used binoculars to examine the German position.

What Dunn saw was not encouraging. The Germans seemed to have bolstered their position with another platoon, possibly two. They formed a defensive L-shaped line, similar to that used in an ambush. The long leg faced the river, and the short leg ran uphill to the east.

"I see two MG42s. One's about ten yards from the west edge of their line and the second is about the midpoint up the hill," Red said.

"I see them. Shit. How many more do they have?"

As if in answer to Dunn's question, a couple of machine guns that were out of his view began firing, their distinctive tearing sound piercing the morning quiet. Dunn looked downhill and saw men on the pontoon bridge duck for cover behind armored vehicles.

Dunn tapped Red on the arm and both men ran back through the woods to their men.

"Goerdt, Bailey, saddle up the 'zooka. Got some more MG42 targets for you." Dunn patted Red on the arm. "Red here will show you where you need to be to get the shot. The guns are hitting the guys on the bridge right this moment, so quick!"

Goerdt and Bailey got their equipment and took off through the woods right behind Red.

Dunn's men were in a semicircle, some sitting with their legs crossed and others kneeling. Their expressions carried the weight of Water's death, the man who had saved their lives just three days ago. Any medal awarded for saving them would be posthumous.

Dunn stepped into the center of the semicircle and knelt, leaning his M1 lazily across his knee. Some of the men glanced at him, and quickly looked away, while the others just stared at the ground in front of them.

"Okay, guys. Look at me."

One by one the men raised their faces and looked at Dunn.

"I'm sorry about Clarence. I feel bad about him, just like you do. I need us, me included, to be focused on our job. We have a task and you know very well that we always complete our assignments. I'm not asking you to forget about what happened to him, but just to put it aside for now. I'm the last guy who wants to remind you we lost three men just a month ago, plus Squeaky losing his leg. We've been through this before and we need to get through this one, too.

"I need you to do a weapons and ammo check. So get started on that."

The men nodded and got themselves into motion, which was Dunn's goal all along. A man with work to do doesn't have as much time to think about the bad stuff.

"Dave, Bob?" Dunn tipped his head for them to join him. "Bob, bring the radio."

Cross and Schneider followed Dunn a few yards away from the men.

"Bob, get company HQ on the line, will you?"

"Sure, thing, Sarge." Schneider set the radio down and got to work.

"Nice speech, Tom," Cross said.

Dunn shrugged. "Hm. I guess."

Farther down the hill, just inside the tree line, Goerdt and Bailey set up for a shot on one of the MG42s. The weapons were currently silent. Goerdt figured they were conserving ammo or cooling the barrels.

Red knelt next to Goerdt and pointed. "That's where one of them is. Can you see it?"

Goerdt looked through the binoculars that Red handed to him. The ugly cone-shaped snout of the MG42 stuck out. "I see it. Where's the other?"

"Come this way maybe twenty-five yards."

Goerdt rotated his head and acquired the second machine gun. "Can you make the shots from here?"

"Well, the angle's pretty steep, but, yes, I can."

"Go for it."

Schneider said, "I have the XO on the line."

Dunn took the handset and said, "Dunn here, sir. The enemy platoon we're facing has received reinforcement by at least one more platoon, but I believe an entire company is there in the rocks. Can we get another artillery barrage?"

The reply was immediate. "Negative."

There were lots of possible reasons, two of which were conserving ammo or other higher priority targets. It didn't matter what the reason was. Dunn knew better than to repeat the question. So he tried another tack.

"We've observed two MG42s firing on the bridge, sir. We are going to try taking them out by bazooka. How about calling in some P-47s? If we can pound them from the air, we might dislodge them entirely."

The XO didn't say 'no' right away, so Dunn thought the man, a sharp first lieutenant, was considering it.

"Okay. I will do that. What are the coordinates? I don't have time to look them up."

Dunn already had them and rattled them off precisely for the XO, who repeated them back correctly.

"Dunn, make sure your men know to stay in the woods. I'm going to mark them as off limits for the Thunderbolts."

"Will do, sir. Oh, sir, how's Lieutenant Carver?"

"We sent him to a hospital. The bullet lodged near his spine."

"Oh, good Lord." Dunn glanced at Cross and mouthed the word 'spine.'

Cross closed his eyes and shook his head. He knew what that might mean for the lieutenant. Paralysis.

"Sorry to hear that, sir. I take it I'll continue as platoon leader?"

"Affirmative, Sergeant Dunn. You are still acting platoon leader."

"Understood. Anything else for me, sir?"

"Negative. Out."

"Roger. Out."

Dunn gave the handset back to Schneider and said to Cross, "Got P-47s coming in. Pass the word. I'll catch Red and Finley. Everyone stay inside the woods."

"Okay. We won't have to tell the men twice on that."

Bailey tapped Goerdt on the helmet.

The rocket screeched away, trailing fire and smoke. The shot was the longest Goerdt had ever made outside of training, about a hundred and fifty yards. The rocket climbed the hill as if following the terrain.

Goerdt and Bailey stood up backing farther into the woods, but keeping their eyes on the rocket. Red was right with them. The explosion sent rocks flying. Smoke covered the area around the target and none of the men could tell whether the result was good or not. Not waiting to find out, they moved a few yards father west and set up for a shot at the other machine gun nest, which was closer.

The Germans started firing at their old position and bullets zipped through the trees behind them, shredding the underbrush.

Goerdt fired the second rocket and watched it strike home. The men moved a second time about ten yards to the west. Goerdt asked Red for the binoculars and raised them to this eyes. Sweeping them across the German line, he found the first target, where the smoke still lingered, but it was clear enough he could see the MG42 still in place. Judging from a small crater in a rock face, he determined he had undershot by about ten yards. He handed the field glasses back to Red and knelt, lifting the bazooka to his shoulder.

"Load me up, Leonard."

Bailey slid the rocket home and tapped Goerdt's helmet a third time.

Goerdt adjusted his aim, allowing for a little more drop than on the first shot. He squeezed the trigger. The rocket flew true and hit the target.

Rifle fire immediately peppered the area around them, and a splinter from a nearby tree struck Goerdt in the left shoulder. The three soldiers beat a hasty retreat. When they were deeper into the woods, Bailey noticed that Goerdt was bleeding and pulled his partner to a halt.

"Hey, Rob. Let me look at that."

"Huh?"

"You're hit."

Goerdt glanced at his shoulder where Bailey's eyes were focused. "Oh. Okay."

Bailey examined the shirt, which was torn. A sliver of wood was embedded in the shirt fibers. He carefully pulled the edges back and peered at the wound, which was merely seeping.

"Looks okay. Just a graze from a wood splinter. I'll patch you up when we get back."

"Okay, thanks."

"It doesn't hurt?"

"Not yet anyway."

Chapter 31

900 meters north of Arry, France, and
1,000 meters east of the Moselle River
11 September, 0625 Hours

Dieter Wittenberg was relieved. The American attack had failed. His men had held up well and driven the enemy back. He ran amongst his men checking for dead and wounded. When he was done, he had four killed, the valuable MG42 teams and the weapons, and two wounded. He made arrangements to get them moved out, and tightened his line by moving men around.

Kneeling between two of his soldiers, he looked at the woods. He could see no movement, but he knew the Americans were there. He turned his attention uphill, to the east. *Perhaps they will try next time to come from there*, he thought. He visualized the American platoon—he was sure that was the enemy strength— moving through the woods just out of his view, and crossing the open area while suppressing fire came from the forest. He'd lost his MG42s, and it would be up to Raupp and Mekelburg to fire on the bridges with their four, the only ones left in the company.

He shook his head. It was an impossible situation. Again. On top of that, he had to deal with Raupp and Mekelburg and their fanaticism.

"Oberfeldwebel?" said a voice behind him.

He turned and found the platoon radioman behind him. "Yes?"

"Call for you." The man, a short wiry fellow, handed over the handset.

"Wittenberg."

"I want you to increase your fire on the bridges." The voice didn't bother identifying itself, but Wittenberg recognized that it was his company commander. "Do you have enough machine gun ammunition?"

"Our MG42s are knocked out. Destroyed by bazooka fire. I lost all four men."

"You lost your machine guns?"

"Yes, and I lost all four men," Wittenberg repeated.

"I don't care about the men! Confirm that you have no MG42s!"

"We have no MG42s. Nothing we could do."

"There's always something to be done. Never mind. I've given the same order to Raupp and Mekelburg. I can depend on them. They haven't lost their heavy weapons."

The phone line went dead. Wittenberg handed the phone back to the radioman without a word, but he shook his head.

He was sorely disappointed in his commander. It seemed there was no limit on the number of idiots available. Raupp's and Mekelburg's blind stupidity must be infectious.

Making his way back to the two squads facing the woods, he checked on the men again, telling them to remain alert because another attack could come any moment. He knelt beside his first squad leader.

"I'm thinking they may try to slide east on us." Wittenberg said, tipping his head in that direction.

"I had the same thought, too, Sergeant."

"I don't want to give away our thinking by moving, but have your men be ready to move farther uphill if I call for it."

"I will."

Wittenberg patted the man on the back and went to a spot behind his second squad so he could see the forest, and think.

Chapter 32

In the woods 1000 yards north of Arry, France, and
1,000 yards east of the Moselle River
11 September, 0645 Hours

Dunn directed his squad to take the left position, with Red's
taking the center and Finley's the right. They were positioned a
couple of yards back from the edge of the woods, with each
soldier taking cover behind a tree.

The Germans had not adjusted their position, and the only
movement Dunn had detected was that of a few men coming in to
replace those who'd fallen.

Dunn checked his watch. According to the radio call he'd
received a few minutes ago, Thunderbolts were on the way. He
was allowed to attack, but not cross over to the German position,
as if he'd ever consider doing that. He'd considered waiting until
after the air attack, but decided that the combination of the two
attacks would create some havoc on the other side, always a good
thing to do.

"Fire!" Dunn yelled.

M1s up and down Dunn's line, almost thirty of them, began firing into the German position.

The Germans immediately returned fire. Bullets shredded tree bark and snapped off tree limbs and foliage around Dunn's men.

Across the way, rock chips flew in all directions.

The American M1 had a much faster rate of fire due to its eight-round clip versus the bolt-action Mauser the Germans were firing. Ordinarily, Dunn would have taken advantage of the firepower difference and moved a squad uphill for a rush against the German position, but he was certain the German leader would slide one of his squads uphill to counter. Dunn didn't want to spread out the Germans, though, because the P-47s were on their way.

Dunn sighted on a German helmet just visible above a rock and squeezed off a round. The helmet disappeared. He saw another go down. He wondered how many in total had been taken out.

Ducking behind his tree, he checked his watch again.

"Cease fire! Cease fire!"

The platoon stopped firing with a few straggling shots until the word was all the way down the line.

The Germans stopped firing.

Dunn gave the next order and the platoon retreated farther into the forest. Dunn and Cross stayed near the edge to watch the coming air attack.

Chapter 33

In fight over Arnaville, 5,000 feet altitude
11 September, 0654 Hours

Captain Benjamin Banks eyed the Moselle River just ahead and below his Thunderbolt. He followed an imaginary line straight ahead extending from the road through Arnaville across the river and up the hill. There were the rocks in which the Germans were entrenched. Just to the north were the woods that had been clearly identified as holding American soldiers. The position of the friendlies forced Banks to alter his typical attack style, which would have been along the German line, to one perpendicular to the line. This merely meant that each of his three flights would come in with the four planes abreast as they dropped their two thousand pound loads instead of in line, then the next flight would roar in.

The call for air support had come in around fifteen after six, and Banks, whose ground crew was already preparing the aircraft for the day's work, had his squadron of twelve planes into the air by six thirty. At four hundred miles an hour, it only took a little more than twenty-three minutes to arrive at the target.

On takeoff, Banks had wondered whether they would have to do a flyover of the target to make sure they knew what they were supposed to hit. He decided that was unnecessary since the rocks and the woods were so clearly demarcated thanks to nature.

"Dogbone squadron from Dogbone leader. Target is clearly identified. Rocky area east of the river. A reminder that the woods to the north are off limits due to friendlies there. I'll take the lead."

Banks tipped *Gorgeous Mary's* nose over and picked his aiming point. A cluster of rocks on the northern edge of the whole target. As his airspeed climbed he held the stick as steady as possible. There was a stiff southerly breeze—the meteorologist had predicted twenty knots—and the plane began to drift slightly left. He corrected with the stick and a little tap on the rudder pedal. This put the nose back on target.

He was close enough to make out human forms in the rocks scurrying around trying to find a hiding place. *Good luck with that*, he thought. Some of the men seemed to be aiming their rifles at him. *Courageous but stupid*, he thought.

He reached the exact point he'd picked and released both of his thousand pound bombs. He pulled back on the stick and the Thunderbolt began to climb.

So intent had he been on his target, he didn't see the twinkling muzzle flashes of a German quad 20mm antiaircraft gun as it began firing from the top of the hill.

His first sign of trouble was when the German shells struck his engine compartment. Smoke poured from the engine. Shells struck the port wing. The stick suddenly felt loose as a control cable was severed.

Banks hollered into his mike, "Taking anti-aircraft fire! Take them out!"

Smoke filled the cockpit.

Oil pressure dropped to zero.

The engine seized.

Banks opened the canopy to help clear the smoke. Able to see better, he realized he was on the east side of the ridge. He moved the stick to the left to come around in a sweeping circle, planning on flying back across the river.

The nose dropped.

The plane only turned slightly left even though the stick was all the way over.

He glanced at the left wing. The aileron hadn't moved with the stick and was stuck in the neutral, or level flight, position. He quickly checked the right and was relieved to see that aileron in the proper position. The cut cable went to the left side. He stomped on the left rudder pedal and the plane's left turn sped up. Soon, the Thunderbolt was heading west.

The nose continued to drop and Banks realized he would never make it back across the river. Decision made, he unbuckled his harness and climbed up through the canopy. Once there, he simply jumped.

He pulled his parachute deployment ring right away and prayed that the Germans wouldn't shoot him as he drifted lower.

From his position dangling from the parachute, he could see the hillside was covered by smoke from the explosions. It looked like his men had been as precise always. The woods were free of smoke and that made him feel happy in spite of his dire predicament.

The southerly breeze blew him northward and he began to wonder whether he'd end up in the trees.

Dieter Wittenberg raised his head and looked around. He could barely hear again. He checked the men nearest to him and they were okay. He crouched and ran down the line to the end of his platoon. He'd found six dead, and three missing; the three boys asking about the new weapons. They'd taken a direct hit from the tub-shaped Jabos' bombs and had been vaporized. He wondered whether they'd had time to feel anything, pain or fear. He hoped not.

An out of breath radioman ran up and said, *"Oberfeldwebel* Wittenberg! The company commander is dead! You're the new commander. Battalion just said so."

"Alsdorf is dead?"

"Yes."

For a brief moment, Wittenberg felt guilty for mentally berating the man earlier. On the other hand, perhaps this was a good thing. He could exert more logical control over the company, and deal with the two Nazi-loving platoon leaders more effectively.

"Thank you. You stay here so I can find you when I need you."

"Yes, *Oberfeldwebel*."

Wittenberg surveyed his company's line. The bomb damage and death appeared to extend far to the south into Raupp's platoon, possibly Mekelburg's. Wittenberg intended to go check on them, but he happened to catch movement out of the corner of his left eye. He looked up and saw a white parachute seemingly hanging in the sky. A man dangled below it. Rage, such as he'd never felt before, suddenly rose in his chest.

He ran back through his line, ignoring men who were trying to stop him and ask questions. His eyes never left the killer drifting to earth.

He got to the edge of the rocks and stopped for a moment. He raised his Mauser and took aim. Probably an easy shot of a little over a hundred meters. He lined up the sights on the man and almost pulled the trigger. His fury prevented it. He wanted to kill the man with his bare hands.

He watched the parachute and tried to estimate its landing point. It looked like it might fall in the open space between the defensive rocks and the forest to the north.

Rage overcame fear and Wittenberg climbed through a gap between boulders and started running.

Dunn watched the P-47s dive in and drop their humongous bombs right on top of the German position. He and Cross were standing at the edge of the woods. They found themselves cheering, hands raised like they were signaling a touchdown.

Suddenly a smoking Thunderbolt streaked overhead, leaving a trail in the sky. A parachute appeared.

Dunn tried to estimate where the pilot would land, and when he finished that calculation, said, "We're gonna have to go get him, Dave. He'll land out in the open. Go tell the men to open fire on the Germans to keep their heads down."

"I'm on it," Cross replied and took off at a run.

Dunn ran through the woods to the east to get closer to the pilot's expected landing point. Behind him, he heard his men let loose a barrage of rifle fire.

Dunn glanced right, through the trees, and was shocked to see a German soldier running up the hill, keeping pace with himself. Suddenly the enemy soldier turned to his left and ran farther into the open, clearly intent on getting to the pilot.

Dunn sped up.

The pilot crashed to earth and rolled over a few times going downhill, entangling himself in the parachute cords.

Dunn and the German were equidistant from the pilot. Both were slowing down from the exertion of the uphill run.

Dunn considered bringing his M1 to bear, but being right handed put the rifle on the wrong side for firing while running. He switched the rifle to his left hand and drew his Colt .45. He flipped off the safety and raised it. He fired four shots. None hit the mark, but the German reacted swiftly and brought his own rifle up and fired a shot that went wide.

Being a bolt-action weapon, the Mauser didn't exactly make it easy to run and fire.

While the German was awkwardly working the bolt, Dunn dug deep and increased his speed.

Dunn raised the .45 and fired three more shots. All missed. Dunn holstered the empty .45 and changed directions. He was almost on top of the German.

The German raised his rifle and fired from almost point blank range. The bullet clanged off the top of Dunn's helmet and he nearly lost his footing from getting his bell rung. His momentum allowed him to charge into the much bigger German and tackle him. Their rifles and helmets went flying.

Just up the hill, the pilot struggled to disentangle himself. He'd drawn a knife and was cutting the cords wrapped around him.

Dunn punched the German in the side of the face and got a ham-sized fist in his left ear in return.

The blow knocked Dunn off the German, who jumped on top of Dunn.

Pinned to the ground, Dunn felt two rough and immensely strong hands encircle his throat. They began to squeeze.

Dunn couldn't draw a breath. He tried to free himself from the German's grip, but the man's hands were locked around Dunn's throat.

Soon Dunn's ears began to roar. His vision seemed to be coming in through a dim tunnel.

Chapter 34

In the open field 1000 yards north of Arry, France, and
1,100 yards east of the Moselle River
11 September, 0701 Hours

Dunn's gasping brain resorted to training and Dunn stopped
trying to pry the German's hands loose. Instead, he used all of his
strength and clapped the man's already painful ears with cupped
hands as hard as he'd ever hit anything in his life.

The sudden increased air pressure in the man's ears hurt too
much and he roared in pain, putting his hands on his ears, rolling
off Dunn to lie on his back.

Dunn took a rasping breath. He got to his knees and followed
up with a right fist to the prone man's solar plexus.

The German gasped as all the air whooshed out of his lungs.
The strike almost paralyzed his diaphragm.

Dunn's next shot, a sweeping undercut to the chin, hit the
sweet spot and the German stopped moving.

A quick glance at the enemy soldier told Dunn several things.
He was knocked out, and he was a sergeant, and well, the guy

was huge, probably around two hundred and ten pounds. *Thank God for a lucky chin shot.*

Dunn suddenly realized he was in no-man's land when a few shots peppered the ground nearby. He rose to his feet and looked around for his rifle and helmet. He spotted them and took off, zig-zagging his way and scooped them up as he ran toward the downed pilot. He jammed the helmet back on his noggin.

Dunn could hear fire coming from his men as they tried to keep the Germans' heads down while he helped the pilot.

When he got to the pilot, who had almost extricated himself from his parachute mess, Dunn hollered, "Hey! Army here to help you."

The pilot glanced up from his work on a last recalcitrant cord around his knees. "Good to see you, ground pounder."

In spite of the sarcastic remark, the pilot's face was set in a grimace, and Dunn deduced he was injured.

As the last cord was cut free, the pilot got to his knees and confirmed Dunn's thought when he put weight on his right leg. It buckled and he fell to the ground, groaning.

"Fuck!"

Dunn slung his rifle and bent over. He grabbed the man under the shoulders and lifted, and positioned himself on the man's right.

"Come on. Got to go."

The pilot put his right arm over Dunn's shoulder and they began the awkward battle of walking and hopping on three legs as the pilot pulled his bad one up like a flamingo.

Dunn guided their path toward the closest point of the woods, which looked like a mile from where he stood.

As soon as they entered the safety of the forest, the pilot said, "God, I've got to sit down a second."

"Okay." Dunn helped lower the man to the ground, unslung his rifle, and took a quick look around. It wouldn't do to let the huge German catch them. Dunn could've just used his knife on the unconscious man, but that seemed wrong, inhumane, which was probably an odd position for a soldier to take, especially after all Dunn had been through and seen. He hoped he wouldn't regret the decision.

An idea popped into Dunn's head.

No one was chasing them into the woods, so Dunn stepped to the other side of the pilot who was rubbing his ankle. Dunn took this position so he could still keep an eye out on the direction from which they'd come. He was still thinking about his idea, but asked, "Roll your ankle?"

"Hurts like hell, so yeah, probably just a sprain. I hear they hurt worse than a break."

Dunn drew his .45 and ejected the empty clip, and then inserted a fresh one, clicking it into place. He charged the weapon by pulling back on the receiver, and then holstered the Colt.

While Dunn was reloading, he said, "Yep, heard that, too. Sir, I need you to wait here for just a little bit. Do you have a sidearm?"

"Yes, I have a Colt, too."

"Make sure the safety is on, that it's loaded, and a round is in the chamber. Then click off the safety."

The pilot obeyed under Dunn's watchful eye.

"It's ready."

"Okay. Keep it in your hand until I get back, not in your holster."

"Aye, aye, captain," replied the pilot with a grin and a mock salute. "Tell me what you're gonna do."

"Going to see if I can carry that big-assed Nazi in here with us. Maybe get some intelligence out of him."

"By yourself?" The pilot looked incredulous.

"My men will keep the krauts' heads down." Under his breath he said, "Hopefully." Louder he said, "Be back soon. Shoot any Germans you see first, ask questions later."

Banks nodded.

"Do you have any extra clips?" Dunn asked.

"Two in my pocket."

Dunn nodded and walked away.

He crept back to the forest edge and located the still downed German. Dunn waited until a barrage of M1 fire forced the Germans to duck, and sprinted across the no-man's land to the unconscious man, still lying on his back where Dunn had left him.

Just as he'd counted on, his men upped the rate of fire to help give him some cover. Cross must have seen him running back into the open. Dunn grinned to himself thinking about what Cross would say later about Dunn's antics.

Dunn bent over and rolled the German over onto his stomach, and picked him up in a fireman's carry, the enemy's right leg over Dunn's right shoulder and his head and right arm over Dunn's left shoulder. He carried the M1 with his left hand and grabbed the man's right pants leg and right uniform wrist with his own right hand. As he took off at a jog, his fastest speed under the circumstances, he thought, *good thing it's mostly downhill.*

His platoon's M1 fire was still keeping the Germans' heads down.

When Dunn was about five yards from the edge of the woods, he allowed a positive thought, *might just make it.*

But of course, he didn't.

Chapter 35

Mess hall – Camp Barton Stacey
Andover, England
11 September, 0610 Hours, London time

Saunders swallowed the last of his second cup of coffee and went to get a refill. He walked past the serving line and eyed the eggs made from powder on the steam table. There was toast, too. His stomach grumbled. He checked his watch. Bloody colonels. Always late. As much as he wanted to fill a plate and start eating, he knew he'd have to wait for the old man. He forced himself on past the lovely sight and smell of breakfast and refilled his cup.

The mess hall was about a quarter filled and so there were plenty of tables where the colonel's breakfast meeting could be held with some privacy.

Saunders' men were still sacked out. They'd arrived back at the base the night before around midnight. After putting away their gear, Saunders told them to get some sleep. He had a hard time falling asleep, though. He'd wanted to call his fiancé, Sadie, but by that time it was near on one a.m. He didn't think even the wonderful Mrs. Hughes would have patience for a call at that hour. After tossing and turning for an hour, he finally drifted off to sleep only to be awakened at five-thirty by his alarm clock after what seemed like only a few seconds of sleep.

Colonel Jenkins and Major Armstrong strode into the mess hall together. Saunders had to suppress a laugh for they made him think of the American comic strip characters Mutt and Jeff due to their mismatch in height.

Jenkins caught Saunders looking his way and headed over to the commando.

"Morning, sir. Major Armstrong."

Jenkins just nodded, but Armstrong said, "Good morning, Sergeant Saunders. You ready to eat? I'm starving. Shall we?"

Saunders smiled at Armstrong's rapid speech. He must be getting used to it.

"I'm ready."

Jenkins waved a hand in the direction of the serving line and said, "After you, Saunders."

"Yes, sir," Saunders replied, a bit surprised by Jenkins' courtesy. He'd noted a change in behavior in their last meeting. He still didn't know what had triggered it.

The men filled their plates and found a table away from everyone.

They ate quietly for a few minutes and then Saunders said, "I have an American friend who smothers his eggs with catsup."

Jenkins raised his eyebrows and Armstrong looked aghast at the idea.

"For that matter, I think he would put catsup on anything."

Jenkins narrowed his eyes. "Ah. Dunn is it?"

"Yes sir, indeed."

"Who's Dunn?" Armstrong asked.

"He's a ranger. I taught him at Achnacarry House some time ago, he and Saunders work together sometimes," Jenkins said. "He's a real pain in the ass, but not as much as his commander, Mark Kenton." Jenkins looked at Saunders as if waiting for confirmation on the American colonel's special talent of getting under Jenkins' skin. "However, I will say, they are bloody good at their job. Don't tell them I said so, Saunders."

"Certainly not, sir." Saunders smiled, thinking he couldn't wait to tell Dunn what Jenkins had said.

RONN MUNSTERMAN

Armstrong put down his fork and looked around before speaking to make sure no one was close enough to hear. "It's still early days, but the items we procured from that radio center will help immensely. You and your men did an excellent job."

"Thank you, Major. I'll pass along the compliment."

"And mine as well, Saunders. You can give the men a two-day pass. Take some time yourself, say, through Saturday. I know your lass is recovering from her injuries and you must want to see her," Jenkins said.

"Thank you, Colonel. Yes, I do."

"Who's the lady?" Armstrong asked.

"My fiancé, Sadie."

"My word. Congratulations. Have you set a date?"

"Coming up soon. The twenty-third."

"Well, that is wonderful news."

The men settled into silence again as they finished the meal. When they were done, Armstrong said, "Well, I must be off. I want to get back to that material." He stood up as did Jenkins and Saunders.

"Colonel, thanks for the help."

"Glad to do it."

Armstrong held out his hand to Saunders, who shook it.

"Thank you, Sergeant. Couldn't have done it without you."

"You're welcome, sir."

The major grinned up at Saunders, and his eyes seemed to sparkle.

"Since you brought it up, Sergeant, I'll leave you with this: Knock! Knock!"

"Who's there?"

"Catsup."

"Catsup who?"

"Catsup with me and I'll tell you!"

This time, instead of groaning, Saunders roared in laughter. "That's a good one, sir. Mind if I pass that along as well?"

"You go right ahead."

The major waved his hand and left, taking his tray with him.

Saunders turned to Jenkins and said, "No sense of humor, sir?"

Jenkins smiled and shrugged.

Saunders was still smiling when he started to pick up his tray.

"A moment, Saunders, if you please?" Jenkins gestured for Saunders to sit.

The men sat back down and Saunders looked at his boss, more curious than anything. Jenkins cleared his throat a couple of times and Saunders realized the colonel was nervous.

"What is it, sir?"

Jenkins looked at Saunders over his long nose for a moment. "I never allow my personal feelings to get in the middle of decision making."

"No, sir, I've never thought so."

"You and your men are extraordinary." Saunders started to reply, but Jenkins held up a hand to forestall the red-headed sergeant. "On your last mission, the one to Insel Riems."

This was the mission where Saunders and his team had been transported by submarine deep into Germany on the Baltic Sea to capture German scientists working on a deadly biological weapon.

"The bombers were under instructions to let loose at a certain time regardless of whether you were off the island or not. I asked if they would be able to delay if you were held up. When I got the answer of 'no' I confess to feeling sick to my stomach. I just wanted you to know that, Malcolm."

Saunders eyebrows went up at the use of his given name. "I appreciate it, very much." So he had been right. Something had indeed happened to alter Jenkins' recent behavior.

Jenkins nodded.

"I take it this is between just us?"

"Yes, please."

"Certainly."

"I'll still be as demanding as ever."

"I would expect nothing less, sir." Saunders smiled and the colonel returned it.

"One other thing. I'm promoting you to Sergeant Major."

This pleased Saunders and he grinned. The tips of his handlebar moustache twitched.

"I appreciate that, too, sir."

"It's well earned. Go back to your men. Give them the news about the passes. Enjoy your time with Sadie. That's an order, Sergeant Major!"

Chapter 36

In the open field 1000 yards north of Arry, France, and
1,100 yards east of the Moselle River
11 September, 0711 Hours, Paris time

The German soldier regained consciousness all at once and began thrashing, trying to get loose from Dunn.

Dunn promptly dropped the man. He took a couple of quick steps back and aimed his M1 between the man's eyes.

The German got to his feet and took a step.

"Halt!" shouted Dunn, as he backed up a little farther. No way was he going to get within arm's length of this brute.

The German stopped and seemed to be sizing up Dunn. He eyed the M1's barrel a few feet away, as if gauging the likelihood of getting to the weapon before the American fired it.

"Don't try it. Halt!" Dunn was wishing he'd learned some basic German from Schneider right now.

The German stared at Dunn, and started to turn away, as if getting ready to just walk back to his own line.

Exasperated, Dunn shouted again, "Halt!"

The man turned to face Dunn again and said in excellent English, "You'll have to shoot me in the back." He turned and took a first step to safety.

Dunn knew the man was right, he wouldn't shoot him in the back. That left one choice.

With a few quick steps, Dunn was right behind the man and he raised the butt of his rifle. With a little extra care, he aimed for a spot behind the right ear. He slammed the butt into the small target and the huge German's legs buckled and he folded up, falling to the ground.

Dunn wondered briefly whether it was really worth it, and set about carrying the man again. This time he made it back to where he'd left the pilot.

"Congratulations," the pilot said dryly as Dunn lowered the German next to a tree. Dunn quickly frisked the man, and found a combat knife, but no sidearm.

"You ready to go, sir?"

The pilot looked surprised. "How are we going to manage this?"

Dunn ejected the round in the chamber and the clip from his M1 and then handed the rifle to the pilot. "Your crutch, sir."

The pilot took the weapon and put the butt on the ground and took a tentative step. "Okay, this will work."

"Good, let's go."

Dunn picked up the German and took off. The pilot followed, the rifle butt making a clunking sound with each step.

Gunfire was still sprinkled every so often, but it seemed both sides were losing interest and it finally petered away into silence.

When Dunn figured he was close, he gave a couple of whistles to let his men know he was coming.

Cross came into view and ran up to take over acting as a crutch for the pilot. Jonesy helped carry the prisoner. The men made their way to a spot where the pilot could be lowered to the ground next to a tree, and the German against another tree.

"Jonesy, better bind this guy's hands and feet right away. Hands first, behind the back," Dunn said.

"Okay, Sarge." Jonesy dug around in his pack and came out with a thin rope about a quarter inch in diameter. He trussed up the German and stepped back. "Done."

"Great," Dunn said, as he knelt beside the pilot. "Tom Dunn."

"Ben Banks."

Banks offered his hand and the two shook.

Dunn pulled a pack of Lucky Strikes from his pocket and offered them to the pilot, who grabbed one and lit it with Dunn's offered Zippo.

"Hm. Thanks, Dunn."

"You're welcome, Captain."

Dunn had spotted Banks' captains' bars on his flight jacket.

"Ah, fuck that, Dunn. You can call me 'Cloud.' "

Dunn's eyebrows raised and he laughed. "Really? Cloud Banks?"

Banks shrugged and chuckled along. "Gotta love nicknames. Goes back to flight school. You got one?"

Dunn, still laughing, shook his head, and said, "Nah. Tom'll do."

"Okay, Tom. You saved my ass. That guy would've killed me. Thanks!"

"Well, I owe some Thunderbolts a 'thank you' myself. Saved our asses when our column got caught in the open by artillery a couple of days ago."

"Really? Was that back about fifteen miles?"

"Yep, it would be about that from here."

"That was us."

"Huh. What are the odds, sir?"

"Cloud."

"Cloud," Dunn said with a smile.

"Pretty steep odds I'd say."

"The leader of the group waggled his wings at us. Was that you?"

"Yeah, it was."

"Well, it was awesome bombing, I have to say."

"We do our best," Banks said with a bit of aw-shucks in his voice.

"Where are you based?"

"South of Paris about ten miles."

"Came through Paris a few weeks ago." Dunn left out his part in saving Paris from a German biological weapon attack.

Banks eyed Dunn's uniform: the five stripes and the Ranger emblem on the shoulder. "Ranger, huh?"

"Yep, almost a year and a half now."

"How'd you come to be here? Isn't this Patton's area?"

"It is. We're attached to the Third Army for a while."

"I see." Banks looked around at his surroundings and noted another Ranger.

"Who's that? The guy who came over to help."

"Dave Cross. My second. We've been together since Ranger school. Say, we have a radio. Wouldn't you like to contact someone?"

Banks smiled. "I sure would. My guys are going to wonder what the hell happened to me."

"Be right back."

Banks nodded.

Dunn went over to Schneider and told him to bring over the radio for the pilot and to assist.

"Will do, Sarge."

When he returned to Banks, Dunn said, "Radio is on the way. I'm going to go check on that German."

"Okay, thanks."

"Goerdt?" Dunn called out.

"Yes, Sarge."

"Come with me. To my surprise, this German speaks English real well, but I might need you just in case."

"Okay, sure. But what about Bob?" Schneider was the primary translator.

"He's helping our friend the pilot with the radio."

"Ah, okay."

The two men knelt on either side of the tied up German. Dunn examined the man's knot behind the right ear. Dunn was worried he'd hit him too hard, especially after being knocked out only minutes prior. Dunn shook the man by the shoulder. When that didn't rouse the prisoner, Dunn started soft slapping his cheeks, left and right. This earned Dunn some fluttering eyelids.

"Tell him 'wake up' in German."

Goerdt said, *"Wach auf!"*

Dunn shook the man again.

The German opened his eyes and blinked as he tried to focus.

"What's your name, soldier?" Dunn asked.

Goerdt translated.

The German stared at Dunn, but said nothing.

"Your name. What can it hurt?"

"Dieter Wittenberg. *Oberfeldwebel.*"

"Tom Dunn. I'd shake hands with you, but," Dunn nodded in the direction of Wittenberg's hands tied behind his back.

Goerdt translated, but then Wittenberg responded in English, "Prudent choice."

Dunn raised an eyebrow, and said, "I thought so. How you feeling?"

"As if you care? You knocked me out twice."

"Well, no choice there on the first one as you were choking the life out of me."

Wittenberg acknowledged this with a tip of the head.

"What's the size of your unit stuck there in the rocks? Can't be all that comfortable in there."

"Dieter Wittenberg. *Oberfeldwebel.*"

"I think you have an understrength company, maybe two hundred men. You had a few MG42s, fine weapon by the way, but we knocked out those, so you're down to your bolt-action Mauser K98s, and maybe some sidearms, although you didn't even have one. Now you can't even bother the guys pouring across the bridge." Dunn knew there were MG42s farther south in the German line, but hyperbole helped make the point.

"So?"

"And just a little while ago you got pounded by an airstrike. What is it you guys call those gigantic fighter bombers? Jabo?"

"So what?"

Dunn shrugged. "I know you guys are scared to death of those things."

Wittenberg shrugged, attempting to lessen the hard truth just spoken.

"Here's what I'm going to offer you. Are you ready to listen?"

"I'm rather captivated."

Dunn appreciated the man's play on words and smiled. He knew English and its nuances very well. Dunn put a hand on the man's shoulder. Gently he said, "The Jabos can be back here anytime I call them."

"You called them in?" Anger rose in Wittenberg's voice.

"Yes, had to."

"You killed my men."

"Yes. And I will continue to do so until your area is clear of Germans. I have artillery targeted on the area up the hill from you and to the south, your only possible retreat paths. I will call in the Jabos." Dunn said this softly, too, but the threat was clear. *Listen to me or all your men will die.* He left out the fact that he probably couldn't actually get the artillery support.

"I'm listening."

"Judging from your rank, you must be high up in the company. Help convince your commander to surrender your company to us and live another day."

Wittenberg shook his head. "Impossible. I am but a platoon leader . . ." he trailed off, his eyes looking heavenward as he realized something.

"What is it?" Dunn prompted.

"Our company commander was killed in your Jabo attack and I am the senior platoon leader, and therefore the acting commander."

"Well, there you go, Commanding Officer Wittenberg."

"No, you don't understand. The other two platoon leaders are party hacks and would never surrender, even if I so ordered it. They are Hitler fanatics. Plus, you're asking me to betray my country."

"No, I'm not. I'm asking you to save your men. You wouldn't be the first German unit to surrender, you know. You do know about the Falaise pocket?"

Wittenberg gave an involuntary shudder. Yes, he knew about the wholesale massacre and capture of tens of thousands German soldiers as they attempted to escape the onrushing, and overwhelming onslaught of the American Army. "Yes."

"Save your men, Sergeant."

"I know I will not be able to convince the other two men. They are too aligned to Hitler, as bad as the SS. You know the SS?"

"I do. Quite well," Dunn replied, thinking of Gestapo Agent Schluter and his platoon of SS troops who tried to massacre the village of Ville di Murlo, Italy. Dunn and Saunders had ambushed the SS, killing them all, and Dunn had a vicious fight with Schluter, who met his demise at Dunn's hands.

"So what can I do? The situation is hopeless."

Dunn shook his head slowly, thinking. "No, it's not. Let's say something were to happen to them."

"I cannot kill them, if that's what you're asking. The men would cut me to pieces."

"No, that's not what I have in mind."

"What then?"

Wittenberg listened without interruption as Dunn spent a few minutes laying out his plan.

"You are certain of this?"

"I am."

"If it fails, then what?"

"It won't fail if you do your part."

Wittenberg thought about Dunn's proposal for several minutes, at times closing his eyes.

At last he said, "Yes. I will do it. Untie my hands so we can shake on it."

Dunn nodded to Goerdt who pulled his combat knife and stepped behind the temporary prisoner. He sliced away the rope, then cut the ones around the man's ankles.

Wittenberg rubbed his wrists, and asked, "May I get up?"

"Yes," Goerdt replied.

The German rose, towering over Goerdt.

Wittenberg extended his hand and Dunn shook it.

"This is the best outcome for your men."

"I agree. How much time will you need?"

"Not long at all."

"Pray that this works."

"It will."

"I wish I had your confidence."

Wittenberg raised a hand in salute and Dunn returned it.

As Wittenberg left, moving toward the woods edge, Goerdt asked, "Do you think he'll do it?"

"I sure hope so, Rob."

RONN MUNSTERMAN

Chapter 37

900 meters north of Arry, France, and
1,000 meters east of the Moselle River
11 September, 0734 Hours

Wittenberg approached his men's position from the northeast and, like Dunn, whistled to get their attention. Several of his men saw him and he quickly covered the rest of the ground. Sliding in between a couple of the boulders being used as cover, he rejoined his men. Along the way, he'd recovered his helmet and rifle.

The men clapped him on the back.

"What happened to you?" asked one of his oldest members, a man close to thirty-five.

"I tried to capture that pilot, but ended up getting captured myself!"

"We saw you get carried off. How'd you'd get away?"

"Got the jump on him in the woods, and took off."

"What about him?"

Wittenberg drew a finger across his throat and made a slicing sound. "Served him right for bombing us."

"What are we going to do?"

The men crowded around to hear, their faces were filled with dread, especially the two youngest, who were just seventeen. Their eyes were sunken, and they seemed to have a hollow look to them.

Wittenberg noted their appearance. He'd made the right choice. It was time for young Germans to stop dying for a man who no longer bothered to make public appearances.

"I'm thinking about our options. You know I have to consider the entire company."

The men nodded their understanding. Everyone knew the company commander was dead.

"I need to converse with the other platoon leaders. You men stay here. Stay alert."

Wittenberg made his way a little west and downhill where he found Raupp with his platoon. They were firing periodically with no apparent effect. Wittenberg shook his head at the wasted ammunition.

"We need to talk about our situation here, Raupp."

Raupp turned to look at Wittenberg. "What's there to talk about?" Raupp clearly had no interest in listening.

"No matter what you think, I'm the company commander. I'm going to go get Mekelburg and then I'll tell you what there is to talk about."

Wittenberg didn't wait for a reply and marched away.

The two young men with the sunken eyes knelt together. One looked around to make sure no one was close enough to hear, and then said in a whisper, "Do you want to do it?"

"Yes. I can't face another Jabo."

"I have a handkerchief."

"Let's go now."

The boys laid their rifles down and stood up. One raised his handkerchief high and they stepped out into the open.

A grizzled thirty-five year-old veteran saw the boys first. His heart raced. *Please, God, let them make it,* he prayed.

Raupp had been angered by Wittenberg's arrival, and his superior attitude. What did he know? Company commander? No way in hell. Raupp's jaws clenched at the thought of the weak man leading.

Something white caught Raupp's eye. He looked that way and was further angered to see two German soldiers marching across the open field with a white flag. *Damn traitors!*

"You men get back here!" he yelled.

When they broke into a run after hearing his command, he raised his Mauser.

Dunn and Jonesy were at the woods' edge, staring at the German position. Suddenly, from their left, Dunn spotted two Germans break into a run toward the woods. One was carrying a white flag of some sort. They were unarmed. Their faces were dirty and filled with fear.

The cracking sound of two rifle shots sounded and both men collapsed, rolling a little downhill before coming to stop in crumpled heaps.

"Sarge? What the hell? Did those bastards just shoot their own men?"

Dunn shook his head at what he'd just seen. "Yeah, they did."

The sound of footsteps came from behind Dunn, and he turned to see who was there.

"Have a call for you, Sarge. It's the CO," Schneider said,

Dunn nodded and took the handset. "Dunn here."

"We want those Germans dislodged. I've requested another airstrike. It should be here in about five or six minutes."

"Sir, can you hold them off? I might be able to get the Germans to surrender. I spoke with their new CO and he's willing."

A long pause met Dunn's revelation. Finally the captain said, "You talked a company commander into surrendering his men?"

"Yes, sir. He's back with his men right now. We're all working on it." Dunn was reluctant to give any more details and hoped the captain wouldn't press him for them.

"It's not that easy to call off an airstrike, you know."

"Please try, sir."

"Dunn, if this goes tits up, we'll both be in for courts martial."

"It won't sir."

"I'm trusting you, Dunn, but those planes are already underway. I'll see what I can do."

"Thank you, sir."

"You contact me right way if you do get them to surrender."

"Will do, sir."

Dunn gave the handset back to Schneider. He checked his watch. Five or six minutes. Shit.

"Bob, leave the radio. Go get Captain Banks." Dunn said. "Hurry."

Schneider took off at a run.

Wittenberg heard the two shots that came in quick succession, but didn't think anything of it. They were on a battlefield after all. He continued toward Mekelburg's position, finally finding him amongst a group of his men, talking. Sporadic gunfire erupted from the American line in the woods and everyone ducked below the height of the surrounding rocks, including Wittenberg, who crouched and advanced.

Wittenberg stepped into the circle of men around Mekelburg. "Sergeant Mekelburg, I need you for a few minutes. Come with me." Wittenberg tipped his head in the direction of the way he'd arrived.

Mekelburg frowned, irritating Wittenberg, but the man nodded his assent.

Wittenberg turned around and headed back to Raupp's position. As he walked, he wondered whether the American had meant what he'd said. On the other hand, perhaps in the end Mekelburg and Raupp would see the sense of surrendering to the Americans.

When Wittenberg returned to Raupp's position the men around the platoon leader all had the same shocked expression. Something had happened while he was gone.

Wittenberg asked Raupp, "What's happened here?"

Raupp turned to face Wittenberg, his expression filled with loathing. "Two of your men attempted to surrender. I dealt with them."

"What? Who were they? Wait, what do you mean, you dealt with them?"

"I shot the traitors."

"You shot my men?" Wittenberg's voice rose, and his face turned red.

"Of course I shot your men. You're a failure as a commander when your men decide on their own to surrender."

"That's not your decision to make, Raupp."

"You were not here, *commander.*"

Deep rage boiled up in Wittenberg. He considered raising his Mauser, but quickly decided against it. He would have to let the American help because, as he had expected, there would be no reasoning with either of these fanatics. He took a few deep breaths, willing himself to calm down, both inside, and outwardly for appearances sake.

He pulled a map from his shirt pocket and walked a few paces away to a boulder about chest high. Using the rock as a table, he spread out the map.

The sporadic gunfire from the Americans had come to a stop.

Mekelburg and Raupp automatically followed so they could see the map.

Wittenberg maneuvered the two men so they stood together to his right.

Both were intent on the map.

Wittenberg removed his helmet and held it in his right hand below the top of the rock.

Mekelburg died first. He collapsed at Raupp's and Wittenberg's feet, shot through the temple.

Raupp turned toward the sound of the shot.

The sniper's second shot struck Raupp between the eyes.

Wittenberg put his helmet back on and raised his rifle. He aimed far above the shooter's location and emptied his clip.

The men around him watched in awe. He was staring down the Americans, daring them to shoot him.

Wittenberg continued to stand, but said to the man nearest to him, "Go get Sagel. Tell him he is platoon leader."

To another man, he said, "You are Raupp's replacement. Stay here with me. We are going to have a brief discussion on our next moves."

"Yes, *Oberfeldwebel.*"

"Both targets down, Sarge," Jonesy said.

"I saw," Dunn replied as he lowered his binoculars. "We'll see what happens."

Behind him, Dunn had withdrawn the platoon so the men were twenty yards deep, just in case things had gone wrong and the Germans had renewed the firefight. He whistled, and watched the three squads approach the tree line, setting up in firing positions. He'd already passed the word that the Germans might be surrendering, but instructed the men to maintain discipline on the line.

With Schneider's help, Captain Banks joined Dunn and Jonesy.

"What can I do for you, Sergeant?"

Dunn explained the problem, and then asked, "Can you contact the squadron and call off the strike?"

Wittenberg knelt behind a different rock, not wanting to stay near the two fanatics' bodies. The new platoon leaders knelt with him.

"We are surrendering to the Americans in the woods," Wittenberg said without preamble. "We are doing it right now. We are under threat of more Jabos and artillery. We have no retreat path open to us, and no way forward. You will order your men to lay down their arms, and form up here. I want this done in two minutes."

Neither man had any intention of arguing against the idea and in unison said, *"Jawohl!"*

The P-47 squadron flying at 6,000 feet was from the same air group and airfield as Banks. They had taken off a little while after Banks' squadron. Loaded with two thousand pounds of bombs each, they had been ordered to attack a German position east of the river, where the Germans were up a hill embedded amongst boulders. The orders had included strict instructions to avoid the woods to the north of the target due to friendlies being in there.

The squadron leader checked his watch. Perhaps three more minutes.

Chapter 38

Northern Hospital at World's End Lane
Winchmore Hills, Enfield, far north outskirts of London
11 September, 0645 Hours, London time

Sadie Hughes sat up and looked at her right leg for the first time in two months. The cast lay in pieces on a cart next to the table she'd been lying on while the doctor cut off the horrible thing. She automatically compared her right leg to her left. She was shocked by how pale and thin it looked.

Sadie's mother, Mrs. Hughes, stood by her daughter's side, holding her hand.

The doctor noticed Sadie's expression of revulsion at her own body part. "Don't worry, the muscles will recover and eventually you'll not be able to see any difference."

"Are you sure?"

"I am. I've done this many times, you know."

"Oh, of course. I didn't mean—"

"Not to worry, my dear," the doctor said with a smile. "Everyone reacts the same way. The main thing for you is to do exactly what your physical therapy nurse tells you."

"How soon will I be able to walk without crutches?"

"That depends entirely on you, but typically within a few days to a week. Both of your breaks, if there is such a thing, were not bad ones. Although in your lower leg both bones were broken, they've healed perfectly. Your femur break, which can be very difficult to repair and heal, was not broken all the way through—I know I mentioned this before—so it healed far faster than if it had completely broken through. In that sense you were very lucky, although I know it doesn't seem like it."

"Thank you for everything, doctor."

"My Sadie is going to be married in a couple of weeks. She wants to walk down the aisle with her father," Mrs. Hughes announced.

The doctor smiled at this news. "Well, then Miss Hughes, you have extra incentive, don't you?"

"I sure do. When can I start with my therapy?"

"You'll start right away. I'll tell the nurse to come in and wash your leg for you, I know it must feel grimy and dusty to you. After that, another nurse will come get you for your therapy, and then off you go. You'll be ready for that walk down the aisle." The doctor smiled and left.

Sadie grasped her mother's hand and smiled. "I can't wait."

"Me either."

Chapter 39

1100 yards north of Arry, France, and
1,000 yards east of the Moselle River
11 September, 0747 Hours, Paris time

"I can't raise them," Banks said. "They must have changed frequencies for this attack."

"Shit!" Dunn checked his watch again. Possibly two or three minutes. He raised his field glasses and examined the German position. There seemed to be a lot of movement, but it was taking too long. He looked to the west, but couldn't see any planes. Although he knew they could appear any moment and would be on top of them in seconds.

There was only one way to save Wittenberg's men.

Cross who was standing next to Dunn and noticed Dunn's expression change. "What are you going to do, Tom?"

"I have to get over there and hurry them up."

"Tom, you can't take that risk. Not for them."

"Sorry, Dave, I have to and I have to go now."

Cross shook his head, but knew he couldn't change his friend's mind. "Okay."

Dunn rummaged around in his pocket and found his handkerchief. He handed his M1 to Cross. "Be back soon."

"You better be."

Dunn smiled at Cross. He turned and ran toward the German position, his left hand held high with a white flag.

Wittenberg had been worried he'd have problems with some of the men in Raupp's and Mekelburg's platoon, but not one man put up an argument about preferring to stay in place and die for Hitler. All it had taken was the comment that more Jabos were coming. Then he'd had to get out of the way as the men dropped their weapons and ran to the position he'd named.

Wittenberg waited until all the men were gathered in the right location before taking another look at the river below. More and more tanks, and their supporting vehicles were crossing the pontoon bridges—the Americans already had two in place—and behind them was a column of infantry that seemed to stretch for a mile past Arnaville. Not for the first time, he wondered, *what were we thinking, that we could defeat America and its industrial might?* And also not for the first time he cursed Hitler's name for all the misery that had befallen his country. The July 20th plotters had been right, Hitler had to die. What a tragedy they had failed.

He wondered if what he'd done, colluding with the American, Dunn, to kill the other platoon leaders, ranked up there with the assassination attempt. Did that make him a traitor? Perhaps so.

Wittenberg shook his head at the dark thoughts overtaking him. Focus, he thought, I need to focus for the men's sake. The remaining boys' sake. Maybe saving their lives offset the killing of Raupp and Mekelburg.

He turned away from the spectacle of the powerful army fighting its way to Berlin. He ran as fast as was safe amongst the rocks, boulders, and dead bodies to catch up with his men. When he reached the end of the line of men, he began working his way through, not an easy feat because there was little room for the men to move aside. Finally, he made it through and was back with his platoon.

He was shocked to see the American, Dunn, running his way with a white flag over his head. Wittenberg frowned. What would cause this? To his men, some of whom had picked up their rifles, he hollered, "Do not fire. Drop your weapons!"

The men looked at their new company commander over their shoulders, but they complied and laid their weapons on the ground.

Dunn slowed to a walk and searched for the German sergeant. Their eyes met. Dunn waved at the man to hurry and join him.

Wittenberg slid between two boulders and ran up to Dunn.

"We have to get your men into the woods. P-47s are on the way and I can't call them off," Dunn said.

Wittenberg looked into the western sky. The morning sun reflected off multiple objects in the air. Were those twinkles of light the Jabos coming to kill his men?

"Come on, get your asses in gear!" Dunn yelled, for he too had seen the shiny dots in the sky. The P-47s were maybe five miles out. Dunn didn't bother to try calculating the time to arrival. He just knew it was perhaps a minute, possibly less. And two hundred men had to cross a hundred yards of open land.

Wittenberg jumped into action, yelling, *"Schnell! In den Wald! Lauft schnell! Die Jabos kommen!"* Hurry! To the woods! Run! The Jabos are coming!

There was a moment of hesitation by the German soldiers. *Run toward the enemy unarmed?* Then Wittenberg yelled again, gesturing with his left arm, pointing to the sky. That did it.

In clumps of three and four at first, then in larger and larger groups, the Germans climbed over, ran around or dashed between the rocks and boulders towards the woods. As the men ran past the American, he pushed them onwards. He was yelling something, but they didn't know what it was. They did notice one thing: he had a very determined expression on his face.

Wittenberg was doing the same thing as Dunn from the other side of the boulders, shoving slow-moving men forward, and continuing to implore them to move faster.

As the first of the German soldiers arrived at the edge of the woods, fear on their faces, Cross and the rest of Dunn's men met them, making sure they were carrying no obvious weapons, and then directed them farther into the woods where the other two platoons would frisk them and get them into a large area amongst the trees where other Americans would guard them.

✪ ✪ ✪

"Squadron leader to Red Eagle squadron. Commence attack. Confirming orders to avoid woods to the north."

The last man ran past Dunn. The line of men going into the woods covered the entire width of the open ground. "Wittenberg! Come on!" he shouted.

Dunn took a peek at the sky. He could clearly make out the shape of the P-47s, the sunlight reflecting off the wings, the propellers, the canopies. They seemed to be right on top of him, although he knew they weren't. Yet.

Battlefield chaos is expected, and somewhat understood, but the sight in front of Dunn eyes was remarkable even to a combat veteran and was outside his experience. Instead of gunfire, there was silence, except for the pounding boots of the German soldiers running from the P-47s and to Dunn's men for safety.

The last of the Germans was almost into the woods, and Dunn found Wittenberg a few yards to his south. The big man was carrying two wounded men, who'd been left behind in the chaotic escape.

Dunn ran to Wittenberg and said, "Let me help." Dunn transferred one of the injured men off Wittenberg's shoulder to his own. "Let's go. The P-47s are almost here."

Wittenberg instinctively turned his head to look. *"Scheiße!"* Shit!

Both men sped up as much as it was possible with another human being strapped to their shoulders, and were about half way to safety when the first bombs struck the hillside behind them.

Chapter 40

Northern Hospital at World's End Lane
Winchmore Hills, Enfield, far north outskirts of London
 11 September, 0700 Hours, London time

The nurse, a vibrant redhead with a dazzling and friendly smile rolled a wheelchair into the room.

"Hello, Sadie!"

"Hi." Sadie smiled in return, the woman's friendliness was infectious.

"I'm Miss Carson," the nurse said. She then leaned forward and whispered, "but you can call me Joyce." She gave Sadie a wink. "I'm going to help you get back on your feet. Are you ready?"

"I am."

Joyce faced Mrs. Hughes and offered her hand. "You are Sadie's mother, Mrs. Hughes?"

"Yes. Pleased to meet you, Miss Carson."

"Joyce, please, Mrs. Hughes."

"Joyce," Mrs. Hughes replied. She already liked this woman.

"Does your leg feel better now it's clean?"

"Oh my, yes." Sadie wrinkled her nose. "It really smelled pretty awful."

"I bet it did, sweetie. Not to worry. They all do. It's not just you."

Sadie laughed. "Thank you, I was worrying a wee bit."

Joyce said to Sadie, "The first thing we'll do is change your shoes. You brought the tennis shoes like you were supposed to?"

Mrs. Hughes lifted a cloth bag. "Yes, we did!"

Joyce took the bag and set it down at Sadie's feet and pulled the white tennis shoes out, setting them aside. She quickly removed Sadie's sensible brown pumps and put them in the bag. After tying the knots, she asked, "Too loose, tight enough, or too tight?"

"They're Goldilocks."

"Just right. Excellent! I like your sense of humor. Okay, let's get you on your feet so we can get you into the wheelchair. I want you to put your weight only your left. Are you ready?"

"Yes."

Joyce held her hand out and Sadie slipped off the examination table. She landed easily on her left foot. Joyce expertly turned her around and maneuvered the wheelchair in place and Sadie sat down.

"Here we go."

Joyce guided Sadie down a long hallway, Mrs. Hughes following, and turned right at the end of the hall. She rolled Sadie through an open set of double doors into a large open space. A variety of exercise equipment populated the room, including a couple of sets of waist-high parallel bars positioned along the right hand wall. Some wooden folding chairs were sprinkled around the room.

Joyce rolled Sadie to the nearest set of parallel bars, right at one of the open ends.

"Here we are."

Mrs. Hughes pulled up one of the chairs and sat down.

Sadie eyed the bars, understanding right away what she would be doing. Joyce stepped in front of Sadie, backing into the open end of the bars. She held out her hands.

"Grab both hands."

When Sadie did that, Joyce asked, "Ready?"

Sadie nodded.

"On three. One, two, three."

Sadie rose from the chair smoothly and rested her weight on her left foot.

"Grab a bar in each hand and hold yourself there."

After Sadie had a solid grip on the bars, Joyce ducked under the right one and walked to a spot right behind Sadie. She placed her hands on Sadie's waist and got a firm grip.

"I have you. I want you to put some weight on your right foot."

Sadie shifted her weight, grimacing in anticipation of pain, but there wasn't any. Relieved, she laughed a little and then said, "It doesn't hurt."

"Well, that's good, but I want you to be prepared for some pain today, Sadie. Your muscles are smaller and will have to work harder." Joyce's tone changed slightly, from friend to taskmaster.

In a small voice, Sadie replied, "Oh. Right. Of course."

"Shift your weight some more so your right leg is holding most of your weight."

Sadie moved.

"How does that feel?"

"It's okay."

"Good. Now, shift your weight back to your left foot and get ready to take a step with your right. When you're ready, take the step."

Sadie shifted her weight and then leaned forward, her hands sliding along the bars, and took a tentative step. Joyce moved with her, keeping a firm grip on Sadie's waist.

"Keep moving, Sadie."

Sadie took another step, and another, and another. Before too long, she made it to the end of the bars. To her surprise, she was covered in moisture.

With Joyce's help, she turned around, and they began the long trek back to the beginning. After ten minutes of walking back and forth, the back of Sadie's dress between her shoulders was soaked through with her perspiration.

"My leg is starting to hurt."

"Just now?"

"Yes."

"Okay. That's good to know. Start again."

Another ten minutes passed and Sadie turned around at the far end. She stared through tear-filled eyes at the parallel bars. The other end seemed a mile away. Her leg pounded, and her ankle hurt, and she felt as though she'd walked miles and miles.

Mrs. Hughes saw the tears streaming down her daughter's cheeks.

Sadie started walking toward her mother. When she reached the end and turned around, Mrs. Hughes stood up and tugged at Joyce's arm.

"Can't she stop? She's crying in pain."

Joyce looked over her shoulder, keeping her death grip on Sadie's waist. "I know this is difficult to watch. Think of a time in your daughter's childhood when you punished her so she would learn." She gave the mother a moment, and said, "Sadie must punish her body so it can learn to walk again. It's that simple."

Mrs. Hughes nodded and sat down, a look of sorrow on her face.

"Let's go, Sadie. Just a little longer, sweetie."

Sadie had used the back of her hands to wipe away the tears, and she was ready.

"So, I heard you're engaged. What's your boy's name?"

"Malcolm." In spite of the pain, Sadie's voice brightened.

"Have you set a date?"

"September twenty-third."

"Oh, I love fall weddings."

"You'll have to come."

"I would love to."

Finally, when Sadie reached the end near her mother again, Joyce said, "We are done. Time for a rest."

She got Sadie seated in the wheelchair and said, "I'm going to go get you a towel, and a glass of water."

"Okay."

Soon, Joyce was back. Sadie drank the entire glass without stopping to breathe. She sighed contentedly and handed the glass back. Then she gratefully took the towel and wiped the sweat off her face, neck and arms.

"Oh my, that towel is soaked," she said.

"So it is," Joyce replied as she took it and laid it on the back of a chair. She then walked in front of Sadie and knelt on one knee. She examined Sadie's face for a long moment and out of habit, Sadie turned her face to the right and raised a hand to hide the scar that ran two inches from her lip toward her right ear.

Gently, Joyce grasped Sadie's hand, and softly said, "No, it's all right." She lowered Sadie's hand and put her own hand near Sadie's cheek. "May I?"

"Okay."

Joyce placed her fingertip on the scar and ran it along the skin.

"Who did the stiches?"

"Doctor Denby."

"He did beautiful work, Sadie. This will fade over time. Just try to be patient." She turned her face to the right so Sadie could see her profile. "Take a look at mine."

Sadie stared at her therapist's face, but found nothing. "Where?"

Joyce raised her hand and touched a barely visible line running vertically beside her left eye. "Just here."

"I can hardly see it!" Sadie said, almost happily.

"Correct."

"How'd you get yours?"

"Car wreck. Glass. Three years ago,"

"Oh, my. Who did that for you?"

"Care to guess?"

"Really? Dr. Denby?"

"Right you are." Joyce stood up and smiled. "See?"

"Yes, thank you."

"Okay, the next thing we'll do is fit you for a crutch, so you can be mobile at home. You will come here every day for a week, and we'll see if we can throw away the crutch. Okay with you?"

Sadie grinned. "Yes!"

After Joyce got Sadie back to her feet, she happened to glance over her patient's shoulder at Mrs. Hughes.

Mrs. Hughes had tears running down her cheeks, but she was smiling. "Thank you," she mouthed and touched her right cheek.

Joyce winked. She handed Sadie the crutch and said, "Okay, Sadie. *En garde!*"

Chapter 41

1100 yards north of Arry, France, and
1,000 yards east of the Moselle River
11 September, 0802 Hours, Paris time

Dave Cross and Bob Schneider were screaming encouragement to Dunn as their sergeant ran across the open ground carrying a German prisoner. The roaring sound of the P-47s in their dive pierced the air, followed by the terrifying whistle the bombs made as air flowed through their four-point fins. Cross's first thought when the bombs went off and Dunn and the Germans went flying was, *how am I going to tell Pamela?*

Cross started running a split second afterwards and Schneider followed to lend a helping hand.

When Cross reached his friend, Dunn was lying face down. He was breathing. Cross checked Dunn's back for blood, and was relieved to find none. He carefully rolled Dunn over. Dunn's eyes fluttered, then opened.

"Welcome back, buddy. Can you stand?"

"Hm, yeah. Think so."

Cross pulled Dunn to his feet and held on as Dunn swayed a little.

Schneider was helping Wittenberg to his feet.

"Können Sie laufen?" Are you able to walk?

In his dazed state, Wittenberg reverted to his native tongue.

"Ja. Ich kann laufen." Yes, I can walk.

Wittenberg glanced at his two downed men. *"Ich brauche Hilfe dabei, sie zu tragen."* I need help carrying them.

"Ich helfe Ihnen." I will help.

"Vielen Dank!" I'm grateful.

Schneider lifted one of the men over his shoulder and Wittenberg the other, although it was clear the German sergeant wasn't quite himself yet. Schneider carried one and used his free hand to steady Wittenberg. Together they started toward the woods.

Cross was steadying Dunn and they ran after Schneider and Wittenberg. Dunn glanced skyward, but couldn't find the P-47s anywhere. Cross caught Dunn looking and said, "Idiot. Told you not to do it."

Even in his muddled state of mind, Dunn understood just how close a call it had been. "Yeah, well, it's done."

Cross grumbled, but said nothing else.

They made it to the woods, and to the area where the platoon was gathered, along with the two hundred German prisoners. Cross helped Dunn get seated on the ground, with a tree as a back rest.

Dunn looked around. The German prisoners were all seated in an opening in the woods. It looked like members of the third platoon were doing the guarding. Some of the Germans were smoking. Dunn wondered if they were American cigarettes.

Wittenberg put down the soldier he'd been carrying with difficulty, and sat down rather hard. He turned to Schneider who had already put down the enemy soldier he'd carried off the field. Schneider looked around the area and spotted who he wanted, and took off at a jog. He tapped the medic on the arm.

"Sergeant Dunn needs to be looked at. He might have a concussion."

The medic stood and said, "Where?"

Schneider pointed toward Dunn. "I also have three Germans who need your help."

"Okay. Tell them I'll be there as soon as I check on Sergeant Dunn."

"Will do."

Schneider returned to find Wittenberg kneeling beside the man the sergeant had carried. Wittenberg's hand was on the man's forehead, and then he slid it downward toward the nose. Schneider realized what had happened: the sergeant had closed the eyes of his dead soldier. Wittenberg's lips were moving. Schneider thought he might be saying a prayer, so he stopped a few yards away as a matter of respect.

Wittenberg finished and moved to the other man, who was awake, but grimacing at the pain. He'd been wounded in the stomach by bomb fragments from the first attack. Wittenberg whispered comforting words to the man for a few minutes. Then the man died. Wittenberg repeated closing the eyes and saying a prayer. When he finished the second prayer, he sat down and looked around at his men. He caught and held the eyes of several haggard men. They nodded, their expressions saying, *they were safe. They had made it through. Thanks to him.* Wittenberg nodded back.

Across the way, the medic checked Dunn for signs of concussion. Dunn dutifully followed the medic's finger around with his eyes, and correctly answered questions like: Who's the president? *Roosevelt.* Which one? *FDR.* What day is this? *Monday.* Where are you? *East of Arnaville, France.*

"Okay, you don't have a concussion. Here're some aspirin. They'll help with the headache. Try to take it easy."

"Okay, thanks, Doc."

"You're welcome."

The medic stood up and looked around until he saw Schneider, who was kneeling beside a German, carrying on a conversation.

"Tut mir leid um Ihre Männer." I'm sorry about your men.

"Danke."

"Kann ich Ihnen etwas bringen?" Can I get you anything?

"Danke, nein."

The medic arrived and repeated his concussion evaluation on Wittenberg, although he had to change the questions around a bit. When he was done, he said, "You appear to have a concussion. You know what this is?"

"Yes, I do."

"You have to be careful. No more knocks to the head. Do you understand?"

Wittenberg shrugged. "I'll try."

The medic pulled a small white card from his shirt pocket and scribbled on it. He used a safety pin to attach the card to Wittenberg's shirt.

"This will tell everyone your condition."

"Thank you."

"You speak English very well, sergeant."

Wittenberg smiled. "So do you."

The medic laughed and patted Wittenberg's arm. He got up and went looking for someone else to treat.

Wittenberg got to his feet without swaying and asked Schneider, "May I visit my men?"

"Um, let me ask my sergeant."

"Where is Sergeant Dunn?"

Schneider pointed.

"I will go ask myself."

"Want me to walk along with you?"

"No, thanks, I can manage."

"You're sure?"

"Ja. Danke für die Hilfe mit meinen Männern." Thanks for the help with my men.

"Bitte schön. Ich hätte mir gewünscht, dass sie in Ordnung gewesen wären." You're welcome. I wish they would've been okay.

"Ich auch. Sie sprechen sehr gut Deutsch." Me too. You speak German very well.

"Danke—Sie auch." Thanks. So do you.

Schneider grinned as he said the last.

Wittenberg chuckled in return, and headed toward Dunn.

Schneider ran back to where he'd left the radio and turned it on, anticipating Dunn wanting to report the capture of two hundred Germans. Schneider took a quick look around him. *Holy crap, two hundred!* he thought.

Dunn saw the big German coming his way and rose. He met Wittenberg half way.

The two men eyed each other for a long moment, sizing up each other.

Wittenberg spoke first, "You were an able adversary."

Dunn shrugged.

"You have an unusual degree of compassion. You could have just let the Jabos kill my men and me. Why didn't you?"

Dunn looked away. Why hadn't he? He turned back to the German. "A few weeks ago we were clearing a village west of Paris. It seemed empty of Germans, but then we found a woman and a little girl in one house, and it turned out her husband was being held hostage to make her be quiet about the presence of four SS soldiers upstairs.

"We did what we had to do, and killed the four SS men." Dunn's jaws clenched and his lips compressed. "But they weren't men, you see. They were boys, just fourteen. But they wouldn't surrender. So . . ."

"You were forced to kill them."

"Yes."

"And now you feel guilty."

"Yes. And angry."

"I would have done the same thing. You had no choice."

"I know that. I would do it again under the same circumstances. I'm angry I was forced to kill children. That your Hitler caused this."

"I have had similar thoughts myself. Not all Germans love Hitler."

Dunn looked surprised. "I thought, I assumed . . ."

"No. We do our duty. But today you gave me the opportunity to save two hundred men from certain death. I thank you for that."

Wittenberg raised his hand in a solemn salute. Dunn returned it equally solemnly.

Wittenberg lowered his hand and then offered it to Dunn. Dunn shook it.

"Dieter, do you like to fish?"

Wittenberg smiled. "From my father's knee."

"And hunt?"

"Yes."

"We're sworn enemies, Dieter, but I think we could have been friends."

"Perhaps in another world. Or perhaps after the war."

"Perhaps."

Wittenberg nodded. "May I have permission to walk among my men, to calm them?"

"Permission granted."

Wittenberg left and Dunn spotted Schneider already working the radio.

Dunn walked in that direction, grabbing Cross on the way.

"Can you raise the captain?" Dunn asked Schneider.

"Should be just a second, Sarge." Schneider was listening on the handset while he spoke to Dunn. "Okay, yes, sir. Here's Sergeant Dunn." He handed over the handset.

"Dunn here, Captain."

"What's going on up there? We saw the P-47s hit the German position."

"We've captured the Germans, sir."

There was a long moment of silence before the captain said, "Repeat."

"We captured the Germans, sir."

"How in the hell did you do that?"

"It's rather a long story, sir."

"I want to see a written report on that ASAP. How many?"

"Two hundred, sir."

"Holy shit! Are you serious? No, of course you are. Okay, I'll send an MP attachment to take them off your hands."

"Thanks for the MPs, sir."

"Did you take any casualties?"

"Yes, we lost three in total, one from my squad, and two from Red's."

"Well, I'm sorry to hear that, but well done, Sergeant. I'll pass the word on up to battalion."

"Yes, sir. Uh, sir, we also have a downed and injured P-47 pilot who needs to get back to his squadron near Paris. Can you send a vehicle for him? They could drive up the hill along the southern edge of the woods from the river road."

"A downed pilot? You have been busy, Dunn."

"Yes, sir."

"Sure. I'll rustle up something. May take a while, as will the MPs."

"Thank you, sir. Do you have any instructions for us?"

"Hold your position and keep an eye on the Germans' former position. Advise us of any change."

"Will do, sir."

Dunn gave the handset back to Schneider and said to Cross, "Some MPs are coming to take the Germans off our hands. Let's get them organized so it'll be a quick handoff. We might get another assignment shortly." To Schneider he said, "Let me know as soon as the captain calls back."

"Sure thing, Sarge."

Cross reached out and removed Dunn's helmet. He held it up and examined the crease from Wittenberg's bullet along the top.

"Damn it, Tom." He shook his head, at a loss for words.

Dunn retrieved his helmet and snugged it back in place. He gave his friend a lopsided grin and then said, "Well, at least we have matching helmets again."

RONN MUNSTERMAN

Chapter 42

1100 yards north of Arry, France, and
1,000 yards east of the Moselle River
11 September, 1015 Hours, about two hours later

Dunn finished making the rounds of the three squads under his command, and double checked security on the Germans. The prisoners had simply found a place to lie down and most were asleep, making their guards' jobs easier.

Just as Dunn was beginning to wonder whether any MPs were really coming, sounds of men moving through the forest making no attempt at stealth filtered through the trees. Suddenly a group of about twenty MPs burst into the opening in the forest.

The leader, a shiny new second lieutenant, scanned the men he saw.

Dunn waved a hand and the lieutenant strode over to him. A master sergeant walked alongside the lieutenant. Dunn and the officer exchanged salutes.

"You Dunn?"

"Yes, sir." Dunn tipped his head toward Cross who was standing next to him. "My second in command, Dave Cross."

The officer nodded. "Lieutenant Glass. This is Sergeant Lowery. So you have a few Germans for us to take off your hands?"

"Yes, sir. About two hundred."

The officer's eyebrows went up. "Wow. You captured a company?"

"Yes, sir."

"I would love to hear the story, but we have to get our asses in gear. Where's their commander?"

"He's over there, but I'll take you to him." Dunn pointed to a group of Germans nearby.

"After you."

Dunn stepped close to Wittenberg, who was sitting, his back against a tree, his eyes closed.

Wittenberg opened his eyes at the sounds of footfalls.

"Hello, Sergeant Dunn." Wittenberg stood up and eyed the officer, noting the white helmet, and the white arm band with MP in black letters. He turned his gaze to Dunn. "Time for us to leave, I take it?"

Dunn nodded. "This is Lieutenant Glass. He's in charge of the MP detail, and they will escort you out of the combat area for processing."

Wittenberg gave Dunn a lopsided grin. "Processing, huh? Sounds so industrialized." Wittenberg offered his hand to Dunn who shook it.

Lieutenant Glass raised an eyebrow, but said nothing.

"Thanks again for making the choice you did and offering us a way out," Wittenberg said to Dunn.

"You're welcome."

Wittenberg looked at the lieutenant. "We think it's a far better fate to surrender to the American army instead of the Russian. We're ready."

Wittenberg saluted and held it.

Lieutenant Glass nodded, and returned the salute. "Have your men form into four columns and prepare to march at my command."

"Yes, sir," replied Wittenberg as he lowered his hand. He nodded once more to Dunn and Cross, and turned to give the order to his men.

Dunn turned to Lieutenant Glass and said, "All yours lieutenant. Thanks for taking them."

"You're welcome. Good job, Dunn. Be careful the rest of the way. Good luck."

"Thank you, sir."

Dunn and Cross walked away.

"Well, this'll be a story for the grandkids," Cross said.

Dunn laughed. "Yep. Might be worth a few beers from Saunders."

"Could be."

"What do you suppose is next?"

"Don't know. I'll tell you one thing, I'd sure like to get back to Colonel Kenton's work instead."

"You and me both."

The two men glanced at each other and said in unison, "But we goes where they tells us!"

They shared a laugh.

Dunn separated from Cross to go check on Ben "Cloud" Banks, the P-47 pilot. He found him sitting close to Schneider and Goerdt. Banks was describing an attack of some sort as he used his hands to represent aircraft, one behind the other; a dogfight. Dunn presumed Banks' plane was the trailing hand. Dunn was proved right when the leading hand suddenly flipped over and crashed into the forest floor. Banks was grinning.

"And that was number nine."

"Wow," Schneider said.

"Incredible," Goerdt said.

Dunn sat down next to Banks. "Sounds like quite a story, sir."

"Always are," Banks replied, his grin widening.

The men talked for a while about where they were from and why in the hell they'd picked the job they had.

After a half hour, they heard the sound of a Willys Jeep. Dunn got to his feet and ran to the edge of the woods. He waved at the driver of the jeep, who waved back. The jeep went into a turn so it could come around facing back the way it had come, and stopped.

"Someone need a ride?" the driver, a corporal, asked.

"Yep, got a downed pilot. Be back in a minute. Smoke if you got one."

"Okay, thanks."

Dunn ran back to the clearing and said to Banks, "Ride's here, sir."

Banks face brightened and he said, "All right. I'm ready."

He got up slowly, and Goerdt jumped up to lend a hand.

"Thanks for listening to an old man's stories, fellas," Banks said.

"Anytime, sir," Dunn said.

"You saved my life back there, sergeant. I can't thank you enough."

"You're welcome, sir."

"No, you can call me Cloud, anytime."

Dunn smiled. "All right, Cloud, it is. Let's get you to the jeep so you can get back to the easy life in Paris."

"Oh, aren't you funny?"

"So they tell me, Cloud."

Dunn took over Goerdt's position on Banks' right side. "Ready?"

"Yeah, let's go. See ya guys."

Dunn got Banks into the jeep and pulled out his package of Lucky Strikes. He handed them to Banks. "Tide you over until you get back."

Banks nodded, and took the gift. "How can I get hold of you? If I wanted to send you something."

Dunn looked aghast. "Oh, no sir. There's no need for that."

Banks lowered his chin and gave Dunn a look that said, *really?*

"Yes, there is."

"Okay. I'm at Camp Barton Stacey. Colonel Mark Kenton's unit."

Banks repeated it and Dunn nodded.

"You got it."

"See ya, Dunn."

"See ya, Cloud."

The jeep roared away, bouncing down the hill to the Moselle River and the pontoon bridges.

Dunn rejoined his men to find Schneider talking on the radio.

Schneider looked up and waved at Dunn to hurry.

"Dunn here," he said, after taking the handset.

"Did the MPs arrive?" The CO asked.

"Yes, sir. Prisoners are on their way. So is the pilot."

"Okay, good. I have orders for you. Get your map."

Dunn cradled the handset between his ear and his shoulder, and pulled out his map. He unfolded it so he could see their current position. "Ready, sir."

"See the village named Marieulles? It's about two miles east of you."

"I see it."

"We think the Germans are still there. I want you to clear and hold the village. I have an armored column heading that way from Arry, but it's slow going at the moment due to antitank weapons."

"Yes, sir. We'll be on the way ASAP."

Dunn and the captain signed off and Schneider handed back the phone. Dunn spied Wickham nearby and called out, "Stan. Go get Red and Finley."

Wickham waved and got to his feet, and ran off in search of the other squad leaders.

Shortly after, the three men returned and Dunn filled in the squad leaders on the new assignment.

"How are we on ammo?" Dunn asked.

"Good enough, I think," Red said.

"Yeah, us, too," Finley said.

"Okay, get the men ready. We're leaving in five."

RONN MUNSTERMAN

Chapter 43

Dunn examined the village of Marieulles from the eastern edge of the same woods his men had occupied for a day and half. The land between the woods and the village sloped away over an empty field. He estimated his position was about four hundred feet higher in elevation than the village. The woods curved both north and south away from his vantage point, forming the rough shape of the letter C, with the village at the bottom tip. A second area of trees came straight west from the village's northern end, and reached almost to Dunn's position, slicing the C in half. One more tree stand ran parallel with the west side of the village. Dunn was glad to see so many trees and thought all three areas would provide the necessary cover for a daylight approach. That the different sections of trees met right at the village was a boost.

Like most French villages Dunn had seen the houses and buildings followed the main road running through the village, which in this case was southwest to northeast. The entire village was no more than five hundred yards long and perhaps a hundred wide. A few Germans were visible and seemed to be running from one place to another in no particular pattern.

Red and Finley were standing nearby doing the same thing as Dunn. All had their binoculars to their eyes.

"Why in the hell are the Germans even bothering with this?" Dunn asked.

"Seems dumb. Our armor can just swing around on the east side and keep on going," Finley replied, disdain in his voice. "Dumb fuckers."

Dunn shrugged. "Orders. As usual. From on high."

"Could be," Red agreed.

Dunn scanned the village once more. He didn't find exactly what he needed, but did locate another possible substitute. He lowered the glasses and looked behind him.

"Jonesy?"

Dunn beckoned Jonesy when the sniper looked up from his task of cleaning his Springfield.

Jonesy joined the three squad leaders.

Dunn put a hand on Jonesy's shoulder and with his other pointed to a spot in the center of the village.

"There's no church steeple in sight, but do you see that three-story building?"

"Sure do."

"Do you think you can work from the roof?"

Dunn handed over the binoculars.

Jonesy took a look at the building. He couldn't see the entire roof, but it was flat. Good enough.

"Yep."

Dunn nodded. "Okay, let's plan on it. You'll have your choice of targets, with higher ranking personnel having more priority. Take Eugene with you as usual. I'll join you to scout out the village."

"Understood. Anything else for me?"

"Not now. Thanks, Jonesy."

"Welcome."

While Jonesy went back and sat down, Dunn said to Red and Finley, "Either of you guys see any Germans toward the north part of town?"

"No," Finley replied.

"Not me. They seemed concentrated in the south," Red said.

"That's what I saw. Here's what I'm thinking." Dunn said, and he told them.

"See any problems with it?"

"Can't think of anything, Tom. Unless we can call in those P-47s again, which I doubt," Finley said.

"Yep, you're right. We're on our own here." Dunn checked his watch. "I have almost eleven hundred hours. We should kick off in five minutes. It'll take us fifteen minutes or so to get to our jump-off point."

"Agreed," Red said.

Finley nodded.

The three squad leaders gathered their men together and Dunn laid out the simple plan of attack.

While the men were getting their gear loaded, Dunn went back to the edge of the woods to check on the village once more. Nothing had changed.

Dunn sighed. His thoughts drifted to Pamela and the baby. He'd previously thought that his wedding day was the highlight of his life, but the moment his wife told him he would become a dad took over first place. He tried to imagine holding a baby. He'd held babies before. His younger sister Gertrude was born when he was six, so he had a pretty clear recollection of holding her tiny body in his spindly arms. This time, though, the baby would be his own. Dunn smiled at the thought. He couldn't wait.

With those pleasant thoughts he turned and rejoined the platoon and got down to the business of preparing for an attack on what might be an equal strength unit.

RONN MUNSTERMAN

Chapter 44

The Hardwicke Farm
5 miles south of Andover
11 September, 1000 Hours, London time

"I feel fine, Mum," Pamela said.

Mrs. Hardwicke, Pamela's mother, ignored her daughter's statement and pulled the young woman into a gentle, but all-encompassing hug. She smoothed her daughter's long blond hair and kissed Pamela's cheeks.

"Come on, let's get breakfast in you. I called Dr. Swails' office and made an appointment for ten thirty, so you have to get on the jump."

"Thanks for making the appointment."

"You're welcome."

Mrs. Hardwicke steered Pamela to the kitchen table, and set about bringing Pamela her tea, eggs, sausages, and toast with orange marmalade.

Pamela stared at her favorite breakfast, and sniffed, breathing the wonderful aroma deep. "This smells so good. I think I've been dreaming of this meal."

"The food not very good over there?"

Pamela shrugged. "Not very. It stops one from becoming hungry at least. And it's hot."

Pamela's supervisor, Agnes, had made arrangements for Pamela to get on a flight back to England for wounded soldiers. The plane had arrived near ten p.m. the night before, and Pamela had ridden to the hospital in one of the ambulances. From there, she called her former roommate, who lived in downtown Andover. The roommate had borrowed a car and driven Pamela home to the Hardwicke farm, five miles south of Andover.

Pamela had tried to sneak into the house, but her two dogs, a collie and a black Labrador, were deliriously happy to see their long lost master, and barked joyfully long enough to wake Mr. and Mrs. Hardwicke. When her parents saw Pamela come in the door, the dad's expression was delighted, but the mom's wasn't. Although she smiled, she instinctively knew something had happened to bring her daughter home in the middle of the night.

The three of them sat on the living room sofa, Pamela in the middle. Mrs. Hardwicke allowed her husband to enjoy the return of their only surviving child and, after a short visit, gently suggested he go back to bed and get his rest for the next day's farm work.

Pamela understood what her mother was doing, and played along cheerfully answering her dad's questions, and giving him another hug and kiss when he went off to go back to sleep.

Mrs. Hardwicke waited impatiently until she heard the bedroom door snick closed.

"What's happened?"

"I'm fine, Mum, and the baby seems to be okay, too."

Mrs. Hardwicke gasped and placed hand in front of her lips.

"I had some bleeding. It stopped and the examination didn't indicate a miscarriage."

Mrs. Hardwicke put an arm around Pamela and pulled her close. With her other hand she cradled Pamela's head and let it rest against her shoulder.

"You're sure?"

"Yes, Mum. I need to see Dr. Swails for another checkup, though."

"I'll go with you."

"Yes, please." Pamela suddenly felt fear like she'd never known before. What if it happened again? What if she lost Tom's baby? "Oh, Mum, what if it's not all right?" A sob escaped her lips and it started a crying jag.

Mrs. Hardwicke just held her daughter tight and murmured comforting words.

Afterwards, Mrs. Hardwicke led Pamela to her bedroom and tucked her into bed. After her mother closed the bedroom door, the fears and tears returned. Pamela rolled onto her right side and curled up. Eventually she fell into an exhausted dreamless sleep.

"You're sure you feel all right?" Mrs. Hardwicke expression was all mother, worried.

Pamela took a bite of her eggs, chewed contentedly, and swallowed.

"Mum, I think I'm all right. I just got so frightened last night, like it all hit me at once."

"I understand that, Pamela. Don't be hard on yourself."

"Oh, I'm not really."

Mrs. Hardwicke looked dubious, but decided to ignore it for now. "Will you stop working?"

"I think I should. I just want to be so careful."

"I wholeheartedly agree. We'll have to tell Dad when we get back from Dr. Swails' office."

"I don't want to worry him."

Mrs. Hardwicke took Pamela's hand in hers and held it. "He deserves to know. He'll want to be able to comfort you."

Pamela nodded slowly. "Okay. After we get back, when he's back from the fields."

"Good. What about Tom?"

Pamela blinked several times, and it looked like she was about to cry, but she didn't. In a small voice she said, "I don't know what to do. I don't want to tell him something like this in a letter, but I never know when he's going to be home. I hate this war!"

"I do, too. Let's see what doctor has to say. Then we can decide what to do for Tom."

"Yes. Okay, that sounds best."

"Finish your meal, and we'll get ready to go."

Mrs. Hardwicke got up, but Pamela still held on to her hand. "I love you, Mum."

Mrs. Hardwicke hugged Pamela and said, "I love you, too."

Chapter 45

The approach to the village had been uneventful for Dunn's platoon. The plan called for Red's and Finley's squads to follow the southern tract of trees, while Dunn's used the one that ended at the north end of the village.

Dunn stopped his squad ten yards from the village, still hidden safely in the trees.

"Jonesy, see the building we talked about?"

Jonesy looked through the tree tops and found his target. "Yes, I see it."

"Like I said, I'll go up there after you and Lindstrom to scout out the village's main road." Dunn turned to the rest of the squad, who were resting on a knee. "Be right back."

The men nodded, keeping their eyes in constant motion.

"I'll follow you," Dunn said to Jonesy.

"Okay, Sarge," Jonesy replied.

The three rangers moved through the last grove of trees and stopped at the edge. Their view was of the back side of the buildings running along the village's main road. There was a five foot gap between the building Dunn wanted to climb and the one to its immediate south. It wasn't really an alley, but it did have a few trash cans strewn about, some tipped over onto their sides.

On the side of the target building was what Dunn had been able to barely make out from his vantage point earlier, a fire escape. He hadn't been certain it was a fire escape, but was grateful it was.

Jonesy pointed at the fire escape and Dunn nodded.

The men checked the windows and did not see anyone. The distance to the building was about ten yards and grass covered. Dunn tapped Jonesy and Lindstrom on their shoulders and the sniper and his protector took off. They ran into the gap, found the hinged ladder and got it to come down. It was relatively quiet, just making a slight *clunk* when it reached its locking point.

While Jonesy and Lindstrom climbed, Dunn kept watch, his M1 aimed generally into the gap.

The men moved fast and were soon at the top floor. Once there, Jonesy found the eight-foot ladder to the roof and climbed it, while Lindstrom waited on the metal grating landing. Jonesy stopped when his head was just below the roof's parapet and he slowly rose until he could just peek over the edge.

He came face to face with a German soldier, who was starting to lean over the parapet, perhaps having heard something after all.

Their eyes met.

The German started to raise his Mauser.

Jonesy's Springfield was still over his shoulder.

In a fluid movement, Jonesy snatched his knife from its sheath and shot his right hand straight up. The knife pierced the enemy's chest just under the breastbone.

The German opened his mouth to scream, but died before making a sound.

Jonesy climbed up a step and shoved. The German collapsed in a heap, taking Jonesy's knife with him.

Lindstrom watched the split-second event take place and raised his rifle.

Jonesy stared down at Lindstrom and waved.

A relieved Lindstrom opened his eyes wide and blew out some air as if saying, *Holy fuck!* He turned and leaned over the railing to give Dunn an OK sign.

Jonesy lifted himself so he could see the roof and was relieved to see that it was clear. He scrambled over the parapet. From a kneeling position he checked for other rooftops that were at least as high. He discovered what Dunn had predicted, this building was the highest in the village. No one would be able to see them. He turned and waved at Lindstrom who climbed the rest of the way and stepped onto the roof.

Jonesy yanked his knife out of the enemy's chest. He wiped the blood off on the man's tunic, and sheathed the knife.

Dunn climbed up and over the parapet to join Jonesy and Lindstrom. He looked at the dead German. He'd had a poor view of the fight and was grateful that Lindstrom had given him the OK sign. He examined the roof which was about forty feet square. The street side had a higher facing, about four feet tall.

Dunn motioned toward the facing and the three men ran across the roof, being careful not to be too loud in case someone was on the top floor. Dunn leaned over the facing slightly to peer down at the street. While there was nothing happening directly below, to the south a dozen or so Germans were busy checking their weapons. The distance to them was about a hundred and fifty yards. Dunn looked to the north. There were no cross streets, although about fifty yards to the north a road coming from the east formed a T-intersection with the main road. He saw no one anywhere. This puzzled Dunn because he'd expected a platoon to be here, although it was possible that some of them had moved to the north. Dunn thought about his plan of attack and decided there was no need to change it.

Dunn asked Jonesy, "You okay?"

Jonesy nodded. "Yeah."

"Okay, good. Take your position so you can cover those Germans down the street. Easy shots, right?"

"Yes, Sarge. Easy."

Jonesy moved over to the southeast corner of the building and laid out his supplies, the extra five-round clips, the suppressor, and the small sand bag for a firm support. He screwed the suppressor onto his 1903 Springfield and tightened it into place.

Lindstrom knelt near his sniper.

Dunn was about to leave to rejoin the squad when he noticed an antenna on the roof. It was about ten feet tall and looked new. Who would need an antenna here? Curious, he moved quietly toward the northeast corner again. He was about to look straight down at the street when motion suddenly caught his eye to the north. He turned his head and squinted. His heart jumped and he lifted his binoculars to eyes. He zoomed in as far as possible on the road coming from the northeast.

"Aw, shit," he muttered.

Chapter 46

Dr. John Swails' office
Andover, England
11 September, 1030 Hours, London time

Mrs. Hardwicke had told her husband she and Pamela were going to run an errand in town, and would need the car. She left out the details. She didn't want to out and out lie to her husband, but she still felt guilty at the lie by omission.

The trip to Andover had taken about ten minutes. Mrs. Hardwicke parked the car in front of a two-story red brick office building across High street from the Star & Garter Hotel, and the two women made their way inside the doctor's office.

Pamela looked around the tiny, narrow waiting room. When had she last been there? She recalled it was when she seventeen. It was summertime and she was just playing with her two dogs, which were very young. They were running around the barnyard in a kind of a chase game, and she'd stepped on a rock the size of a potato. She'd rolled her ankle and hit the ground hard. Dr. Swails had checked her out, taking some X-rays to make sure it wasn't broken, and showed her how to wrap it properly after the swelling went down. Looking back, Pamela suddenly realized that was the moment she'd become interested in nursing. She smiled to herself. Life was funny.

There were no other patients waiting. At the far end of the room, a woman with gray hair and glasses sat at a small desk and was writing on a notebook. Pamela remembered her as being a friendly, outgoing person with a smile for everyone.

Behind the desk was the door to Dr. Swails' office and the examination room.

Pamela and Mrs. Hardwicke walked over to the desk.

"Excuse me," Pamela said.

The woman glanced up. Her face registered surprise, and then she broke into a warm smile. "Pamela!" The woman stood and ran around the desk to hug Pamela. They disengaged and she said, "What are you doing back here? I heard you were in Queen Alexandra's service." She frowned. "Everything all right?"

"Hi, Mrs. Spivey. Yes, everything's fine. I . . ." Pamela suddenly realized how hard it was to tell someone else about her problem aside from her mother. "I'm here to have a pregnancy checkup. I had some spotting yesterday."

"Oh, dear. Right. Let's get you checked in. You are next, as I'm sure you noticed."

Mrs. Spivey wrote Pamela's name on the patient register. "Why don't you make yourself comfortable?" She looked at Pamela's mother and said, "It's good to see you, Mrs. Hardwicke."

"You, too."

A few minutes later an older man using a cane stepped through the door and stopped at the desk.

"You're looking as beautiful as ever, Mrs. Spivey. You sure you can't have dinner with me tonight?"

Mrs. Spivey smiled. "That's a lovely idea, Mr. Colby. I just don't think Mr. Spivey would be happy about it."

Mr. Colby sighed. "One of these days you'll say yes."

"Bye, Mr. Colby."

"Until next time."

As the man walked by Pamela and Mrs. Hardwicke, he paused in front of Pamela's mother.

"Don't you look lovely today?"

"Mr. Colby, be on your way! Don't bother every woman you meet," Mrs. Spivey shouted.

He winked at Pamela's mother and went out the front door, whistling.

Mrs. Spivey shook her head and rolled her eyes. "Incorrigible, that man."

Pamela and Mrs. Hardwicke laughed.

A few minutes later, the nurse stuck her head out the door and said, "Pamela?"

Pamela and Mrs. Hardwicke followed her into the examination room, where the nurse asked Pamela to sit on the foot of the table and Mrs. Hardwicke to be seated in a chair nearby.

After the nurse weighed Pamela, and took her pulse, blood pressure, and temperature, she gave Pamela gown to put on, and left.

Dr. Swails entered a few minutes later, to give Pamela time to change. He smiled at the two women.

"Mrs. Hardwicke, how are you?"

"I'm well, thank you."

Swails stepped close to Pamela and said, "Congratulations on your wedding. I'm sorry I couldn't be there. Someone was ill at the time."

Swails was in his mid-sixties, and a bit portly. His nose was perhaps a bit too large for his round face, and crooked from a few breaks in his rugby days. His brown eyes tended to come across as soft, but he was an intelligent man, finishing first in medical school.

"I also hear congratulations are in order for your pregnancy."

Pamela gave a demur smile, partly because she, like virtually all women, wasn't quite ready for the use of the blunt and accurate term *pregnancy* by a man, even a doctor, and partly because she was worried.

"Thank you."

"Let's do another quick check of your vitals." Swails repeated what the nurse had done, carefully checking his numbers against the nurse's. They were close enough. "Good. Good. Your numbers are in good shape."

"Oh, good."

Swails raised his stethoscope and placed it on the upper left of Pamela's chest. He held it there for a few seconds then moved it to the right side. He listened to her heart from the back, and said, "Take some deep breaths."

As Pamela breathed he listened. He moved the stethoscope around to all four quarters of her back.

"Breathe normally." He listened from one spot for a few seconds, and while taking the earpieces out and letting them come together at the back of his neck, he said, "Everything sounds good."

He walked around in front of Pamela. This allowed Mrs. Hardwicke to easily see him also.

"Tell me what happened yesterday," Swails said with a reassuring smile.

Pamela recited the events slowly and precisely; to her it seemed as if she was being clinical about herself.

Swails nodded periodically, to encourage Pamela to continue.

When she was done, Swails asked, "How did you feel afterward?"

"Feel? I was very tired. I was scared."

"Those things are good to know. How about your body? Other than feeling tired, how did it feel?"

"Oh. Well, I didn't hurt as bad, more like a tummy ache, if that's what you're asking."

"No pain like when it started?"

"No. Much less severe."

"Your head nurse examined your pelvic area, yes?"

"She did. She's the one who said I hadn't miscarried."

"Hm. Right. Well, how far along do you think you are?"

"About ten weeks now, I'd say."

Swails nodded. He turned to Mrs. Hardwicke and said, "I'd like to do my own pelvic exam now."

Mrs. Hardwicke stood. "I'll wait for you just outside, dear."

"Okay, Mum."

Mrs. Hardwicke left the examination room and stepped into the waiting room. She sat down in the chair closest to the back rooms.

Swails was thorough in his examination of Pamela and when he finished he told her she could sit up, which she did.

"I'd say all is well," Swails said. "I do recommend as much rest as you can stand for the next two or three weeks. Hm. Let's make that three. No heavy work or lifting. Stay off your feet. I know you're a nurse, but," he shook his head, "you'll have to give that up until baby comes."

"I understand. I expected as much."

"Do you want to calculate the due date?"

"Oh, I already did that. Late April or early May."

"Very good. Advantages of being in the medical field, eh?"

Pamela laughed. "Yes."

"Well, I'd like to start seeing you once a month from now on."

"Oh, any concerns?"

"No, I'm just trying something new with my pregnant patients. I want to see them often before they have the baby and maybe we'll have healthier babies, and mothers, too."

"I like that. Thank you."

"See you next month."

"Yes, Doctor."

Swails left the room.

Pamela changed back into her clothes and then joined her mother.

"Everything's fine, Mum!"

Mrs. Hardwicke closed her eyes and said a quick prayer of thanks.

After Pamela make an appointment for mid-October, they left. On the drive home, both women were smiling and chatting and laughing.

"At least we have good news to give Dad and Tom," Pamela said.

"Too right we do!"

RONN MUNSTERMAN

Chapter 47

Marieulles, France
11 September, 1137 Hours, Paris time

Dunn ran across the roof and said to Jonesy, "Four tanks coming in from the northeast. They're buttoned up right now, but when they make it into town, they might pop up, so take out anyone in an open hatch."

Unflappable as ever, Jonesy merely replied, "Will do, Sarge."

"If you can't make the shot, return to the original plan, but wait for Rob's bazooka fire."

"Okay."

Dunn patted the men on the back and ran to the ladder.

Jonesy and Lindstrom got their gear together and moved to the northeast corner, where Jonesy settled into a kneeling firing position and sighted the tanks. Dunn was correct, the hatches were closed. Jonesy noted he would lose sight of the tanks for a short time as they first entered the village. The road approached from the northeast and shortly after reaching the village, it turned south to go past the sniper. Some buildings and trees would hide the tanks. They would reappear just one hundred yards from his position.

Jonesy explained the situation to Lindstrom and then said, "Go back to the other position and keep an eye on what's happening to our south. Be very careful if you use the binocs. Gotta watch out for sunlight reflecting off the lenses."

"Okay, Jonesy," Lindstrom replied. He scrambled back to their original spot and got situated.

Dunn made his way back into the forest unseen and when he reached his squad, they were kneeling in their attack positions, a tight line facing the buildings. The men all looked at him, waiting for the word.

"Change of plans." He looked at Goerdt. "Rob, we've got four tanks coming in from the north. Should be here in five minutes. How many rounds do you have left?"

"Three."

"Can you stop four tanks with those?"

"Sure, Sarge," Goerdt replied. He patted Bailey on the arm. "We'll find a way."

"Jonesy will take out anyone in an open hatch, but if they're still buttoned up, it's up to you guys."

"Got it, Sarge," Goerdt said. "On our way."

Goerdt and Bailey stood up, picking up the bazooka and the satchel carrying the last three rockets. With a wave of their hands, they took off winding their way through the trees.

Dunn watched them leave, already working on what he'd do if they failed to stop the tanks. The truth was, not much could be done. Other than let them go on through. They were probably on their way to reinforce Arry to the south.

"Hmm," he said aloud.

"What?" Cross asked.

"Well, we could just let them pass on through and advise battalion. Maybe some Thunderbolts are around."

Cross looked at his boss and frowned. "Really, that's your plan? Let someone else handle it?"

The other men in the squad watched Dunn for his reaction, their eyes a bit wide.

Some leaders would have become defensive, angry even, but Dunn did the opposite. He laughed. "Okay, you got me. Just thinking out loud. After Goerdt and Bailey take care of things, Jonesy will start firing on the south."

Dunn paused to look at the small group of men. After the loss of Waters, and with the sniper and assistant on the rooftop, and the bazooka team off on their assignment, Dunn only had Cross, Wickham, Schneider, and Martelli in front of him.

"I found something interesting on the roof: an antenna. So after things get started, Martelli, you and I are going to enter the building's first floor and see what we see. There's a handy back door so we'll bust in through it. Dave, you take the others and follow the original plan."

Cross nodded. He recognized that Dunn was taking a risk, checking out the building, but it might be worth it. Or not.

Goerdt and Bailey found an opening between buildings about fifty yards north of where they'd left Dunn and the rest of the men. As they ran through it, Goerdt suddenly stopped, holding out his hand to warn Bailey.

Bailey looked at Goerdt and nodded, as if saying, *Yes, I can hear them.*

The tanks were already pretty close. Goerdt took off again and when he neared the street side of the opening, slowed to a walk. He edged himself along the wall of the building on the north, his left, and peeked around the corner.

The four Panzer Mark IVs turned left and were headed straight down the street in a column twenty yards away. They were all buttoned up. Goerdt sized up his position and wasn't all that thrilled. Their escape route was the narrow opening they'd arrived through and it was a good fifty feet to the back of the buildings.

The fact that he only had three rockets for four tanks factored in only as a problem to solve, not as a weakness. He estimated the distance to the street at only five yards. He could practically spit on the tanks as they passed by. He pictured where each tank would be at the time of the first shot, and where he might have to move to for the other shots. He also established the firing order for the three tanks he would shoot. Another consideration was his rate of fire versus the reaction time of the trailing tanks' front gunner. Most bazooka teams could fire five or six rounds per minute. He and Bailey would have to do better.

"Leonard?"

"Yeah, Sarge?"

"You've got to be super-fast on the reloads. Understand me?

"I do."

"Okay. Here's what we're gonna do." Goerdt laid out everything.

Bailey listened closely, and when Goerdt got to the interesting part, Bailey's mouth dropped open. "Are you kidding me?"

"Nope. Any other questions?"

"Can you really do that?"

Goerdt shrugged. "I guess we'll find out, huh?"

"Yeah, I guess so."

"Load me up."

Goerdt lifted the bazooka to his shoulder.

Bailey pulled a rocket from the satchel and, suddenly feeling superstitious, kissed it, and slid it in. He tapped Goerdt's helmet. Bailey pulled out the last two rockets, holding one in each hand, and kissed both of them, too. *Can't hurt,* he thought.

Jonesy examined all four tanks carefully through the Unertl sight. "Damn it." All four were still closed up tight. He lowered his weapon and ran across the roof to join Lindstrom.

"Scoot over, Eugene."

Lindstrom moved over to give the prime location to his sniper. He did a three sixty, looking for any threats to Jonesy. Satisfied all was clear, he faced the south to wait with his sniper.

Dunn and Martelli ran across the open area behind the building and stood with their backs to the wall next to the door. It opened inward, which was good. They could kick it in.

The first Panzer slowly rumbled by the bazooka team, just fifteen feet away. It was enormous. Goerdt waited. And waited some more. The second tank was about twenty feet behind the first. As it clanked by, Goerdt continued to wait, and he realized his breathing was getting too rapid so he took a couple of deep breaths to calm himself. He prayed that he hadn't miscalculated the angle.

The third tank was right in front of him, which put the lead tank about fifty feet away, its engine heat rising from the rear.

Goerdt stepped out from the safety of the space between the buildings and knelt. He fired the rocket.

As it sped away he ducked back between the buildings.

The rear of the first tank exploded and the tank halted immediately, fire roaring from its rear. A second later, the ammo aboard ignited and the explosion blew off the turret.

Bailey pushed the next rocket in and hit Goerdt on the helmet.

Goerdt stepped back out and knelt, but this time he was facing north, aiming at the trailing tank. He pulled the trigger and dived back to safety just as the tank's coaxial machine gun began firing. The bullets stitched a line into the pavement exactly where Goerdt had been.

The rocket struck the drive sprocket on the tank's right tread and the Panzer spun around on its left tread before the driver could stop it. The tank was at a forty-five degree angle to the street facing southwest.

Unfortunately, that was right at Goerdt's and Bailey's position.

Ronn Munsterman

Chapter 48

Marieulles
11 September, 1141 Hours

When Jonesy heard the first tank explode, he calmly sighted on a German soldier he thought might be a leader based on how he had been interacting with other soldiers. A gentle squeeze of the trigger and the Springfield fired. The round struck the soldier in the chest and he collapsed. While Jonesy was working the bolt, weapons fire came from the south, and several more of the Germans dropped. The survivors started running for cover.

Goerdt immediately got back to his kneeling position and Bailey loaded the last round. A tap.

Goerdt stepped out and aimed at the second tank's ass and fired. The round exploded in the engine and, like the first tank, the ammo exploded with the same result, a turret flying off.

Goerdt dove back into the gap expecting the last tank's machine gun to fire at him. He got back to his knees and when no shots came his way figured the gunner might have been knocked around from the rocket.

Dunn put his hand on the doorknob and twisted. To his surprise, it turned. He looked at Martelli and winked. He pushed the door open and stepped inside, Martelli following.

Jonesy targeted a running soldier and shot him. The Germans were heading his way, trying to get inside a building, any building, but the fire from Red's and Finley's squads was heavy, and they were falling left and right. From below, Jonesy heard the weapons firing from the rest of his own squad. The Germans had been caught in a deadly crossfire, Dunn's intention all along. Some made it inside and were breaking out windows. They began to return fire.

Jonesy had no more clear targets. He watched as five members of Red's squad peeled off from their position and ran across the street under fire. Jonesy sighted on the windows.

He found a Mauser sticking out of a window, but the soldier was hidden by the wall. Jonesy lined up a shot guessing where the soldier would be behind the wall and fired. The Mauser fell out of the window. Jonesy smiled to himself.

Goerdt's remaining problem was the third tank, which was still alive, but stopped. It was penned in on the narrow street by two immobile tanks. Suddenly the engine roared and the tank began to reverse. Goerdt glanced to the north and realized that when the last tank veered to the right, it left a space on the opposite side. The third tank commander had spotted it and was going to bulldoze his way past the last tank, even if it meant tearing down the front of the building on the other side of the street.

Goerdt dropped the bazooka and pulled three grenades off his shirt.

"Leonard, run! Get out of here! Take my rifle."

Before Bailey could respond, Goerdt ran into the street for the interesting part.

Dunn and Martelli were in a large room at the back of the building. A door faced them on the opposite side. They ran over and opened it.

Four Germans were at the windows to the street peering out at the action, a reverse of kids looking in the candy store. A radio sat by itself on a table against the south wall.

Dunn grinned and winked at Martelli again.

Dunn whistled and raised his M1.

Goerdt pulled the pins to all three grenades as he ran alongside the Panzer, careful to stay out of the way of the tread. Thankfully the monster was moving slowly as the commander guided the blind driver in reversing to safety. Goerdt eyed the spot he needed. The drive wheel had six spokes. He bent over and slipped the grenades through one of the spaces between two spokes. The grenades settled in, falling a little behind the wheel. Goerdt spun around and ran south.

The four Germans twisted around and shock covered their faces when they saw two Americans standing there with weapons aimed at them. One of the soldiers reflexively moved his hand toward a pistol at his waist.

Dunn took a couple of quick steps and aimed the M1 between the man's eyes. *"Nein."* The man stopped and raised his hands.

Dunn motioned for the men to disarm themselves and each one carefully lifted the flap on the holster and with a finger and thumb only, withdrew their weapons, and put them on the floor at their feet.

Goerdt looked to his right. There! Exactly what he needed. With no hesitation, he dove through the front window of the store. He rolled as he landed inside and covered his neck with his hands.

The grenades exploded within milliseconds of each other and shredded the drive wheel. Hot shrapnel ripped into the corner of the building where Goerdt had been earlier, and some tore through the window frame he'd just shattered.

Outside, the last tank came to a halt.

Red and Finley and their squads began moving up the street, clearing buildings as they went, and finding little resistance.

Jonesy had no other targets, so he removed the suppressor and tucked it in his travel bag. "Let's head down and see if we can help out."

"Right behind you, Jonesy!" Lindstrom replied.

Dunn motioned with his rifle for the Germans move to his right and to be seated on the floor. Martelli followed their every move with the muzzle of his M1. After they complied, Dunn kicked the pistols in the opposite direction. He walked over and opened the front door carefully.

Dunn peered through the crack and was rewarded with the sight of four motionless and burning Panzers. The two lead tanks were completely destroyed, their turrets crumpled and askew as if they had been blown off. The two tanks behind were also a mess. It looked like Goerdt had knocked a tread off each of them. He raised an eyebrow wondering how he'd taken care of the fourth tank. Hatches suddenly popped open on the last two tanks and the crews climbed out, clearly shaken.

Dunn opened the door a little farther and movement to his left caught his eye. Goerdt and Bailey were standing next to a building on the west side aiming their weapons at the tank crews. Goerdt must have been yelling instructions because the crew members, all ten of them, climbed down and lay down on the street, arms outstretched.

Dunn stuck his head out just a little and looked down the street to the south. Red's and Finley's squads were only twenty yards away, each on opposite sides of the street. It looked like there were a couple of buildings left to clear.

Dunn closed the door and faced the Germans. That was when he noticed the rank on the oldest of the four, a man with gray hair and a square jaw.

Dunn made an assumption and said, "Hello, general. Kind of a bad day for you guys, huh?"

The general stared at Dunn through angry blue eyes. He said nothing.

"Well, that's okay if you don't want to say 'hello.' I'm just being friendly. You care to get on that radio over there and tell whatever men you have left here to surrender?"

"Go to hell."

Dunn grinned. "So you *can* speak English. And I'll take that as a 'no.' That's okay. We'll be done soon. I'm sure you heard your tanks getting blown up." Dunn shrugged. "So much for your reinforcements, huh?"

A sound behind him caused Dunn to glance that way. Jonesy and Lindstrom stepped into the room. Dunn turned back to the Germans, but said, "Eugene, go get Schneider and the guys and meet me in the back with the radio."

"Roger, Sarge."

"Al, you and Jonesy keep an eye on our new friends here."

"Will do," Martelli said.

Dunn lowered his rifle and left the room.

A couple of minutes later, Schneider and the rest of the squad arrived.

"Schneider, you're with me. The rest of you guys go north on the back side of the buildings and help Goerdt and Bailey. Looks like they captured some more tank crews." Dunn grinned.

"Holy shit! Those guys are fantastic indeed," Wickham said in his Brit-Tex accent.

"Get going," Dunn said with a smile.

Wickham and Cross took off.

"Bob, Call up the CO," Dunn said.

"Right away."

A minute later, Dunn was talking to the company commander. "Yes, sir. The village is just about secure. Any chance of getting some more MPs? We've got some more prisoners including a general."

"You're kidding. Okay, I'll see what I can do. Out."

"Dunn out."

Schneider took the handset back from his leader with awe in his eyes. "Really, you got a general?"

Dunn smiled and tipped his head toward the building. "Go see for yourself. Talk to him. See if you can get his name."

Schneider picked up the radio and went inside. Dunn followed and watched as his interpreter spoke to the general. It appeared to be a short conversation because Schneider laughed and turned back to Dunn.

"He won't tell me his name. Told me to stick my radio up my ass."

"Well, that's original."

"Ha. Yeah, that's what I thought."

Dunn went to the front door again and opened it. He was surprised to see Goerdt and the rest of the squad marching the tank crews toward him. He looked to the south and spotted Red only a few feet away, looking up.

"Hey, Red."

Red looked down in surprise. "Oh, hey, Dunn. Looks like we've got the village. We're gonna check these last few buildings, but I don't think anyone's there. We've picked up a few . . ." He glanced down the street. "What the hell? You guys took out four tanks? And captured some crew?"

"What can I say? Here, come on in for a minute."

Dunn stepped back to let Red in.

"Say 'hi' to the general there." Dunn pointed.

"Huh. Fuck. You got to be kidding me." Red shook his head and looked at Dunn. "You've been busy."

"Ah, just lucky."

"Yeah, right. Okay, we'll take care of the mop up."

"I already called the CO. He hopes to send more MPs our way."

"Okay. See you later."

"Yep."

An hour later, the first vehicles of the American column entered a secured Marieulles. Dunn filled in Captain Stafford, the company commander, including the destruction of the tanks and the capture of the crewmen.

The captain stood with Dunn, Red and Finley outside the radio building. Moments before, the German general had saluted the captain, finally gave his name, and then boarded a truck with the rest of the prisoners. Schneider and Wickham had gathered the radio set and papers together and handed them off to two MPs, who promptly put them in the cab of the prisoner's truck, a deuce-and-a-half.

"Sir, didn't you want to get more from the general?" Finley asked.

"Nah. We'll let the intelligence pukes take care of that. I didn't recognize his name, so I don't give a damn who he is.

"I'm not much on math, boys, but I think you're in the neighborhood of two hundred and thirty captured Germans. Not a bad days' work. Good job. Word has already been passed along on your earlier exploits."

He stepped back and the three men saluted him, which he returned.

The sound of a fast-moving jeep caught everyone's attention, and they turned to the south. The jeep pulled to a smooth stop next to the captain's jeep and the battalion commander jumped out, a colonel.

The colonel returned the salute of the four men. He eyed the three squad leaders for a moment, and said, "Hellava job, boys. Which of you is Dunn?"

"I am, sir," Dunn said.

The colonel examined Dunn for a little while. "You dreamed up the capture of that company? Back there on the hill?"

"Oh, well, it was all of us, sir."

"It was him, sir," Red piped in. "It was all his idea. We just did what he planned."

The colonel stared at Dunn. "Great work, Dunn. I wanted to say thank you for that. You're an example of the kind of leadership we need. I wish you could stay with us longer."

Dunn frowned. "I don't understand, sir. Why can't we stay with you?"

"Didn't I say? Well, Colonel Edwards, you know him, right? On General Patton's operations staff?"

"Yes, sir, I know him."

"He called me earlier. You and your squad have been recalled to uh, Barton Stacey. You leave within the hour. There's a small field southwest of Arnaville that we set up for small aircraft. I've got a truck coming for you. You wait right here."

"Yes, sir. Thank you, sir."

"Colonel, you may be interested to know that one of Dunn's men killed four Panzer Mark fours, and captured ten crewmen. All together, he's responsible for seven tanks and three intact crews," Captain Stafford said.

The colonel stared at the captain for a moment, digesting the news. Then he asked Dunn, "What's the soldier's name?"

"That's Sergeant Rob Goerdt and his teammate, Corporal Leonard Bailey."

"You tell them 'well done' for me. And I want a full report written by Goerdt about how he did it. Might be a valuable training tool. He can do it after you men get back to England, but make sure he does and get it sent to me right away."

"I will do that, sir."

"That's all."

Everyone saluted again and the colonel returned to his jeep and took off, continuing north.

Captain Stafford was the first to speak. "Dunn, the colonel's right. You've been a big help to us. I do wish you could stay, but," he shrugged.

"It's been our honor to serve with you, sir." Dunn turned to Red and Finley. "And with you."

The men all shook hands and Dunn stepped back inside the radio building. His men were sprawled out, taking a well-earned rest.

"Gentlemen. Have something to say." Dunn waited until all eyes were open and on him. "We're heading back to Barton Stacey. Get packed up. A truck'll be here soon. The captain and the battalion CO pass along their thanks. Rob, Leonard, the colonel says 'well done.' Rob, he wants an after action report on all the tanks you took out. Do it as soon as we get back and give it to me to forward to the colonel."

"Right, Sarge," Goerdt replied. Bailey patted him on the back and Goerdt smiled.

"Okay. Hop to, everyone!"

Chapter 49

American airfield, XIX Tactical Air Command
20 miles south of Paris
11 September, 1940 Hours

Ben "Cloud" Banks used his new crutch to hop and slide his way outside his tent. Facing west, he had a great view of the setting sun, which was growing larger and more orange by the minute.

The docs had confirmed what he'd already known: his ankle was sprained, not broken. They'd wrapped it, and given him a container of aspirin and a crutch. Said he'd need the crutch for a week. Oh, and by the way, you're grounded until we clear you, so pay attention to what we tell you.

His squadron had been happy to see him, fearing the worst when they saw his parachute open and his Thunderbolt crash to the earth. They gathered around him in the dimming light. He told them about the crazy sergeant who'd run out and got him to safety all the while capturing a very big German soldier along the way. He described the fight between the two with a few embellishments, *what good story isn't enhanced*, he thought.

Saving the best for last he continued, "So this Dunn guy, the one who rescued me, decides to talk the German he knocked out into surrendering."

"I thought he already surrendered?" Holden asked, looking puzzled.

"Well, he was captured, but Dunn was after a bigger fish. He found out the guy was the acting company commander and Dunn talked him into surrendering the *entire fucking company!* You might be wondering how."

The men all nodded as they leaned closer.

"Well that's where we come in. See, we'd already hit them and they had some losses. So this Dunn character says 'I've got you pinned down with the Jabos and artillery.' Told him there was nowhere to go. So either give up or die in those rocks.

"So then the kraut says he's got a problem with a couple of fanatical platoon leaders. Then I lost track of the conversation because Dunn lowered his voice. The kraut guy nods his head and they *fucking shake hands.*

"Well, not long after, I hear a couple of rounds go off on our side, a few seconds apart, and right after that the krauts come streaming out of the rocks with their hands up. They looked like ants coming out of the wood work. Quite a lovely sight I have to tell you. You know what I think happened?"

A few of the men said, "No, what?"

"Well, see, there was this one fella with Dunn's bunch. Had himself a sniper rifle, don't know what kind, had a bolt action."

"Springfield," Holden said.

Banks snapped his finger. "Yeah, I bet that's right. I think this sniper killed those two problem platoon leaders for the kraut so he could surrender the company."

"How many?" Holden asked.

"Final count was two hundred and six."

"Wow," said one pilot.

"Holy shit!" said another.

"Holy shit is right. And you know what? You should'a' seen the expressions on the krauts' faces. They were all the same. You know what it was? It was relief. They were glad their war was over. Probably looking forward to their first hot meal in months, if not years."

This draped silence over the group of pilots as they considered what it would mean if they were shot down and captured by the Germans. They knew they wouldn't be treated as well as the ones this guy Dunn had captured, that was for sure.

"So that's my story. You guys have an early mission in the morning. Don't stay up too late." Banks got up with the help of his new friend, the crutch. His men stood.

"Glad you made it back, Cloud." Holden said, speaking for the others. "Really glad."

Banks nodded. "Yeah, me, too."

Banks left the tent area and walked toward the mechanical crews' area. He found the chief alone in his tent.

"Hey, chief, mind if I come in for a spell?"

The chief started to rise, but Banks held up his hand and the grateful man stayed put.

"No sir, come in." The chief was lounging on his cot, wearing only his light brown skivvies.

Banks sat down in a folding chair. "I need a favor. I owe a guy back in England my life, so I want to send him a gift. Any way we can make that happen so it's at his colonel's office at Barton Stacey in the morning?"

The chief pulled a clipboard off his nightstand, an empty wooden ammunition box standing on end. He flipped a page and read the next one. "We're due for parts first thing. I can ship back your gift on the return flight. Would that be okay?"

"It would."

"What are we shipping, sir?"

Banks told him and the man's eyes lit up.

"I have some extra for you and your men, as well as the air crew taking the delivery back."

"I'm very grateful, sir. Where is the box to ship?"

"You'll find it in my tent along with the box containing the extras for you and your men and the air crew. Come by any time after sunrise, if you would."

"We'll be there, sir. Thank you, sir. The men will appreciate the gesture. As do I."

"You're welcome, and thanks, too, for the air delivery."

Banks got up and stepped out into the cool French night. The stars were driving off the sun and the sky was becoming dotted with bright lights. Banks stood there a while just gazing at the sky where he lived most of the time.

He understood he'd been extremely lucky to have come down within yards of an American unit, and especially one whose leader would rush out and tackle an enormous German to complete the rescue.

He had been pleased and surprised when Dunn had been smart enough to make the threat of the Thunderbolts returning to finish off the German infantry company.

Banks glanced down at his ankle, and then leaned down to rub it. The pain was still there, but he thought he could get back in the air where he belonged sooner than the doctor had said. With that thought in mind, he started crutch-walking back to his tent.

He was thinking about the blue sky and patchwork earth from ten thousand feet. A picture he never tired of seeing.

Chapter 50

American prisoner of war gathering point
5 miles south of Verdun
11 September, 2004 Hours

Dieter Wittenberg stared around him. A sea of German soldiers filled his view. His two hundred men seemed a mere drop in the bucket. He guessed there were five thousand German soldiers inside the hastily erected horse wire fences, topped by barbed wire.

Somehow the Americans had been able to feed everyone in just a few hours, so Wittenberg and his men had a hot meal for the first time in a long time.

Wittenberg wondered whether he'd done the right thing. Should they have stayed in place and fought? He knew the story of Stalingrad. Not the one the Nazis showed in Göbbels' films, but the real one that said over a quarter of a million men were lost. If that's what staying in place would have meant for his men, surrender was the best choice. At least life was now possible.

A man sidled up next to Wittenberg and the acting CO looked to see who it was. He couldn't think of the man's name on the spot, but he was a member of Raupp's platoon. Wittenberg wondered whether the man knew what Wittenberg had done, in essence, colluding with the American commander, Dunn, in the deaths of Raupp and Mekelburg.

"Evening," Wittenberg said.

The man was Wittenberg' height, but thinner. He turned his blue eyes to the CO.

"I believe you did the right thing."

"Which thing is that?"

"Surrendering."

"You do, eh?"

"Yes. There was no way to escape, thanks to our idiot battalion commander and his selecting that horrible place in the rocks."

"I agree."

"The Jabos would have finished us off."

"Yes, they would have."

"I'm glad Raupp and Mekelburg got killed. They would never have agreed to this."

"My thinking, too."

"Where will the Americans send us?"

"To America."

"It's an enormous country."

"Yes."

"Maybe it'll be a place called Texas."

"Could be."

"Take care of yourself."

"You, too."

The man moved away, leaving Wittenberg alone in a sea of captured Germans.

Chapter 51

The John Russell Fox Pub
Andover, England
11 September, 2240 Hours, London time

Dunn was to meet Saunders at the same pub where Dunn's bachelor party had been in July, the John Russell Fox Pub. When he'd checked in with Kenton by phone, the colonel had told him to take the night off, sleep in, and to come see him the next afternoon.

The pub was dark, and there was an abundance of cigarette and cigar smoke. Dunn found a small table by the front door and sat down facing the door. A waitress came over right away and Dunn ordered a pint, and one for Saunders. She returned quickly with two dark British ales.

Dunn had given his men the night off and they had all gone into Andover, too, but to a different pub on the north side of town. This suited Dunn. He felt like he needed some privacy, or maybe it was just a need to be away from the men for a short while. He loved his men, but being alone with his thoughts was something he was beginning to treasure more and more. Of course, being alone with Pamela was not the same as being alone alone. It was far better. They had learned to just be together. Sometimes they wouldn't talk for a while, just content to be in each other's presence. When conversation resumed, it was if they'd picked up right where they left off.

He planned to go out to the Hardwicke's farm after the meeting with Kenton, just to say 'hi' and see how they were doing and whether they'd heard from Pamela. Army mail was pretty damn slow, so he hadn't received anything lately. He doubted he would stay the night, since Pamela wouldn't be there, and would instead go back to the barracks.

The door opened and in stepped Malcolm Saunders. He immediately spotted Dunn and walked over to the table. Dunn got up and they shook hands, and then they sat down. Saunders smiled at the sight of the beer. He picked up the glass and held it out for Dunn to touch with his own.

"Cheers," they both said.

"Good to see you, mate."

"You, too, Mac." Dunn had taken to calling Saunders that because it was what Sadie called him.

"You got back tonight?"

"We did. How about you?"

"Late last night. Midnight or so."

"Where you been?"

"We took a ride to Belgium. Loads of fun."

"I bet. We stayed with Patton's Third Army until today. Made it all the way just past the Moselle River. Thought we were gonna go into Germany with him, but Kenton called us back. Don't know what for yet."

Saunders looked around the pub, which was populated half and half, army and civilian. It was loud, but bearable.

"Seems like it's been a long time since I've seen you."

Dunn looked at the ceiling as he thought about it. "Yep, I'd say it was breakfast with you and Sadie. Was that a month ago?"

"About, yeah."

"How's Sadie getting along?"

"I haven't heard. Last time I saw her was a couple of weeks ago. I'm heading over to see her tomorrow in Cheshunt."

"Good. Any other news?"

Saunders' face lit up. "Oh, right. You don't know. We finally set a date, the twenty-third."

"Congratulations!" Dunn grinned and stuck out his hand and Saunders shook it again.

"Thanks. She hopes to have the cast off and be able to walk down the aisle with her father."

"That's good news. I hope that works out the way she wants."

"Oh, believe me, it will. My Sadie's a tough girl." Saunders took a deep swig of his beer and swallowed, a contented look on his face. "Anything new with you two?"

"Oh, yeah, there is. I ran into Pamela in France a couple of weeks ago. Can you believe that?"

"With you, yes."

Dunn pulled a couple of cigars from his shirt pocket. He handed one to an unsuspecting Saunders, who was just delighted to have one. "We had dinner in Paris and she told me she's expecting!"

"Dunn, you're going to be an old man. Congratulations!"

Dunn smiled. "Looks like a May baby."

"Well, this is just great news. Light me up."

Dunn fired up his Zippo and lit both cigars. The two men added their smoke to the room.

"Things are looking up for us," Saunders said.

"They are."

Neither man wanted to say much more than that out of fear of jinxing their luck.

"Guess what my men and me did in Belgium?"

"Found some Belgian chocolate."

Saunders rolled his eyes. "No. Captured a bloody general is what we did."

"No kidding?"

"Nope."

"Nice."

"So what'd you do?"

Dunn got an ornery look on his face.

"I'll see your general, and raise you an entire company of Germans."

"You did not! A general and a company?" Saunders tried to look angry, but it came across as a grin instead.

"And you remember Rob Goerdt?"

"Aye."

"Knocked out seven panzers, him and his loader. Used hand grenades on the last one when he was out of bazooka rockets. Blew out the drive wheel."

"Bloody hell. I would love to have seen that."

"Yep."

"You gonna get him a medal?"

"Already wrote it up. Giving it to Kenton tomorrow. The battalion commander wanted Goerdt to write up how he did it and send it to him."

"Is that a record?"

Dunn shrugged. "Don't know. Could be. Oh, and one other thing."

Saunders chuckled. "Of course."

"Saved a Thunderbolt pilot from the Germans."

"You've been fooking busy."

"Yep."

Saunders finished his beer and nodded at Dunn. "Drink up and order another pair. I'll buy because you won the capture game."

The beers arrived and Saunders said, "Had an interesting talk with Colonel Jenkins. Seems he thinks you are bloody good at your job."

"He said that?"

"Aye. Although I was sworn to silence" Saunders held his hand up like he was taking an oath. "And of course I said I would obey." He winked.

Dunn grinned and lifted his mug. Saunders clinked it.

The two friends talked another hour, sharing stories, beers, and their cigars. They shared future plans, each one of them knocking on the wood table.

Just in case.

Chapter 52

The Hughes' house
Cheshunt, England
12 September, 1312 Hours

Saunders shut off the car and stared through the windshield at the Hughes' front door. He'd told Sadie on the phone he'd arrive by one thirty, and he had beat that by quite a bit. Speeding would do that for you.

He got out and walked across the green grass in the front yard. He knocked and Mrs. Hughes answered the door.

"Mac! So happy to see you. Do come in. Sadie's in the living room."

Saunders stepped in and Mrs. Hughes immediately drew him into a hug. When she let go, she smiled and said, "She's missed you terribly."

Saunders grinned. "Me too, Mrs. Hughes."

"The mister is working, but he'll be back half five if you can stay for dinner."

"I wouldn't miss it for anything. In fact, I've a few days off."

Mrs. Hughes clapped her hands together in glee. "Oh good." She lowered her voice, "Let's surprise Sadie with that news."

"Right. Sounds fun."

"Come on, then."

Mrs. Hughes led Saunders into the living room and stepped to the side.

Sadie was sitting in her wheelchair with a blanket over her legs, her right leg still on the horizontal support for the now removed cast. Saunders grinned wide and strode across the room. He knelt and wrapped his arms around Sadie, and then kissed her. He pulled back and just stared at her face for a moment.

"You look beautiful, Sadie."

And she did. Her color seemed to be back and her eyes were practically ablaze.

Saunders' heart did a flip flop as he was reminded how much he loved this woman.

"I do love you, Sadie, dear."

She put a hand on his cheek. "I know you do. I love you, too."

Saunders glanced down at Sadie's hidden legs. "How are things?"

"Oh, pretty good. Soon, doctor says."

"I can't wait."

"Me either. Say, would you mind helping mother with the tea?"

Saunders stood up. "Sure. Be glad to."

Saunders followed Mrs. Hughes into the kitchen.

Mr. Hughes stepped in from the dining room where he'd been hiding. He quickly removed Sadie's blanket, revealing a white skirt. He held out his hands which Sadie grasped and pulled herself upright. Hughes handed her the crutch he'd been carrying and moved out of the way.

Sadie walked across the room to stand by the front door and she turned around to face the living room. Hughes winked at her, and went back into the dining room to hide once more.

A moment later Mrs. Hughes walked in carrying the tray for tea, Saunders following her, still wondering why he'd been asked to help. She obviously hadn't needed it.

He glanced over the shorter woman's shoulder and spotted Sadie standing by the door. He stopped in his tracks.

Sadie walked across the floor toward her future husband, her skirt swaying with her movements.

To Saunders' eyes, she somehow managed to make using the crutch look graceful. He took a step toward her, but she held up a hand.

When she reached a point right in front of Saunders, she stopped and looked up expectantly.

Saunders pulled her close and kissed her again, for a long time.

When they pulled back, he said, "You said the doctor said 'soon.' I thought you meant the cast to come off."

Sadie gave him a mischievous grin. "I know. A little subterfuge."

"I'm so happy to see you on your feet. You look terrific."

"I'm delighted to be on my feet. And thank you. I should be able to get rid of this crutch by Friday. Will you come back and take me for a walk?"

Saunders glanced over at Mrs. Hughes and grinned. "I don't have to come back. I can stay until Saturday."

Sadie squealed in delight and hugged Saunders again.

Mr. Hughes stepped into the room.

When Saunders saw him, he said, "So, the conspiracy is complete."

"It took us all to pull it off."

"We'll done, then."

At the dinner table, after the meal, the Hughes family and Saunders sat around chatting, Sadie's three little brothers hanging onto Saunders, literally. Sadie sat next to him.

"I have some happy news about Dunn and Pamela."

Sadie glanced over at Saunders and knew immediately what it was.

"She's expecting."

"She sure is. May, he said."

"You congratulated him, didn't you?"

"I did. He's a happy man."

"I'm so glad. They will make beautiful children."

Saunders leaned over and whispered in her ear, "And so shall we, my darling."

Chapter 53

Colonel Kenton's office – Camp Barton Stacey
12 September, 1445 Hours

Colonel Mark Kenton shook hands with his number one squad leader and said, "It's really good to see you."

"You too," Dunn replied.

"Have a seat."

Dunn sat down and Kenton went around the desk to sit.

Kenton's aide, Lieutenant Sam Adams, was off the base on an errand for the colonel, so it was just the two men.

The two men, friends really, looked at each other a moment.

"You've lost some weight over there."

"Have I? Probably the grub we've been eating for a few weeks. Not the best."

"No, it's not."

Colonel Mark Kenton had been Dunn's boss for some time. They'd first met in Italy, at Anzio. Later, Kenton called on Dunn to join his unit of special mission operations. Dunn and his squad joined Kenton at Barton Stacey. Dunn and the colonel had developed a more collegial relationship over time and respected each other very much.

"How's your son?" Dunn asked.

Kenton was about old enough to be Dunn's father. Kenton's eighteen-year-old son had just entered West Point.

"His first letter was brief. Up at sunrise running. Work hard all day. To bed at sundown. Seems to be okay."

"Glad to hear it."

"How's Pamela?"

Dunn's face lit up. "She's expecting, sir."

"Congratulations. She still at that British hospital in France?"

"Yes, sir. Although, I actually ran into her. A lucky set of circumstances led me to go to the hospital and there she was. We had dinner in Paris. That's when she told me."

"I still remember when my wife told me she was expecting. I don't think my feet touched the ground for weeks."

Dunn chuckled. "Sounds about right."

"You made platoon leader, I heard."

"Ah, yeah. The lieutenant got shot at the Moselle River. CO needed someone to take over for a while."

"Of course. Sorry to break you away from that. Sounds like you were doing outstanding things, like you always do."

"I think the men are ready for something a little different."

"Sorry about Waters."

"Yeah. Bad break for the kid. He was just settling in. Saved our bacon out there when some artillery rounds were walking up on us at breakfast one morning."

"Does it warrant a medal?"

"I'd say so. Here, I wrote it up for you." Dunn pulled the paper from his pocket and handed it over.

"By the way, Rob Goerdt deserves something, too." Dunn told the colonel the story of killing seven tanks and capturing three crews intact.

Kenton raised an eyebrow. "Incredible. Write it up for me and I'll get Lieutenant Adams to work on both of them as soon as he gets back."

Dunn smiled and pulled another folded sheet of paper from his shirt pocket, and handed it across the desk. "Already done, too."

Kenton smiled and leaned forward to take it, but he set it aside. "I'll look at it later." He sat back, a thoughtful expression on his face.

"Something on your mind, sir?"

"Some of the higher ups have been asking me about you. Don't worry, it's all good."

"Would these be the same 'higher ups' who wanted us to name our squad something catchy, like Merrill's Marauders?"

Kenton grinned. "Since you ask, yes. However, I did not tell them what your choice was. 'Dunn's Dummies.'"

"Prudent of you, sir."

Kenton nodded. "So anyway, would you ever consider going the officer route?"

"Not a chance, sir. That's not for me. I want to be with the men."

"But you proved yourself leading that platoon and capturing all of those Germans. You're a very capable soldier and leader, Tom."

"You know I just did what needed to be done, sir. Anyone would have done it."

Kenton sat forward. "Oh, bullshit, Tom. No one would have talked those Germans out of there like you did."

"How'd you know that?"

"I have ears everywhere." Kenton smiled.

Dunn shook his head. "Well, anyway. No, sir. I don't want to become an officer. Besides, you said it yourself once, that I'd have to leave the unit."

"That's correct. And yes, I recall saying that. Okay. I'll tell them to leave us alone and let us do our job. Let you do yours as a sergeant. Although, I might have to promote you again. I might need someone to lead a larger unit on a mission. Maybe down the road."

Dunn shrugged. "Whatever you need, sir."

"Speaking of missions, I have a few to choose from. I thought I'd give you the opportunity this time to pick the one you want. Sound okay?"

"Yes, sir."

Kenton opened a drawer and pulled out four brown file folders. All were stamped with the red Top Secret marking. "Here you go."

Dunn read all four of the folders, then held one up. "This one."

"Good choice." Kenton put the other three away, and wrote Dunn's name on the one he'd selected. "It's the one I guessed you'd pick."

Dunn just smiled.

"Take some time off. The men, too. Come back next Monday."

"Will do, sir."

Kenton nodded. He stood up and Dunn started to rise, but the colonel held out his hand. "No, stay seated."

He bent over and picked up a large wooden ammunition box sitting next to his desk. He walked around the side of the desk and put in on the surface.

"Came for you this morning to my attention. Open it. It's from some guy named Cloud Banks. Really 'Cloud?' "

"Yes, sir. Flight school, he told me. Pilot humor."

Kenton shook his head and chuckled.

Dunn opened the lid and looked in. He reached down and picked up one of the items. It was long and wrapped in brown paper, like a butcher would use. Dunn knew what it was by the feel of it, but unwrapped it anyway revealing a dark green bottle with gold foil wrapped around the neck and a white label trimmed in gold. He turned it in his hand. "Champagne, sir. Moët and Chandon."

"Impressive. Who's this Banks guy?"

Dunn told him.

"Well, no wonder he sent you a crate of champagne. I'd do the same damn thing, you save my ass."

"I would, too." Dunn handed the bottle to Kenton. "Why don't you have a bottle, sir? The men won't miss a couple of them." He lifted another from the box. "You mind keeping it here until the weekend? Don't want the men to drink it all at once."

"Sure. What're you doing with that one?"

"I'm going out to see Pamela's parents. Thought we'd celebrate the baby news together."

"Very good, Tom.

Chapter 54

The Hardwicke farm
5 miles south of Andover, England
12 September, 1520 Hours

Pamela Dunn sat at the kitchen table where she'd eaten breakfast most of her life. A blank sheet of beige stationary lay on the table. She had a pen in her hand and she was nibbling its top, uncertain how to write what she wanted to say.

She'd been relieved by the news from Dr. Swails that the baby was fine. Although she had to be careful and not get overtired.

She stared at a picture of Dunn on the table. He was wearing his uniform, of course, and his boyish grin was there, as was the sparkle in his eyes.

God, I wish Tom were here, she thought.

She sighed and started writing:

My dearest Tom,

How I wish you were here with me. I have some news. Everything is okay, but I had a bit of a problem recently. It's called spotting, and sometimes, but not this time! it can mean a miscarriage. I am home now and have seen my own doctor, a kindly man, Dr. Swails. He assures me that all is well. I did stop working, Miss Cohn was very understanding.

Pamela continued writing her letter, turning the page over. She was so intent on the paper she didn't hear the dogs barking when a vehicle drove into the barn yard. She didn't notice her mother walk right past the table to the door and open it.

She wrote a little bit more and then signed the letter:

With all my love, and baby Dunn's too,
I love you very much!
Pamela

Dunn leaned over Pamela's shoulder, reading what she had just written.

"I love you, too!"

Pamela started and the pen went flying across the room. She turned around. Her mouth dropped open and she jumped out of her chair into Dunn's arms. They kissed.

"What are you doing home?" Dunn asked, finally, after coming up for air.

Dunn had made the leap of thought that Pamela didn't want him to make.

"Is everything all right with you and the baby?" He looked down at her tummy, a worried expression on his face.

"Everything is fine. Come on, let's sit down and I'll tell you what's going on."

They sat at the table, Dunn to Pamela's left. He folded his hands on the table and looked at Pamela expectantly.

"May I get you some tea, Thomas?" Mrs. Hardwicke asked.

Even in his worried state, Dunn remembered not to say 'no.' "Yes, please."

Pamela's mother got the tea pot off the stove, poured a cup, and placed it in front of her son-in-law.

Quietly, she left the kitchen so the couple could have some privacy.

Not wanting to worry him any longer than necessary, Pamela began her story. Dunn didn't interrupt except at the point in the story when she had fainted he grasped her hand and held it tight.

She finished with, "So have to take it easy for three weeks, I can't lift heavy things, and I had to stop working. I already told my supervisor, Olive Cohn, yesterday after doctor's appointment. She was very nice and wished us well."

Dunn's face had turned white a couple of times in the telling, but it was returning to a normal color.

"That must have been quite frightening. All of it. I'm sorry I wasn't there to help."

"Oh, don't be so hard yourself. Everything is fine."

"Hm. Okay. Well, I'm glad you got home so quickly." He tapped the letter, which was still upside down. "This tells me what you just said?"

"It does. Oh, I'm so relieved to be able to tell you in person."

"I'm glad, too."

"How long are you home? Or do you know yet?"

"I picked out our next mission, Colonel Kenton thought we'd earned that right, so I did."

"I don't suppose you can tell me where it is?"

Dunn smiled. "I'm sorry, no. Maybe someday I can."

"That's okay. When do you leave?"

"Meeting the colonel Monday morning. I'm off duty until then. Care to take a short trip?"

"Where?"

"Just to Andover. Stay at the Star and Garter?"

Pamela giggled. "I would love that."

Dunn blushed as he asked the next question, "Are you still able to, you know, make love?"

"As long as we stick to traditional positions, yes. Nothing wild, boyo," Pamela whispered.

Dunn glanced around the kitchen in fear that Mrs. Hardwicke might have heard, but she was still elsewhere in the house.

"Ah. Okay that's good to know."

"So when are we leaving?"

"Huh?"

"When are we leaving?"

"Oh, well, anytime you're ready."

"Take me home, Tom."

"We are home."

"You know what I mean."

Dunn jumped to his feet and held out his hands. "Boy, do I!"

Author's Notes

It seemed a natural thing for us to follow Dunn across France and I think it made for some interesting insights into what being on the front line was like. Here in America, (and perhaps elsewhere) we tend to think of the Germans who fought in WWII as being evil because of what we learned about all of the horrors associated with the Nazis and their bloodthirst for world domination. And let's not kid ourselves from the safety of seventy-one years, that's exactly what Hitler wanted to do, along with Tojo of the Empire of Japan.

This fifth Sgt. Dunn novel explores the concept of the evil Nazi soldier versus the typical German soldier adhering to the idea of duty by revealing life on the front line from both sides. I hope I have treated the subject with honesty and fairness. I tried to allow us to get a deeper glimpse into the lives of Dunn's men, and some of the funny occurrences (the snake on the Meuse River) were there for that reason. Here's the snake that Goerdt took care of care of for the screaming city boy, Martelli.

http://www.planetepassion.eu/snakes-in-france/Common-adder-France.html

There's quite a bit more humor in this book and it's meant to illuminate how the men and women who lived and served during WWII handled the stress of survival against all odds, of not knowing what would happen on any given day. Major Armstrong's penchant for knock knock jokes comes from my family. One of my wife's favorites is the banana / orange exchange. My personal favorite is the long mosquito exchange. I learned this at the age of thirteen at Boy Scout camp and thought it was the funniest thing ever. Still do . . .

Writers do weird things accidentally, or maybe it's just me, but in the first draft, I had the orange / banana knock knock joke backwards. While video chatting with our son, Nate, and his family who live in Egypt, he pointed this out to me, very nicely, I might add.

I had fun introducing Benjamin "Cloud" Banks and the P-47 Thunderbolt.

https://en.wikipedia.org/wiki/Republic_P-47_Thunderbolt

This aircraft excelled at attacking the Germans on the ground, whether it was trucks, trains, artillery positions, or personnel, it was indeed deeply feared by the German soldiers. They called it Jabo, which is short for *Jäger-Bomber*. Try to imagine twelve of the monstrous six-ton aircraft coming at you at over 400 miles per hour and dropping a combined total of about 24,000 pounds of bombs on you. As for "Cloud," that was too good to resist. Thanks go to Steve Barltrop for the nickname. He also loaned me a great book on the aircraft, *P-47 Pilots The Fighter Bomber Boys* by Tom Glenn.

https://amzn.com/B00ETOSR7Q

You may have noticed Dunn's rank change in this book. In previous books I have him as a Sergeant First Class. While researching something else, I stumbled onto the fact that from 1920 to 1948, the five-stripes were for the rank Technical Sergeant. Sergeant First Class was reinstated in 1948 and remains active today. I decided to go ahead and correct the error and explain it.

The dialog between Pamela and her patient, Cooper, where he purposely mixed up Iowa with Ohio is based on real experiences I've endured, as have many other Iowans. Idaho is also often used in place of Iowa. Ben Banks' hometown of Wathena, Kansas, is a real place and my wonderful wife's hometown. Her dad, Max Elder, a WWII veteran (Burma), worked at Armour meatpacking. Sgt. Kinney's irrational behavior is based on stories of men who just come unglued at some point. Dunn's sister Hazel's revulsion to cottage cheese is exactly how my daughter in law, Jessica, views it. Dr. John Swails is based on the small town (Wathena) doctor who delivered my wife and all of her siblings—at home.

The premise for the big capture Dunn made comes from an article I read while researching ideas for the book. I figured if the OSS could do it, Dunn would be able to figure out an interesting way to accomplish it, too.

http://articles.sun-sentinel.com/1988-06-09/news/8802030446_1_french-resistance-oss-commandos

The Rock Island Arsenal where Gertrude works is a real place.

http://www.riamwr.com/

They really did produce the M1 Garand rifle among many other weapons. M1 Grand rifle serial number 2 is in their museum collection.

http://www.arsenalhistoricalsociety.org/museum/highlights.html

The Dunns' running family joke about where they got their brains is based on a friend from years ago, Al Yonelly, whose wife did that to him. Often.

A can of peas (20 ounce can) really did cost sixteen rationing points out of forty-eight as mentioned in the Dunns' Sunday dinner chapter. The chapter where Clarence Waters saves the squad from artillery is based on a true story told to me by my late Uncle Amos. He received the Silver Star for his actions that day (although he failed to mention that detail at the time). In case you're wondering, like my son, Nate, the use of Fahrenheit in chapter eight when Saunders asks Chesley about the forecast is correct. England didn't switch to Celsius until 1962. While writing the sentence "His last waking thought was, *I'm a lucky man*," I was listening to Emerson, Lake, and Palmer's 2010 London concert and the song *Lucky Man* came on!

I'm a big fan of *Band of Brothers*. I enjoy the interviews of the men and the exchange between Dunn and Wittenberg comes from comments made by Shifty Powers:

"We might have had a lot in common. He might've liked to fish, you know, he might've liked to hunt," Powers said. "Of course, they were doing what they were supposed to do, and I was doing what I was supposed to do. But under different circumstances, we might have been good friends." ~ Darrell

"Shifty" Powers, HBO's Band of Brothers interviews (at the 11:32 mark, although watching the whole segment is worthwhile).

https://www.youtube.com/watch?v=AMUbF0ItdT0

The scene where young German soldiers ask Wittenberg about the secret weapons promised by Göbbels comes from Albert Speer's book *Inside the Third Reich*, page 410.

http://amzn.com/0684829495

As for Sgt. Dunn number 6, I already know what Saunders and his bunch are doing, and for Dunn, I have an idea that I'm noodling which might be the right choice.

I really would love to hear from you. Please email me at sgtdunnnovel@yahoo.com. You can also sign up for my infrequent newsletters so you'll be among the first to know when something new is coming.

RM
Iowa
May 2016

Please consider following me on my blog and or Twitter to get up-to-date info on what's happening with upcoming books.

www.ronnmunsterman.com
http://ronnonwriting.blogspot.com/
https://twitter.com/RonnMunsterman
@ronnmunsterman

The Sgt. Dunn Photo Gallery for each book:
http://www.pinterest.com/ronn_munsterman/

About The Author

Ronn Munsterman is the author of five Sgt. Dunn novels. His lifelong fascination with World War II history led to the writing of the Sgt. Dunn novels.

He loves baseball, and as a native of Kansas City, Missouri, has rooted for the Royals since their beginning in 1969. He and his family jumped for joy when the 2015 Royals won the World Series. Other interests include reading, some more or less selective television watching, movies, listening to music, and playing and coaching chess.

Munsterman is a volunteer chess coach each school year for elementary- through high school-aged students, and also provides private lessons. He authored a book on teaching chess: *Chess Handbook for Parents and Coaches*

Munsterman retired from his "day job" in December 2015. In the latter half of his career he worked as an Information Technology professional with everything from Microsoft Access to PowerBuilder to web development and finally, with SAP. His new "day job" fulfills his dream: to be a full-time writer.

He lives in Iowa with his wife, and enjoys spending time with the family.

Munsterman is currently busy at work on the sixth Sgt. Dunn novel.

RONN MUNSTERMAN

RONN MUNSTERMAN

Made in the USA
Las Vegas, NV
03 February 2023

66824410R00184